down when time comes-

xx while

THE
FLAT
BUREAUCRAT
A CIA SATIRE

Also by Susan Hasler

Intelligence

Project HALFSHEEP

To Eldon,
immortal
poet,

THE FLAT BUREAUCRAT
A CIA SATIRE

[signature]

Susan Hasler

Bear Page Press • Asheville

The Flat Bureaucrat

Published by Bear Page Press, Asheville.

Bear Page Press and the Bear Page Press logo are trademarks of Zreil Global Marketing, Inc., or its affiliates.

Cover design by Susan Hasler

ISBN-13: 978-0-9965779-0-8

First Edition: August 2015

In memory of
Betty Hodges,
a woman of letters

A Note on Terminology

It is impossible to pin down the real CIA, even after working there for a couple of decades. The place is so large, so varied, so full of secrets that no one can understand the whole of it. My novels chronicle a version of the CIA I call the Mines. The terminology is my own, taken from mining vocabulary and whimsy. I call the corridors of the Mines tunnels, the analysts alchemists, the operatives sharpers, et cetera. I wanted to give a sense of an insider language full of acronyms and cant. I chose not to use the real terms, because some are classified and others change when the bureaucracy periodically reorganizes. I have provided a glossary at the end of this novel to help keep things straight.

Acknowledgments

I would like to thank Janice Lierz of Bear Page Press for her support in all aspects of the writing and publication of this book. I thank Martha Woodroof, Chris Bolgiano, and Cindy Storer for reading and offering comments on drafts of this novel. Joyce and Phil Richardson have been the best writer friends a person could have. I thank Judi Hill and my fellow Wildacres Writers for all of their advice and for many laughs over the years. Finally, I am indebted to my husband, Stephen White, for everything.

THE FLAT BUREAUCRAT

A CIA SATIRE

Out of the Blue

Death comes out of a clear blue sky. I learned that lesson all too well when the big planes hit the towers and again last May, when tiny planes turned a baseball park into a killing field. Those events, those astounding intelligence failures, will be yesterday forever. I can never again trust a lovely day, or the even smell of almonds or fresh-mown hay, which might be cyanide or phosgene, respectively. After thirty years in this intelligence agency, known to its familiars as "the Mines," every innocent, light, joyous thing is tainted. Yes, as Simon sang, there's an IED in the baby carriage.

I feel so old.

I drive through the crisp morning shadows of the willow oaks that line the perimeter road and park in one of the spaces reserved for the Four Horsemen. Not the Four Horsemen of the Apocalypse, the Four Horsemen of the Mines. It's a subtle difference. We are the most senior officials, next to the Boss of Mines and his deputy. We head the four main shafts: the Black Mines, the White Mines, the Paper Mines, and the Smithery. I, Shelby Wexler, am the Boss of the White Mines, where alchemists interpret raw intelligence for the busy policymaker. Note, the adjective "busy" must always proceed the noun "policymaker," for there is no other type. The less they accomplish, the busier they are. The ones who do nothing at all are like whirling dervishes. All you see is a blur.

That threatening sky is as blue and ass-warm as a new-laid robin's egg. It has only one fluffy cloud, hovering high over the Potomac. I glance at it as I slam the door of my truck and throw my hip against it to engage the latch. To my thirsty eye, that cloud resembles a whiskey bottle on its side, spilling out the last sad drop.

I lower my gaze to my destination, and suddenly I see it as if through a stereoscope, with its flat features taking on an unreal depth. I see it as if I were looking at it for the first time, or perhaps the last. It's an eerie feeling. In the foreground, steel posts block the drive that leads up to the front steps. A grass quadrangle occupies the middle ground. On a college campus, such a patch of grass would attract sunbathers, dogs, and frisbees, but here it is empty. Beyond the grass, the long horizontal expanse of the Old Shafts Building forms a wall seven floors high, punctured by hundreds of windows. The windows in the center of the uppermost floor belong to the Boss of Mines or BOM (pronounced 'bomb'). The building features a helipad on the roof for convenient disposal of dead BOMs and other senior officials. Out front, a few smokers cluster near the bronze statue of Nathan Hale with the noose around his neck—our institutional icon.

I shake my head to dispel the unreality. Meanwhile, another Horseman drives up: Arthur White, the Boss of the Smithery—where techies make spy devices. I move out of the way to allow his silver Corvette to pull into the reserved space next to mine. Arthur is the quintessential techie. Everything he owns is shiny. I suspect he has stainless steel balls. He is the vainest human being I've ever met. A graduate of MIT and former President of MENSA, Arthur builds Rube Goldberg-style apparatuses in his spare time. For his last Christmas party, he constructed a room-sized device featuring a chain-saw, Jello-filled balloons, a dozen vintage Slinkies, a xylophone, a robotic shark, a drone, several thousand dominoes, and an aquarium full of albino bull frogs. Its purpose was to deliver a single olive to a cocktail. "It's no wonder three wives have left him," my wife whispered as the falling olive splashed vermouth in my eye.

Arthur parks as far as possible from my pickup. He unfolds himself from the low-slung car with the smooth precision of a satellite deploying in space. He is tall, lean, fit, ironed, and polished—the polar opposite of my short, lumpy, rumpled self. I hate him, not passionately, but still, I hate him. I hate all of the other Horsemen, and they hate me.

"You left a smudge on my cover yesterday," he says with a galling prissiness. "You're lucky you didn't ding the finish."

"One should not expect to go through life without a few dings," I point out.

"One should if one owns a 'vette." Arthur pops the trunk of the car.

I shrug. "I used to own a 'vette.'"

"You owned a *Chev*ette, Shelby, not a *Cor*vette. I doubt you understand the difference. Here." He pulls the canvas cover out of the trunk and shakes it out. "The least you could do is help me get this on." I take the other end, and we tuck the baby in. As he picks up his briefcase, Arthur glances at my well-dented pickup.

"You keep that thing just to annoy me, don't you?"

"Yes."

Arthur's face puckers as he peers into the back of my truck. "I thought I smelled something foul. Is that shit?" he asks as if he had never seen or produced the stuff.

"It's black gold," I tell him. "Rotted horse manure. I get it from a stable near Middleburg. It's the best thing possible to amend that nasty, hard-pan subsoil the developer left when he scraped off my topsoil to sell to someone else. It's gardening season. Look at the weather. If I didn't have to be in this building, I would be out with my tiller working in the manure and I would be a happy man."

"You have strange, disturbing tastes, Shelby." Arthur glances up at the blue sky and the large white cloud. "Lacunosus."

"What?"

"That cloud is a altocumulus lacunosus."

"Hmph, looks like a bottle to me."

"I'm not surprised." Arthur makes a show of sniffing.

Okay, so in the last few months I've drifted toward alcoholism. I have a good excuse for it, and it's not like I don't have a lot of company in this place. The Mines drives a man to drink. At least I didn't have to walk.

As we proceed toward the building, I pin my eyes on the asphalt, and tuck in my chin. I hope my body language will discourage any further conversation. I wish I had gas so I could cut a big one, but for once, I do not.

Of course, Arthur continues talking.

"Did you know William Sibley?" he says and then adds, unnecessarily, "The man shot at the gate yesterday."

"Yes." I swallow the knot that rises in my throat. "He worked for me. Used to be a sharper, but he left that a while back. He headed my Foreign Liaison Visits Division. He was a friend. Can't imagine why he would do what he did."

"Friend? My condolences. Greyson thinks the thing was suicide by security patrol. Sibley refused to show his Mines tag, refused to stop, had a gun on the passenger seat. He put his foot on the accelerator and drove through." Arthur waxes philosophical. "Why are people so impatient to die? All they have to do is wait, and stress, poor diet, the Beltway or the terrorists will do it for them."

I don't answer. There is a chance, albeit slight, that silence will be met with silence. But Arthur likes to fill gaps in speech with his own insight and logic, as one might fill empty Tupperware containers with pasta and dried beans. He gives me a curious look. "You know why the guards were so trigger happy. It was your fault. You were the one who called the bomb puppies out for a sniff over. They didn't find a thing. You put everyone on alert all over town. Why?"

Some questions never find their answer.

We pass into the shade of the long concrete portico in front of the Old Shafts Building. I take a few last steps, then ... a blood-curdling auditory assault—an excruciating, high-pitched, rapidly-pulsing shriek that penetrates my tympanic membranes like an ice pick. Arthur looks up, yells something I cannot hear, and is gone. I look up and see the concrete ripple like water. I want to run, but I can't move. The wave breaks over me. I gasp and breathe in dust. The world tilts. Darkness pricked with stars. Weight. Things explode around me and inside my body. Capillaries in my eyes and face erupt in a thousand tiny bursts. Ribs crack in rapid succession. Air hisses from my lungs into the pleural cavity. Organs rupture. The weight of all the Mines and its history crushes the wall of my chest. A last word rises in my mind: viscera. I convulse.

And my story ends.

Or not.

2

The Wrong Punctuation

I assume I'm dead because my hemorrhoids aren't itching. I'm feeling no pain, and yet I'm not drunk. I was hit by a few tons of concrete. My body must be as flat as a pancake. No, I'm definitely dead. Yet I'm still here in some sense, without senses, wherever here is. I can't tell you how awkward it is for an atheist to discover an afterlife. I really thought death would be a period, not three dots. I would be happier with a period. I'm not an ellipsis kind of guy. I want to be done with it. Period.

And if I was wrong about the afterlife, then where's the damn light? Am I not supposed to be heading for a light? It's just dark.

Frankly, I thought I'd see it coming. I am—or was—an alchemist, which is Mines' jargon for analyst. An alchemist is supposed to see into the future and, in particular, to be alert for threats. What happened? It wasn't a bomb. It was sound—rhythmic shrieking ungodly sound—tearing through headquarters. Right before it happened, I remember looking at the building and thinking it suddenly looked unreal, but that was the only indicator. Or was it?

Yes, I had raised an alert and asked for the bomb-sniffing dogs to go over the compound, but that was to appease my Chief of Alternative Analysis, Maddie James. So many alerts had come to nothing. I didn't think this one was any different.

I should have seen it, but a certain willful blindness had overtaken me, and not only me. For many of us, blindness had become a survival skill.

I hear nothing, but the Mines must be vibrating with noise. How can it be that the place that was my whole world is crashing down right now, and I hear nothing? I feel no physical manifestations of anxiety: no thumping heart, sick stomach, chills up the spine. The absence of those things somehow makes the angst worse.

What was my role in this catastrophe? I can think of nothing I did wrong …

Damn the ellipses.

The light seeps back, dull and artificial. Not the sort of heavenly brilliance one would wish for under the circumstances. It acquires the harsh focus of an interrogation. My inchoate surroundings resolve into a room with split vinyl chairs, dust, and low tables of tattered news magazines. I see a familiar framed photo on the wall, an image of a blackened tree sticking up through a cracked bed of igneous rock. Now I know where I am: the polygraph waiting room. The polygraph division is in one of the "out buildings," or off-campus facilities tucked away in the anonymous Northern Virginia suburbs. Like all Mines employees, I come here once every five years for a re-poly.

"We're ready for you, Shelby."

I jump and turn to see the same guy who gave me my last polygraph. He's pot-gutted and stooped. Hairless head, long chicken neck, and bulging, rheumy eyes lend his physiognomy a scrofulous look.

"Hello, Shelby."

He extends his hand. I grasp it reluctantly, then pull away at the cold touch. "Excuse me," I stutter, "I've forgotten your name."

"Virgil."

"You are kidding me," I say, thinking of Dante, but then I remember that this man's name is, indeed, Virgil.

Virgil wears a black golf shirt with the red, white, and blue Mines logo on the pocket. Below the logo it says "Mines Retired." They sell those shirts in the Company Store. He must be working on contract now.

"It hasn't been five years since my last test," I say.

"You know that employees have to be polygraphed after any major change in status: marriage to a foreign national, return from overseas, death, et cetera."

"I didn't know the Mines conducted postmortem polygraphs."

"I don't work for the Mines any more," Virgil says. "Not since I died."

This is very bad news. I take a closer look at his shirt. It doesn't say "Mines Retired." It says "Mines Expired." Where did he buy that?

"Am I in Hell?" I ask. Surely an eternity trapped in the polygraph room with Virgil would qualify as Hell.

He shrugs. "Heaven, Hell … it's not black and white like that. You should understand. Don't you alchemists deal in shades of gray?" He lapses into a spasmodic laugh, a high "heep, heep, heep" ending in a moist snort.

I look around for any sign of life in this room, which is usually crowded with employees waiting for a polygraph examiner to come and say, "We're ready for you." It's just me and Virgil, and we're both dead. If I were alive right now, I would be sweating. But I'm not alive, and I'm not nearly as dead as I should be.

"This is ... astounding," I say. "I didn't even believe in a life hereafter, much less a one that would function like the Mines."

He sucks his teeth and rolls his eyes over the room. "Shelby, the afterlife isn't like this for everybody. It's tailored to the individual, a reap-what-you-sow system."

"That is ... bad news."

"Tell me about it," he says. "You think this is my idea of heaven? No beer, and even the soda in the machines is flat. Well, get in here. I haven't got all day ... Oh wait, I do have all day. I have all eternity." Again the heeping, snorting laugh.

I start to follow him into the polygraph room, then stop when I notice the sign above the door: ABANDON HOPE ALL YE WHO ENTER HERE. I squint to read the small print underneath: *We Have No Close of Business*.

"Yes," Virgil says, "that's new."

The polygraph room itself hasn't changed since my last test. During my long career, I spent hours being polygraphed. This despite the fact that I had no lifestyle or loyalty issues. I stayed out of debt, never took mind-altering drugs after entering underground, never cheated on my wife with a man or foreign national, never got friendly with reporters, never played fast and loose with classified materials, took no secret trips overseas, never even remotely considered handing over secrets to a foreign security service. Yet the poly was a bitch every time I took it. Why? Because, like any good alchemist, I could never accept that questions could be answered with a simple yes or no.

I don't need to look around. I know every wretched inch of this room. In the center is a large black vinyl chair, scratched on the arm as if some unfortunate had tried to claw his way out. I think of all the sweating done in this ratty piece of furniture. It probably weighs five times what it did new. Next to it is a table with the machine. Styluses, as delicate as spider legs, hover over a clean stretch of paper. The polygraph examiner has a straight wooden chair in the corner. The black chair faces a two-way mirror, which is marred by ... no that can't be ... but it is—a comet of bird shit streaked across the surface as if thrown there by centrifugal force. Was some large bird caught in the room? Did he circle desperately hoping for escape? But we are nowhere near an open window. I sit down and see my reflection beneath the spatter: a grumpy bald man with three chins, a stain on his tie, and a jacket too tight around the middle.

"I don't know how you're going to conduct a polygraph," I say. "I can't feel a thing: no heartbeat, nothing. I can't sweat. You won't get any electrical sensations from my skin. Nothing your sensors can detect. I'm completely disconnected."

Virgil waves his hand over the apparatus. "This is a crude tool, Shelby. Just for show. I really don't need it, but it makes people uncomfortable, so I keep it around."

I stare anxiously at the dull glass in front of me. "So who's behind the mirror? Jesus Christ, Allah, the Buddha? I suppose I was wrong about God, but who was right?"

Virgil's moist lips slide into a smirk. "No one."

I stare at myself glumly as Virgil makes a show of hooking the machine's sensors onto my visible, but somehow nonexistent body. I get a wire around the chest, one around the belly, a sensor on the finger, the usual. Then he bends over and reaches through his legs to pull his chair under his butt. It's a graceless maneuver I remember from our last polygraph.

"How does that feel, Shelby?" Virgil asks. Polygraph examiners resemble car salesmen. They use your name repeatedly, insistently until you want to club them to death. I decide to reciprocate.

"It doesn't feel like anything, Virgil. What do you think?"

"Ah, but are you comfortable, Shelby?" he asks slyly.

"Of course, I'm not comfortable, Virgil. I'm intensely uncomfortable."

Satisfaction suffuses his hideous face. "See? You don't need a body to be uncomfortable, Shelby. So I can successfully polygraph you." He flips on the machine. "Shall we begin with a few test questions, Shelby?"

"Shoot, Virgil."

"You know the drill. There will be four types of questions: irrelevant, diagnostic, relevant, and those I ask simply because I'm a sick bastard."

I feel an odd satisfaction. "I knew it! I always suspected it, but I've never heard a polygraph examiner admit to the fourth type before."

Virgil picks up a pencil to mark the chart. "Okay, Shelby, answer truthfully with a simple 'yes' or 'no.' Is your full name Shelby Isherwood Wexler?"

"Yes." From the corner of my eye, I see the styluses come to life, dancing madly over the paper. "Does that damn thing think I'm lying?"

"Ignore it, Shelby," Virgil says. "Just answer the questions correctly. Was your position Boss of White Mines?"

"Yes." The styluses swoop like birds.

"Shelby, are you dead?" He waits, then raises his

voice. "Shelby, I said, are you dead?"

"Damned if I know."

"Yes or no, Shelby."

"Apparently, it's not a yes or no question," I argue. "How can I say I'm dead when I'm still conscious? How can I say I'm alive when my body is kaput?"

"Yes or no, Shelby."

"Yes."

The styluses swoop. Virgil shakes his head with the gravity of a grim reaper, and his voice comes out an octave lower than usual. "The machine detects prevarication, Shelby. Let me repeat the question. Are you dead?"

"No." In the mirror, I see red splotches bloom on my face, but I feel no sensation.

Virgil scowls. "Now, Shelby, the machine doesn't like that answer either."

"See what I mean?" I forget about the sensors and throw up my hands. "You people are all about absolutes when there are no real absolutes in the world. Alchemists know that. That's why we never say 'certainly,' we say 'almost certainly.' I have yet to meet a polygraph examiner who could understand that."

Virgil leans forward to readjust the wires. "I hate alchemists. Shelby, didn't we have this same argument the last time you were here?"

"Probably."

"Then let's not do it again. I'll skip that question. Okay, yes or no, is your tie blue and yellow, Shelby?"

The words "Shelby, Shelby, Shelby" echo in my head. I forget to answer. He repeats the question. I finally say, "Yes," knowing that the answer will not satisfy him or his wretched machine.

"The machine detects prevarication, Shelby."

Anger takes over, and my voice rises with each word. "Well, Virgil, that's because I don't know if I can even call it 'my tie' anymore since I'm dead, or at least almost certainly dead. Do dead people really own ties, Virgil? If dead people can own ties, Virgil, then yes, the tie is blue and yellow. If not, then it's NOT MY FUCKING TIE!"

He points. "That tie in the mirror, Shelby, is it blue and yellow?"

"Yes."

"Are you an atheist, Shelby?"

"Oh my God."

"Yes or no."

"I was. I don't know now. Who's behind the mirror? I can't answer this, Virgil. I won't. It's not yes or no. You're killing me with that yes or no."

Virgil slaps his thigh and laughs with a heep, heep, heep, snort. "'Killing me,' good one, Shelby. Okay, I think that's enough test questions. Perhaps we should get to the meat of the session now."

"Why do you even need to polygraph me? Doesn't whoever or whatever is behind the mirror know it all, already? Why must we go through this charade?"

"Sorry, but you don't have a need to know the answer to that question."

"The hell I don't!"

"Another good one, Shelby." Virgil laughs, leaning back enough to give me a view up his gaping nostrils. A driblet of snot, poised to run down his upper lip, retracts when he closes his mouth to suck in a breath.

Kill me now, I think, and then, *Shit, that won't help.*

"There's a way out of this room," Virgil says.

"What is it?" I allow hope to raise its gullible head like a mole about to be whacked.

His finger indicates a point on the wall near the ceiling. It's an inscription I hadn't noticed before: "Ye shall know the truth, and the truth shall set you free."

It occurs to me that worse might await. "Where do I go when I leave this room?"

"Depends."

"On what?"

"No more questions from you. It's for your benefit, Shelby. You don't know the truth about yourself now, but you will before we're done. Then I think you'll be ready to accept the judgment. Now—"

"This process is too black and white, too dualistic, with its yes or no answers," I argue. "Is that really the way the universe runs? Does that mean we're under a Manichean system?"

Virgil rolls his eyes. "I hate alchemists. You guys haul out the fifty-dollar words and over-analyze everything. Just answer the damn questions yes or no."

"Wait. I have a few questions. I need to know what happened to the Mines." Virgil holds up a hand to stop me, but I continue. "Come on. I have to know. I worked there thirty years. My God, all the people. Thelma, my secretary. If you don't tell me what happened to anyone else, tell me about Thelma. She's the best person I know. She put up with me for twenty years, and I have to know what happened to her."

Virgil leers. "What sort of relationship did you have with Thelma, Shelby?"

"Not that kind!" I say indignantly.

"No fantasies, ever?"

"Oh, come on, Virgil, you dirty bastard. I lived and breathed the Mines. You have to tell me what happened. Please. Thirty years can't end like this. What did we miss?

Why did it happen? Was it ... Did I ... Did some of the blame rest with me?"

"Shelby, do you really want me to focus on the attack and why it happened? This isn't just a poly, it's a trial, a judgment day. Think about it hard. You can be judged on your entire life or only on the part leading up to the attack."

"If I say 'my entire life' will I find out what happened at the Mines?"

"No."

"If I say the attack?"

"Then we'll go into it in detail as we would in a trial. I don't think this would be to your advantage, however, when it comes to the final judgment. Frankly, Shelby, you soured. You started out with good intentions, good ethics, decent values, and then, near the end, you became an alcoholic, and even worse, an ice-cold cynic like me. And look where I ended up." Virgil's hand sweeps around to indicate the cramped room. "Do you really want to be judged on the final few weeks of your life? You know the sins of commission from your youth are easier to forgive than the sins of omission from your final months."

I would be holding my breath if I had any breath to hold. I served a year in the Peace Corps before I came to the Agency. I taught children in India and, what's more, I came to love them. I corresponded with one girl for years and sent money to help out with school. That would be a lot of brownie points towards securing a more comfortable hereafter. It might at least partially offset the rest. But then I would never find out what happened at the Mines. That in itself would be Hell. And it would be cowardice.

"Well, Shelby?"

I look into Virgil's thin, asymmetrical face. I hate how his nose veers off to the side. I hate the moist, smirking lips. He'll have no mercy on me.

"I've given a great deal of money to charity recently," I say.

Virgil is unimpressed. "You got your deductions from the IRS, didn't you? Don't expect any from me. Come on, Shelby, give me an answer. Your whole life or just the past few months?"

Images race through my mind: the faces of colleagues, the stars on the memorial wall. Faces and stars merge, multiply, and explode until I feel dizzy. A cry rises from my chest. "The Mines. I want to know what happened. Who lived? Who died? Who attacked us? Who was responsible for missing the signs?"

Virgil looks to the ceiling in thought; then a snaggle-toothed grin breaks out on his face. "I'm going to send you back."

Hope, stupid, blind hope rises again. "Thank God. Can I change anything?"

"Too late." Virgil grins as if this were a joke. "We'll give you most of your senses back to help you pick up on clues you missed the first time. You'll have sight, hearing, and smell—no taste. Touch will be according to my whim. You'll be a passive observer—not that you weren't passive to the point of being barely conscious when you were alive—but this time you'll really be a fly on the wall. Or perhaps I should say, a fly in the brain."

"Whose brain?"

"Depends."

"I'll be able to hear their thoughts?

"No. That wouldn't be helpful. No thoughts, just their angle of view. The angle of view is everything, you know."

"Will—"

"No more questions."

The injustice of it all clots in my throat, almost like a physical sensation. Coughing doesn't help. I struggle to get my words out. "Who do you think you are, anyway? This is ridiculous, just ridiculous."

Virgil heeps, snorts, and hawks a glob of saliva into my eye. "When the subject uses the word 'ridiculous' for the first time, the fun starts."

3

The Last Happy Hour

In an instant, the polygraph room is gone, and I arrive in a skull not my own. It doesn't take me long to recognize it. It's Spartan, masculine, and gamy. I smell hints of locker room, bacon, and the green waters of the Potomac. I'm in the past, months before my death. I'm in the head of the soon-to-be-late Boss of Mines, Brick Mason.

That head was about to explode.

It was happy hour. "Happy hour" was a euphemism in the Mines for the daily five o'clock meeting of senior officials in the BOM's office. Happy hour was never happy; it lasted more than an hour; and there was no alcohol. I remember this particular happy hour well—the police questioned me about it extensively. Now it looks like I will have to sit through it again, this time staring from the eyes of a doomed man.

Those eyes were wandering. I remember at the time thinking that Brick was having some trouble focusing as if he were on medication. Now, from inside his skull, I have a dizzy view back and forth across the standard government decor: blue carpeting, dull gold curtains, dark-paneled walls, and stiff portraits with flags in the background.

Finally, those eyes fixed one by one on the faces in the room. First there was Greyson Earl, the sly and untrustworthy Boss of the Black Mines or BOBM (pronounced bob 'em). Greyson ran the sharpers or spies. He was a towering figure who moved noiselessly and gave off a strong essence of cat. His dark eyebrows were preternaturally thick and spiky. A streak of white bisected the left one. The effect was so startling that I couldn't help but suspect it was deliberate. It amused me to picture him in front of his bathroom mirror, applying peroxide to his brows and then coaxing them into devil points with a tiny comb.

I have already described Arthur White, the supercilious Boss of the Smithery (BOS). His eyelids were drooping. He was narcoleptic, and I suspect he was about to fall asleep.

Salvador "Slinky" Nardovino was the Boss of the Paper Mines (BOPM, pronounced bop 'em). Slinky was a man of many hyphens, the product of an African-American mother and Irish-American/Italian-American father. He was thin and wiry, with broad cheekbones and salt-and-pepper hair. He had lost his left arm below the elbow in the first Gulf War, where he served as a logistics officer. In its place was a Hosmer hook, which he operated with great dexterity. Slinky had so many physical tics that "Twitchy" would have been a more apt nickname. He was the best BOPM in a generation because of his unbounded enthusiasm for every detail of his work. He bored the rest of us, but we admired his ability to get a job done, no matter how many—or how odd—the obstacles.

Finally, Brick focused on me, Shelby Wexler, the lumpen Boss of the White Mines or BOWM (pronounced bow 'em). It is probably a good thing that I won't be privy to his thoughts. I can well imagine what he thought of me. I looked like a pile of crumpled laundry if laundry can be said to be sullen. I had no idea. I remember peering out of that body thinking of myself as distinguished, stoic, almost heroic in my patience with the great irritations of life, including daily "happy hours." But the resentment, the impatience, the *thirst* in my face was clearly evident. I wanted to go home and drink.

It was an awkward moment. Brick watched us fidget. An odd collection of items cluttered the coffee table: a well-worn canoe paddle, a Russian Matryoshka doll, and a yellowed file folder stuffed with three inches worth of material. Brick's eyes focused on the last item, on a printed label partially covered by an old photo of a very young, athletic-looking man. It was Brick's personnel file.

"Shelby," Brick said. I jumped. It was not a good sign to have my name be the first word spoken in the meeting.

"Do you think I should resign?"

Panic leaped in my eyes. I couldn't believe he would ask the question. Election day was approaching, and it was almost certain that a new president would ask for Brick's resignation as soon as he took office. The worst had gone public. The Mines faked intelligence tying Iran to the terrorist attack on Burton Oil Park. The outgoing administration had ordered the forgery—in an indirect, deniable way—but that was no excuse. Frankly, I couldn't believe that Brick hadn't resigned already.

He watched my chins joggle as I tried to swallow. "I believe it would be customary." There was an excruciatingly long pause as Brick's eyes rolled back and forth over the office.

Finally, he said, "Customary to resign at the end of an old Administration or customary for a disgraced BOM to resign?"

"Well … both."

"I know what you're thinking," Brick said, "You're thinking that I should have resigned before I agreed to disseminate that report."

That was exactly what I was thinking, and feeling smug and superior as I did so. I had found out about the forgery at the stadium attack hearings. I wasn't BOWM then; I was the Boss of Congressional Affairs. Being blindsided by this news infuriated me. Sharon Pendergast was BOWM, but she resigned shortly afterward. The other Horsemen claimed ignorance of the faked intelligence, but I was sure that Greyson must have known.

Abruptly Brick went to the table, leaned over, braced one hand on the corner, and slammed the other down on the personnel folder.

"MS-5 file clerk," he said. "I was a goddamn nineteen-year-old MS-5 file clerk when I started out at this place. All I had was a high school education, but I worked my ass off. In return, the Mines promoted me, paid for my education, sent me all over the goddamn globe." Brick picked up the folder and began to leaf through performance appraisals loaded with perfect sevens and envelopes with award citations.

"You can't find a bad performance report in here," Brick said. "Not even a mediocre one. For more than thirty years, I walked on water. Jesus Christ himself didn't do it that long. I checked all the boxes, paid my dues, and less than a year ago, I ascended to this office—a destination I set for myself when I entered underground. A lot of men have had that goal, but I made it, and at no small cost."

The room went silent except for the accelerated rasp of Brick's breath. He put the personnel folder back on the table. He picked up the Matryoshka and began to disassemble it, unscrewing each wooden doll at the waist, removing its smaller sisters, screwing it back together, and setting it down. It took some time because this was a large, elaborate Matroshka. At last, nineteen gaudily painted dolls of graduated size stood on the table.

"Anyone here see anything more than dolls?" he asked. "Greyson? Arthur? One of you should be able to figure it out."

The Boss of Black Mines leaned forward, picked up the tiniest doll, and rolled it around in his massive hand as he examined it. He rubbed his thumb over its surface, scratched it with a fingernail, even lifted it to his nose and sniffed. Meanwhile, Arthur squinted through his glasses, examining another of the dolls. Brick sat back, watching without the ghost of a smile on his face.

Finally, Greyson said, "I give up. Why don't you tell us?"

Brick's eyes fastened on Greyson's face. "You give up much more easily than the KGB. They worked on the problem for years. You see, this doll sat on the shelves of a store in Moscow. The cost was prohibitive for most Russians. About twice a month, I walked into the store and asked to see it. I would take it apart, put it back together, thank the snarling salesgirl, and leave. Our Russian counterparts must have put this thing through every test imaginable, trying to figure out if it was a dead drop, a code system, or whatever. The only thing there for them to find, however, was the faint scent of herring."

"A red herring," Greyson said.

"Exactly. When I left Moscow, I bought the thing and brought it back here to remind me how much of our trade is sham exercise." With the back of his hand, Brick swept the nineteen wooden dolls from the table.

One landed on the notebook in my lap. Brick watched as I struggled with the awkward dilemma of what to do with it. I didn't want it staring up at me with those creepy wide blue eyes, but I was afraid if I set it back on the table, he would throw it at me. Moving as inconspicuously as possible, I nudged it off into the space on the couch between Greyson and me.

Brick picked up the paddle. "You're all familiar with the canoe pool," he said. Of course. The canoe pool was famous in the Mines. Several men took the ferry to Sycamore Island and paddled across the Potomac every day just after sunrise. They chained the canoe to a hickory, crossed over the parkway, and showered in the gym. Brick had been a regular whenever he was at Headquarters.

"My hours haven't allowed me to participate since I became BOM. So I keep my own canoe chained to an oak down by the river. Sometimes I still take it out, which irritates my security detail no end." Brick sucked his lips inward while we waited for him to continue. "I should have gone out more often. It might have saved me if I had. When you sit on the dividing line between water and sky, choices seem simpler. I do my best thinking there. Before I attained my current position, I used to think about how I would do things. Whoever was the BOM at the time, I believed I would have done things better, cleaner." Brick lowered his eyes to the carpeting where they lingered until his vision grew fuzzy. Only the faint buzz of florescent light fixtures marred the silence.

Finally, when the moment had become unbearable, Brick's head snapped up. "Get out," he said.

We Horsemen hurried to comply. Brick watched me collide with Arthur as we made for the exit.

"Stooges," he muttered as the door closed. He stood for some time allowing his eyes to light on this or that symbol of power: a flag, an award citation, a thick bronze medal in a velvet-lined box. Then he picked up his personnel folder and returned with it to his desk. Starting with his yellowed application to the Mines, he fed the papers into the shredder he kept near his right knee. His movements were slow as if a sedative ran through his veins. Sometimes he stopped to read something and shake his head. The shredder jammed. Brick took a new burn bag from the pile in his bottom desk drawer and shook it out. He emptied the receptacle of the machine into the bag, folded the top over twice, and stapled it every two inches, per Mines regulations. He filled two more bags as he finished his personnel file and emptied papers from the drawers of his desk. The process took some time.

The voice of his secretary, Daphne, came over the intercom. "Brick, do you need anything before I go home?"

"No, have a good evening. Who else is left in the office?"

"Only Huey. I think the poor guy would like to go home to his new bride. How late are you going to be here tonight? I'm sure your driver would like to go home, too."

"Not much longer. Send Huey in before you go, would you?"

"Sure. See you tomorrow."

"Right," Brick said. "Daphne?"

"Yes?"

I can only imagine what was going through Brick's head during the long pause that followed. Daphne had been his secretary for twenty years, following him around the globe to a string of dangerous posts. She had a reputation for unflappable courage, loyalty, and kindness. And through all those years she had been in love with Brick Mason. Everyone knew it. It shone from her eyes. And everyone knew it was unrequited. To Brick, Daphne was like a sister.

"Daphne," Brick finally said, "take care of yourself."

"Of course." She sounded puzzled. "I always have."

"Don't forget to send Huey in."

Before long a hesitant knock sounded at the door.

"Come in. I don't bite," Brick said in a voice gruff enough to belie his words.

Huey was the junior SCUDO, or Security Patrol Uniformed Duty Officer, in the BOM suite. He was a big man with an open, innocent face. Perhaps he was still awaiting permission to be an adult. He was uncomfortable in his uniform and hesitant to set foot on the thick carpeting of power. "Yes sir?" he said.

Brick pulled out his wallet and selected a few bills. "Get me an order of hot wings from Charlie's."

Panic showed in Huey's eyes. "But I'm not supposed to leave the office while you're here."

"Are you supposed to disobey direct orders from the BOM?" Brick added enough menace to his voice to turn the young SCUDO's face deadly pale. "Are you?"

"No, sir." Huey approached warily to collect the money.

Brick added the rest of the bills in his wallet. "Get yourself something while you're at it and eat it there. Take your time. It's going to be a long night. Leave the change as a tip. Always leave a good tip. When you go to meet your maker, the sins you answer for shouldn't be petty."

"Yes, sir."

When Huey had left, Brick carried the burn bags over to the chute in the wall near his desk. He flipped the latch and opened the square metal door. He threw in the bags and listened for the faint sound of the impact seven floors down. He didn't bother to close the door.

Brick sat back down at his desk and grabbed a pen and a notepad with the Mines seal at the top. He wrote without hesitation as if the words had been on his mind for some time. "The Mines now makes her living on her back. My lifelong ambition was to be her BOM, and I turned out to be her pimp. I can't live with that." He added his slashing and almost unintelligible signature and tore off the sheet. He stepped outside the door and stuck the note on the trident of a small bronze statue of Poseidon that sat on a credenza. When he wanted Daphne to see a note first thing in the morning, he always left it there.

Brick closed the door, went back to his desk, and sat down. He opened his upper drawer and took out an old Russian Tokarev pistol. I don't know much about guns, but I recognized this one because a friend of mine owned one just like it. The KGB had used these pistols, and a lot of old Sharpers collected them out of a twisted nostalgia. Brick ran his thumb over the Communist star pressed into the black Bakelite handle. He steadied his elbows on the desk. From Brick's eyes, I can't see exactly where on his head he aimed the gun, but I do see the spasmodic movement of his arm just before the shot rang out. So loud. The room seemed to jump and blur, and then slowly came back into focus. The blotter was red with blood, but Brick was still alive. That last-second jerk of his arm must have thrown off his aim.

When the shot went off, Brick had dropped the gun. Now he scrambled to pick it up with shaking hands. He put the barrel in his mouth and depressed the trigger, but the gun jammed. He tried again and again, then threw the thing down.

"Need time to bleed out." Brick pushed his chair back from the desk. The view through his eyes was blurry, red at the edges, pulsing. It swept back and forth in drunken arcs. At last, Brick focused on the open burn shoot. With inhuman grunts he stood, stumbled a few steps, and threw his upper body into the opening. Brick's torso briefly rested on the threshold of the chute. The balance of his weight tipped, and he fell. I felt rushing darkness and heard the hollow banging of bony knees and elbows against the sides of the chute. Brick got hung up before he reached the basement. He lived for half an hour jammed in the chute upside down.

I curse Virgil for leaving me in that shattered skull as the blood dripped down. The smell of urine, and excrement, and sweat was overwhelming. Brick muttered from time to time, but his words were unintelligible. He fell silent. Shards of light reeled before his eyes; then faded to the most impenetrable darkness.

The artificial light of the polygraph room comes back slowly. I turn a look of hatred on Virgil. "You bastard. What was the point of leaving me with him while he died?"

He gives me a smile that is almost sweet. "I don't need to have a point. Tell me, what struck you most about Brick's death?"

I feel stupid as the obvious answer comes to me. "His death was unlike any version of it I heard. It didn't match the story told by the press, the Horsemen, or anyone else in the Mines."

"Yes," Virgil said. "So many things are like that."

4

The Clean-Up

I smell menthol cough drops and pencil lead. I'm in a different head. This host was moving rapidly through an empty basement tunnel, muttering. I recognize the voice of Slinky Nardovino.

The words came out in a rapid staccato. "Damn it, damn it, damn it. Of course, they send me to do this. I tell them to call the police, but do they listen to me? No, they send me to do their crap work." He stopped by a door labeled "Burn" and reached into his pocket to pull out a slip of paper with a combination number, cipher, and security code. He held this with his hook while he worked the locks. The black leather glove on his right hand made it more difficult for him. He had to spin the combination three times before the wheels and notches aligned, and the fence fell. Slinky punched in the cipher, opened the door, and stepped inside to enter the security sequence on the keypad next to the door. A green light flashed. He entered a few more numbers. It flashed again and turned to red, indicating that the system was disarmed and would not begin to blast an alarm. Red and green had counterintuitive meanings in the Mines. Green meant everything was locked up and safe—you could not proceed.

Red meant open and dangerous—you could proceed.

Slinky expelled a breath and turned on the lights. A large dumpster stood under the chute to catch the falling burn bags. He emitted a child-like whine of reluctance and complaint. He looked back toward the door, took a step in that direction, stopped. He turned and took a few quick steps to the dumpster. He gripped the lip with a gloved hand and a hook. Slinky wedged the toe of his sneaker into a ridge along the side and pulled himself up. He looked in, sucked in a breath, blinked. He saw a blood-spatter sun superimposed over mounds of burn bags, some split and spilling their contents. No body. He glanced at the chute protruding from the ceiling and saw the clotted drops clinging to its edge. He banged his hook on the dumpster. "Damn. He must have gotten stuck up there."

Slinky secured the vault and muttered to himself all the way back to the seventh floor. I had never heard him utter anything more than a mild curse before. Now, he used all conjugations of the verb "to fuck" interspersed with the names of the Horsemen and the late BOM and a host of obscene synonyms for same. He stopped swearing when the elevator reached the seventh floor. He passed through the BOM's outer office, ignoring Huey, who leaned against a credenza, pale and miserable.

Slinky went into the inner office and slammed the door behind him. Greyson and Arthur, interrupted in mid-argument, turned. Like Slinky, they were dressed in casual clothes and gloves. "Well?" Greyson said.

"Lots of blood and no body. He stuck in the chute." Slinky scanned the room. His gaze fixed on the pool of blood on the desk, then moved to a bit of gore on the carpet. "This is a chunk of bone, isn't it?" He got down on one knee to get a closer look. "It's got hair on it. It has to be part of Brick's skull. Do you think he could cross the room and throw himself down the burn chute with a wound like that? Are we looking at a murder?"

"Could be." Arthur squinted at the hairy chunk with the same prissy look of revulsion he had aimed at the horse manure in the back of my truck. "We won't know until we can examine the body."

"But then why would a murderer throw Brick's body down the burn chute?" Slinky asked. "That makes no sense."

Greyson's face broke into a toothy grin. "It's what I would do. Just for the rich, delightful humor of it."

Slinky straightened and focused on Grayson's face. The BOBM yawned and ran his tongue over his upper lip. "Did you do this?" Slinky asked. "Was this your shortcut to being the next BOM?"

"Of course, not," Grayson said. "I was just trying to put myself in the mind of the murderer."

"So you think it was murder?" Slinky said.

"As I keep pointing out," Arthur said, "we need to look at the wound before we can make that determination. So the next order of business is recovering the body."

A series of small disturbances at the periphery of Slinky's vision indicated that his eye tic was acting up. He cleared his throat in three nervous blasts. "We don't do the recovery. The police do that. Have you called them yet?"

Greyson took a menacing step in Slinky's direction. "I told you; we are not going to have police crawling over this place. Suppose this was murder? It wouldn't just be the police. The Internal Investigative Organ has jurisdiction over crimes in a federal workplace. They'd have a field day.

Big time. They'd be in here for months demanding access to all sorts of things, unspooling their crime scene tape and blocking off our access while they pawed through our secrets. God knows who they'd choose as suspects. Probably all of us."

"Great," Slinky said. "The security system in the burn bag room will have a record of my entry. If we don't call the police now, that will look damned suspicious. You're talking about obstruction of justice. It doesn't matter whether it's suicide or murder. We can't cover it up."

"Maybe not, but we could divert attention." Greyson began to make slow circles in the air with his gloved hand, a characteristic gesture indicating that the wheels were turning, he was thinking, planning, scheming. He crossed the room, pivoted, and stopped. Slowly a smile spread across his face. "All right, listen to this." Greyson's hand continued to circle. "We take Brick's paddle and his canoe and throw them into the Potomac. Arthur, you call in one of your paper experts and have him repair that tear in the suicide note where Brick stuck it on the trident. We put it in an envelope, address it to Alberta, and slip it in the office's outgoing mail. Meanwhile, we clean up and replace the carpeting tonight. Do you have more of this carpet, Slinky?"

"I always keep an inventory of carpet and padding, but—"

"Good." Greyson took off pacing again. He spoke faster. "Tomorrow morning Daphne comes in. She waits for Brick a while, and then calls Security. We let them muck around a bit looking for him; then we point out that Brick's paddle is missing and suggest they go down and check his canoe. That puts the focus of operations on the river. Eventually, the canoe shows up in the river somewhere, but they never find the body."

"But maybe Alberta has already called the police," Slinky said. "She might have called when Brick didn't come home last night. She must have called Security already."

Greyson's lips slid into a sleazy grin. "Alberta is at my place, asleep. She told Brick she was at an offsite."

Slinky threw up a little into his mouth.

"Ugh," Arthur said. Greyson's decades-long affair with Alberta was an open secret on the seventh floor. Even Brick knew. "Ugh" was the universal reaction to it.

"Won't they look for Brick's footprints going down to the water?" Slinky asked.

"They will and they will find them." Greyson went to a cabinet, opened the door, and pulled out Brick's gym bag. He unzipped it and rifled the contents until he located a key attached to a bottle opener. "The canoe is chained to a tree. This is the key to the padlock." Greyson dug in the bag again. "His Tevas are in here and all the clothes we need. Huey is about the same size and weight as Brick. We dress him up, give him the paddle, and send him down to the river. He puts the canoe in the water and paddles downstream a bit." Greyson paused, thinking. "Arthur, how do we get him out of the water without leaving a trace?"

"We have him take off the shoes and throw them in the river. If they're found, all the better. Then he abandons the canoe and swims to the rocks under Chain Bridge, where we have a car waiting to pick him up."

Slinky's breath came faster, even his tic seemed to speed up. "No," he said. "Stop. Think about what you're doing. You guys are getting in the zone. I've seen it before. You get so caught up in your schemes you forget everything else: legality, morality, consequences, common sense. You're so caught up in what you can do that you forget to ask whether or not you should do it. I say no."

Greyson pointed a finger at Slinky. "This, asshole, is why you're head of admin. No imagination."

"And what about the body?" Slinky asked.

Arthur took off his glasses and began to clean them with a chamois he kept in his pocket. "We can send a camera down, figure out exactly where it hung up. We could use a grappling hook to get it out." Arthur stopped wiping. "No, that might spread his DNA around too much. I think it would be better to get a pole and jab at it until it falls to the burn room. It will land in the dumpster. We cover it with a tarp and wheel it to Medical." Arthur put his glasses back on. "I'll call in a doctor I trust to do a discreet autopsy."

"But what do we do with the body?" Slinky said. "We can't just throw it into the river after we've done an autopsy."

"Cremate it," Greyson said. "Throw it in with the burn bags. Who would know?"

"Don't you think Brick deserves a decent funeral?" Slinky said.

"Nah, he was an asshole." Greyson swiped his tongue over his lips. He was up to his elbows in intrigue and having a ball.

"I agree completely," Arthur said. "This is no time for sentimentality. Look, Slinky, this is a done deal. You don't get a vote. You want to call in the police? As you said, there's an electronic record of your entry into the burn bag room."

"You told me to go down there."

"That's not what we would tell the police," Greyson

said.

"Of course, not," Arthur said.

"Fine." The resignation was heavy in Slinky's voice. "I'll change out the carpet. I want you to know that I hate you guys."

"We hate you, too, Slinky," Greyson said. "Sincerely, we do."

5

Back in Kansas

Leaving Slinky, I slide back into a skull as comfortable as a rump-sprung recliner. It is my own three-dimensional, pre-concrete skull. I want to breathe a sigh of relief, put up my feet, and have two fingers of Scotch, but I realize that I'm just a visitor now, a parasite. I can't control a thing. All I can do is watch while the past repeats itself.

It was dark. My lids were shut. A soft, familiar hand grabbed my shoulder and squeezed. I didn't respond, so she squeezed again, this time with her fingernails biting my flesh. My eyes popped open to see my wife Esther bent over me. Her skin, still embossed with the pattern of the chenille bedspread, was already washed and dusted with powder. Her beryl eyes, magnified by bifocals, were sharp and unforgiving. I glanced at the digital clock on my bedside table. It gave both the hour and the day: 5:53 a.m. of the day after Brick's suicide. As yet, I knew nothing about it.

Esther was always up first, even though she had never worked outside the home. Things had been strained between us of late, but she still rose before dawn, turned the radio to a morning talk show, and made my breakfast—bacon, eggs, toast, and juice. If you had tried to tell her that there were other foods that could serve as breakfast, she would have asked, "Why?" My wife was a key factor behind my cholesterol and heart problems, but I don't blame her. After all, it wasn't my heart that killed me.

"Shelby." Esther's voice had an edge. She would cut me no slack.

I always awoke like a reluctant third grader, whiny and argumentative. I looked at the clock again. "I have seven more minutes," I said.

"Greyson Earl is on the phone."

"If ever there was a reason to go back to bed, that's it. Tell him I'm in the shower. I'll call him back later." I pulled the cover over my head.

Esther tugged it off again. "He says it's urgent." She thrust the receiver into my hand. We had the good old-fashioned type of phone. I refused to relinquish it for one of those new ones that do everything but reliably convey a clear conversation, which is the only goddamn reason to have a phone.

"What the hell do you want?" I growled into the receiver. Esther frowned and wagged her finger at me. She hated when I was rude. She didn't understand that with Greyson, rudeness was a necessity.

"We have a problem here," Greyson said.

"When is there not a problem there?" I asked. "I suppose you want me to get in early."

"On the contrary, it would be better if you took a sick day. Or two. We'll handle it."

"What's going on?" I asked.

"Trust me, Shel. The day will come when you will

thank me for this. Go back to bed. Sleep off whatever you drank for dinner last night."

Of course, I should have questioned him further. I should have gone to work to see for myself. I should have done this and I should have done that. Instead, I hung up and told my wife I wasn't feeling well. She didn't believe me, but she went out to the living room and called Thelma for me anyway. Thelma was already at work. She lived way out in the suburbs and came to work before dawn to avoid the traffic. I heard Esther talking softly for some time. They were probably plotting against me for my own good. The alliance between my wife and secretary annoyed me no end.

I went back to sleep. An hour later, Esther shook me awake again, despite my efforts to ignore her. "Shelby, the phone."

"I don't want to talk to Greyson."

"It's not Greyson. It's the hospice. The nurse says she doesn't have much more time. You have to go."

So I hauled ass out of bed and flew to Kansas City.

It was the fourth time I had stood at the entrance to a tunnel I call the "cancer tube." I watched my maternal grandmother and grandfather, my older sister, and now my mother slide down to a subterranean river smelling of bodily fluids and antiseptic. I always pictured the tube as being made of a pale rubbery latex, damp and dripping inside, throbbing with pain, feverish, but with a cold wind blowing through. It always unnerved me to stand at the mouth of that tunnel looking in.

Now I am well down the tunnel, looking out. I am in

my mother's head—a fearsome place full sharp edges and shadow.

She was trying to focus on my face, but it floated oddly in her field of vision.

I had rushed to her side out of guilt. I knew I wouldn't mourn Beulah Wexler when she died. She was a sour, hypercritical, doom junkie. She fretted endlessly over the possibility of electric fires, theft, pandemic, fraud, tornados, termites, terrorism, dry rot, drought, and insect infestations. Oddly, she never spoke of cancer, the thing that so devastated our family. She continued to worry over other things, even as one tumor coiled around her esophagus and others bloomed on her liver.

In her last waking hours, my mother was strangely obsessed with Brick Mason's suicide. "They'll drag you off to jail for killing him," she said in a cracked voice. "Then who will take care of me?"

I saw a look of impatience come over my blurry face. "I didn't kill him, Ma. I've told you that. He killed himself out on the river. It was in the newspapers."

"He didn't," my mother said with more strength than I thought she had. "I know what happened. I know."

"I've got the newspaper right here, Ma." I picked up the local paper from the floor. "Here, let me read it to you:

MISSING SPY CHIEF'S CANOE, SUICIDE NOTE FOUND

AP, Langley, Virginia, 20 September. Late Tuesday afternoon, local authorities found a canoe belonging to Brian "Brick" Mason, head of the Central Intelligence Agency, washed up on the right bank of the Potomac, near Roosevelt Island. Authorities confirmed that a suicide note was sent to his wife, but declined to release its contents. Sources in the intelligence community say that a security camera caught pictures of Mason leaving the compound via the George Washington Parkway exit. He was on foot, dressed in river gear, and carrying a paddle. The gate was locked and unmanned at that hour, but a member of Mason's security detail admitted to opening it for Mason. The Mines declined to release the name of the security guard.

I put the newspaper down. "See, Ma? He committed suicide."

"Bullshit," she said. "You murdered him. They'll drag you off to jail, and then who will take care of me?"

My blurry face kept repeating, "Don't worry, Mom, I'll take care of you," until her eyes closed.

Toward evening, my mother's lids opened again. This time my face through her eyes was more floaty and indistinct. She roused herself enough to accuse me of being a vulture waiting to get her money when she died. "But you have none, Mom," I told her. "I've been paying your bills for years." She used her waning strength to ream me out for my ingratitude, disrespect, and insolence. Then she found my Achilles heel. "You ruined my grandson," she said. "It was your fault." From her eyes, I watch the living Shelby suck in his lips and bite back the pain. Her eyelids closed, and all I see is the dull red of the light shining through the thin veil of flesh.

I had counted her breaths: twelve per minute, still

normal although they had removed the feeding tube two days earlier. I longed to be out of the room, to get away from that dreadful sucking cancer tube that I feared would be my own destiny. I wanted to see life as the stuff flowing up through a tree—able to branch and spread. Instead, I inherited an immutable fatalism that saw life as a long, straight tunnel, shrinking to the cancer tube.

We were in the University of Kansas Hospital, where other family members had died. The last one was my sister, who succumbed to breast cancer in room four doors down from my mother's room. For the first time, I had no one else to wait alongside me. Blood relations were dead or estranged, and Esther stayed in Virginia because my mother hated her, called her "the Jesus freak." So I waited alone.

At two a.m., my mother's eyes popped open. I was just a fuzzy blob in the corner, illuminated by a book light. I was reading *The Jewel in the Crown*. I had first read it by flashlight sitting on a sack of Hollytone behind the furnace in our basement, where I retreated from the parental discord. I read it so many times that the smells of fertilizer and curry were linked in my mind. It's the book that ignited my fascination with India and foreign affairs and set my sights on a career in the Mines. I snapped it shut when I realized that my mother was awake.

She paid me no attention. I was just a blob in the background. Another face was moving into view: my dead sister.

I remember how my mother's head abruptly rose from the pillow as if someone had jerked a string attached to her nose. Her eyes fixed on what I had thought was an empty space behind the IV pole. I see now it was Norma standing there, clearer and more in focus than me. It was the teenage Norma, a slight, dull-eyed girl with lank hair and vicious acne.

My mother began to speak in a querulous growl. "You left me," she said. "You abandoned me, so don't you show up now with apologies." Poor Norma, she was so cowed by my mother that she never left home, got married, or lived. "Don't use that tone of voice on me, I'm not senile," my mother said. Her hand rose a bit from the blanket, pointing at my sister. Beulah Wexler liked to point at her children, aiming that long index finger between the eyes. As a child, I imagined it spinning like a drill. She loved the expression "drill it into your head," as in "I'm going to make you understand even if I have to drill it into your head."

Norma cringed as my mother's voice crackled in the gloom. The separation between Ma's words grew as the night wore on. She spoke to Norma, to her own mother, to my father, but mainly to Norma, who was her favorite child, although you wouldn't know it to hear my mother's side of the conversation. "Norma ... stand up straight ... you look like a hunched crone ... you plan to wear that ... to my funeral? Slovenly. So disrespectful."

Wendy entered the room with a cart. She was my favorite of all of the amazing nurses who worked on the Hospice floor. She maintained a positive attitude in the face of an entire ward of patients slipping toward death—like skipping across a California hillside during a mudslide. She had been at it for fifteen years, yet cheer shone from her heavily freckled face, with its broad, high cheekbones, and wide-set eyes.

All my mother saw was a looming shadow that blocked her view of her firstborn. "Norma," she said as she tried to look past the shadow, "It's time for my funeral."

Wendy took mother's hand. "You head for the light. It's okay to go now, honey. Nothing left to be done. Nothing else to cross off the list. Just go toward that pretty light and everything will be heavenly."

Mother closed her eyes. Her breathing continued. I had counted the breaths as I held my watch under my book light. Twenty breaths per minute, each one rasping and awful. She opened her eyes and this time she looked at me. "You ruined Edward," she said. She saw the distress on my face and said again, "You ruined him." Her lids closed and her loud, ragged breath abruptly stopped. Grotesque shapes flickered before her eyes. A moment later her breathing started again. One, two, three more breaths. Then nothing.

Through my mother's eyes, I look for the light but see only darkness.

6

The Interregnum

I'm almost happy to see the polygraph room. As much as I hate this place, at least there's no blood on the floor, no corpses. No, I'm wrong again. There are two corpses, Virgil and I.

"Why don't you play dead like a good stiff?" I ask.

"You wish." He begins to crack his knuckles. I jump at the first crack because it's too loud, as if artificially magnified. Nine more cracks reverberate in the small room.

"You have sound effects now?" I say.

"I have whatever I need to get at the truth." Virgil crosses his legs, leans back in his chair, and studies my face for some time. Perhaps he's waiting for me to start sweating and has forgotten that I can no longer do so. I glare back, but this only amuses him.

"So, you came back from your mother's funeral and you didn't ask questions. The whole world was talking about Brick's suicide, except for Shelby Wexler, who shrugged and had nothing to say. That's amazing."

"You make it all sound so sinister," I say. "It was just ... I went into a sort of depression after I buried my mother."

"Get off it. You didn't miss her."

"No," I admit, "but I lost interest in things, couldn't see the point of anything anymore."

He nods. "You got a strong whiff of mortality and the smell turned your stomach."

"Yes. That's exactly what happened to me."

"You wish," Virgil says. "We both know what really happened to you, but we won't go into that now. You're not ready to face it. Let's go back to the machine, Shelby." He scoots his chair over to the polygraph. The wooden legs screech against the floor like amplified chalk on a blackboard. He waits with pencil poised ready to mark two points: the one where his question ends and the one where my response begins.

"Shelby," he says, "would anyone in your office have any reason to say that you were so out of your gourd drunk and depressed that you wouldn't know your asshole from a hole in the ground, much less guess what had transpired in the BOM's office?"

"Oh, come on," I say. "That's not fair."

"You're looking for fairness?" Virgil's naked brows arch into a series of folds. "Seriously? You think you deserve fairness?"

"I think every human being deserves fairness."

"Actually, they don't." Virgil repeats his earlier question, and I respond with a meek "yes."

"Shelby, did you ask any questions aimed at getting to the truth of the situation?"

I push back for some stupid reason. "Look, Virgil, you know how it is in the Mines. It's rude to ask people questions that you know they can't answer, that will force them to lie. Haven't we had enough of this? Why are we focusing on Brick? When are you going to tell me about the Mines attack? What happened to Thelma?"

"Patience, Shelby. You have somewhere else to go? Yes or no."

"No." I slump in my seat.

"Sit up straight, Shelby. You're pulling the wires. There. Now, where were we? Brick. Let's jump ahead. The police, needless to say, didn't find a body. No one noticed the slight charred-Spam smell coming from the Mines burn facility two days after the disappearance. Meanwhile, Brick's apparent suicide was red meat for media hounds and conspiracy theorists. They couldn't get enough of speculation, the wilder, the better. They kept bringing up the fact that Brick was the second Boss of Mines to drown during a canoe ride. They tried to draw a connection between Brick's death and Carnaby's, but sometimes a coincidence is just a coincidence. What exactly happened on that last canoe ride? Maybe Brick put down the paddle and stuck a gun in his mouth." Virgil forms a pistol with his hand and mimes the act. I see his uvula glisten as he pulls the "gun" out. He swipes his moist finger across the Mines seal on his shirt and continues. "Or maybe Brick slit his wrists and bled out into the river. Or maybe he downed vodka and pills and jumped over the side. Or maybe he was abducted by terrorists or Iranians or Iraqis or Taleban or Chechen extremists or Russians or anti-government activists or an old rival in the Mines itself, or hell, maybe it was aliens. Some loony reported seeing Brick splitting a sausage pizza with Elvis in Dupont Circle."

"Why are you going on about this?" I ask. "As far as I can tell, Brick's death had nothing to do with the attack that killed me."

"But it did," Virgil says. "One thing always leads to

another. An alchemist ought to know something as simple as that. Brick's death gave the terrorists their opening. It led to a longer interregnum than usual. Interregnum. It was one of you alchemists who taught me that one. I don't usually go for the high-priced vocabulary words, but I like that one. It sounds like interrectum, which would be the space between assholes, which is exactly what an interregnum is." He laughs. The heeping and snorting continue for some time. Virgil is bowled over by his own lame joke. Finally, he arrives at his point. "The interregnum is a dangerous time at the Mines, isn't it? Things slip through the cracks. It was particularly dangerous in this situation since Brick had no deputy at the time of his death. When did old George Fellows croak? About two weeks before Brick died, wasn't it? Had a heart attack standing in front of the vending machine. They found a mashed Ho Ho under his body. Downright funny the way some people die, isn't it? I mean you getting flattened like a squirrel on the pavement? Hilarious." He laughs again.

I listen to the infernal heeping and snorting and wonder what I've done to merit this hell. Then I remember that I will probably find out, and I sink deeper into depression.

Virgil finally gets hold of himself. "So, anyway, after Brick disappeared, it was Greyson Earl who was running things until a new President was in place to appoint a new BOM. And Greyson was preoccupied with covering up the true circumstances of Brick's death."

"Okay, we both know all of this, Virgil. You're just playing with me like a cat with a fat, dead mouse. Eventually, you'll swallow me whole. Will you just tell me what happened during the interregnum to set the wheels in motion? Did the Mines hire someone we shouldn't have?

Did a terrorist penetrate our defenses?"

"Would you like to meet him?" Virgil asks with a smile so sweet and dead that it lowers the temperature of my corpse another ten degrees.

I feel a shiver in the void. "No, I would not."

Loop

The first thing I smell doesn't say "terrorist" to me. It's what they like to call "product" these days. The word covers a range of substances that I, for one, would never use or abuse even if I still possessed my own naturally greasy hair. Ridiculous, pricey froth. Smells citrusy like something you would rub into furniture or dollop on a fruit salad. Other odors begin to intrude: stale smoke, men's cologne, beer, sweat. I have no idea whose head I've landed in until the odors pull a word from my memory: Loop. Short for Fruit Loop.

Loop was the nickname the bomb dissectors in the Counterterrorism Unit gave to Gordy Grant. Grant was the Internal Investigative Organ's liaison to the CU until he made a few critical errors: compromising a safe house, removing classified documents from the building, being caught after hours with his pants down on a conference table with a summer intern who was the daughter of the head of the unit. And he had a camera set up to film it, which in the view of the Mines, if not the head of CU, was the worst offense. Photographic equipment was strictly forbidden inside Headquarters.

Yes, Gordy was a piece of work. The Mines kicked him out of the building and insisted that the Organ fire him. If not for that, the Organ probably would have fired him, but they kept him on just to piss off the Mines. They did demote him to a humiliatingly low-level position. Everyone thought that would make him leave, but he stayed on.

He was sitting at a small round table in the corner of a dimly lit bar. No, not a bar, this was a British pub. Dark wood dominated the room from the coffered ceiling to the paneled walls and furnishings. The wood had the patina of real age and not the faux age you find in American reproductions of a British pub. A bright light concentrated on a mirrored wall lined with bottles. A dimmer bulb lit a vitrine of pork pies, Scotch eggs, and other ungodly dense and tasteless examples of British fare. That left the rest of the place, with its handful of working-class customers, in shadow. If any doubt remained as to the location of the bar, the pint of beer sitting on the table in front of Gordy was bereft of condensation. It was genuine warm British beer.

A crack of light split the opposite wall as a man entered. He dressed like a middle manager but wore his hair rather long, covering his ears. It had an incongruous sixties pop look to it that matched nothing else about his person. His ethnic origin was likely the Indian subcontinent. The expression on his face had a practiced, pleasant blankness. The man pointed at a slice of something unidentifiable in the vitrine and sat down with it to read a newspaper.

Gordy moved quickly, grabbing his pint, crossing the room, and slipping into the chair opposite the newcomer.

A streak of pure malevolence flashed in the man's

eyes, but he extinguished it with a blink. "I don't believe I know you," he said in a clipped, ice-cold British accent.

"I know you, Fahad, and we have an important goal in common, one I can help you achieve."

"I can't imagine anything in my life that would require that help of an American. Who are you?" This time the man injected his words with venom, but there was no mistaking the trapped-animal panic in his eyes.

Gordy's voice went syrupy and soothing. "I'm a man who hates the same place you hate. A man who would like to see it crumble. A man who spent two years inside those walls taking notes, taking pictures, fantasizing about bringing the place down. I have the knowledge. You have the means. I know someone with influence and money. You need money right now, don't you? You lost your main donor."

"If this is some sort of trap—" Fahad tensed up as if to run, but what would be the use?

Gordy took a sip of his beer, playing it cool even though he was sitting opposite a man with mass murder in his heart. "With what I know I could have had you and your friends arrested ten times over. You've been so careful to act the part of the perfectly assimilated Paki, right down to your choice of eating establishments." Gordy's gesture encompassed the room. "But everyone slips up now and then. You should thank me. I got the information first and kept it out of the hands of the Mines' Counterterrorism Unit."

Fahad's leaned in and whispered, "Where did you get this so-called information?"

"All you need to know is that working with me is not optional for you. You shouldn't resist. I can help you get the screamers where they need to go."

Fahad's eyes went dark. "Don't even say that word. If you really want to help us, don't use that word."

"Fine. I won't say it, but we're working together."

"I could have you killed."

"Then the people who investigated my death would find out all about you. I've arranged it that way."

"I'm supposed to trust you?"

"Yes, and don't even think of aborting the operation or leaving the country."

Sweat glossed Fahad's face. He swallowed whatever answer was forming on his lips and gave Gordy a hostile, penetrating glare that would have terrified any sane man.

Whether Gordy was a sane man or not was clearly in doubt. He reached inside his jacket and pulled out a computer disk in an unlabeled cardboard sleeve. He pushed it across the table. "I want you to trust me, to get on with the operation as before but with better information, access, and funding. Watch this. It will reassure you. If the contents went public, I'd be fired and disgraced. I'm willingly giving you leverage over me so you'll carry through with this thing. It's that important to me."

Fahad picked up the disk. "What's on it?"

"Myself and a couple of lady friends and a former IIO agent who is now in jail for espionage. You'll see. I have unusual sexual tastes."

Fahad dropped the disk as if it had burned his fingers.

"You don't have a choice here," Gordy said. "Go home and think about it. If you take me up on my offer, I have another disk for you, one with photographs taken inside the building that will help you with your project." Gordy drained his pint and stood up. "I'll be in touch."

When I get back to the polygraph room, I have a few questions for Virgil, but I only get to ask one. "So who was this influential man Gordy was talking about?"

Virgil grins. "A member of Congress. Would you like to meet him?"

I hesitate long enough for Virgil to change his mind. I can see another idea sparking dull red in the back of his pupils. The man is easily distracted, like a child with Attention Deficit Disorder. Instead of an orderly tour of the events leading up to the attack on Mines Headquarters, I'm getting Mr. Toad's Wild Ride. No telling where he will send me next.

"No," he says, "I've changed my mind. That can wait. I'm going to put you back in your own head."

8

The Raven

I was growling. The 337 budget request form in my hand had turned my afternoon sour. I glanced at the figure at the bottom of the page, then the signature of the requester. Maddie James had her nerve. The infernal woman hadn't been back in the building for a full day and she was already making ridiculous demands. I crumpled the form into a ball. I wanted to fling it across the room, but the blasted thing was classified. I stuffed it into a burn bag instead.

"Jesus fucking Christ," I said too loudly.

From the outer office, Thelma called, "Watch your language!"

What was the point of holding one of the highest positions in the Mines, if you were still going to be treated like a child by all the women in your life?

Nothing good could come of having Maddie James back in the Mines. She was wounded, dangerous, and fanatical. She was the bomb dissector who should have stopped the Stadium Attack. She had sounded a warning before the attacks, but she couldn't provide a time and place. She and her "canary crew" came close, but they couldn't pull everything together in time.

A pain shot through my head, and I pinched the bridge of my nose hard. The Stadium Attack. Those three words alone were enough to cause extreme distress to anyone in the Mines. As if to rub our faces in it, the Mines Fine Arts and Historical Preservation Committee or MFAHPC (pronounced em-fop-see) had put up an exhibit. At the morning meeting Greyson, the Acting BOM, had decreed that we Horsemen must go see it by close of business. I looked at my watch. I couldn't put it off any longer.

"Thelma," I called. "I'm going downstairs."

The MFAHPC put on its periodic exhibits in one of the broad, first-floor tunnels. I hated all of their damn exhibits. History didn't need dramatic lighting and poignant captions. It was devastating enough on its own.

I hurried past a collection of grim artifacts, dramatically lighted and artfully displayed. They included passport photos of the terrorists, a section of bent fencing, and other items trampled by the crowd. Some furnishings and computer equipment from the terrorists' living quarters completed the display.

The exhibit completely ignored the political aftermath of the attack. The Administration quickly labeled the thing a highly-sophisticated chemical attack and blamed it on Iran. They pointed to a Mines report proving the link. The US almost went to war over it.

It was Maddie who outed the faked report before the Mines Oversight Committee. Well, technically it was her boss, but Maddie made it happen. The resulting scandal turned the national political landscape toward the left. It ruined careers and drove Brick Mason to suicide.

To punish us, the MOC insisted that Maddie James

be Mines Chief of Alternative Alchemy. She was as welcome as Typhoid Mary. As I passed through the exhibit, I couldn't banish the image of her sitting before the MOC, calmly sticking a knife deep into the heart of the Mines.

I was not entirely unsympathetic to Maddie. I admired her courage in taking on the powers that be, but at the same time I felt she had damaged her employer more than necessary in the process. And damaging the Mines was the same as threatening national security. She didn't need to make such a public spectacle of her revelations. It was spite on her part.

At the time, I was Boss of Congressional Affairs. I spent my days fielding angry phone calls and threats from the Hill. I jumped to fulfill requests. I spoke softly, humbly. I promised and cajoled. Nevertheless, I began to doubt that the Mines would come through the storm intact.

Then the Mines chose a scapegoat. The BOWM, Sharon Pendergast, fell on her sword and resigned. Brick chose me to take her place. It was the job I had aimed for my entire career. I occupied it for less than a week when my son ...

But no, I will never use Edward as an excuse for my bad behavior. I started drinking to excess, and it was my fault.

I would need to drink more than ever with Maddie James back in the building. I had done my best to delay her return. I had Security slow down her reinvestigation. I took my time about finding her office space. But I couldn't put off the inevitable forever. She now sat in the smallest office on the seventh floor. It was a former utility closet.

I passed through a doorway cut through a gigantic photograph of carnage. Suddenly Maddie James was there in the flesh, standing before the last image in the exhibit: a screen capture of the Stadium Attack's first and youngest victim, taken right before she died.

Maddie was as still as that little girl in the photo, frozen in time. Maddie looked older than I remembered. Her sharp-boned face was slack, and her eyes glistened. She looked like a widow at a funeral in her plain black suit. I grew still watching her, even as my instincts told me to get away from her as quickly as possible. The strangeness of her posture held me transfixed. The woman had always been a perpetual motion machine. Now she was slump-shouldered and broken.

"*One too many terrorist attacks,*" I said to myself. "*One too many attacks she didn't stop.*" I made a mental note to request an appointment with a psychiatrist in Medical to talk about the long-term impact of stress on the bomb dissectors.

The Strikes will always be yesterday in the Mines. The Stadium Attack will always be yesterday in the Mines. A good alchemist must maintain a cold, objective mind. Maddie's brain was overheated and weary. How could anyone trust her? She had grown too emotional, too unreliable. She was a wounded animal who would thrash around and damage God knows what in the process.

At last, Maddie broke her stillness and took a gulp of air. She turned around and saw me, lunged for me. I turned and fled as fast as my stiff knees could carry me.

Virgil leans back on two legs of his chair and gives me a look filled with amusement, scorn, and accusation. "You underestimated Maddie."

"She was too emotional to do her job," I say.

"You underestimate emotion. It has its uses."

"Emotion doesn't belong in the Mines."

"As if you could banish it," Virgil says. "Wasn't it emotion that made you flee from Maddie? That doesn't seem like a rational way to behave."

"Fleeing Maddie James was completely rational."

"Let's examine why you can't deal with emotion, with pathos. Your mother liked to club you over the head with it, didn't she? She loved to talk about her feelings and how you hurt them."

"Are you saying that my ignoring Maddie had more to do with my mother issues than with the fact that she was teetering on the edge of breakdown? That's ridiculous."

"I love it when the subject uses the word 'ridiculous.' I suppose I could quiz you on your mother issues, but that would be boring and it would take way too long. Instead, let's return to Gordy's influential friend. I think you'll be surprised."

The Influential Friend and the Unwitting Source of Funding

I am in an old and angry vessel. It smells strongly of men's cologne, Listerine, and Werther's candy—all of which don't quite cover the sour stench of decay. I hear blood rushing like a storm-swollen stream, beating a loud, arhythmical tune as it courses over rough deposits of plaque. A vicious clacking and sucking suggest that the teeth are false. I am looking through thick, silver-framed glasses, but they are smudged, and this man's eyesight is poor. Still, surroundings come slowly into focus: heavy polished furnishings and a wall crammed with photos of important-looking men shaking hands with other important-looking men. From the tall ceilings and style of architecture, I realize I'm in a Senate office building, perhaps the Rayburn.

The windows were dark, and the quiet oppressive. A large flat-screen flashed with the gaudy red, white, and blue graphics of election night coverage, but the sound was muted. The face of the Democratic candidate appeared on the screen, and a caption indicated that he was the new President Elect of the United States.

A gavel spun toward the screen and hit the corner, knocking it cockeyed. A high-decibel squawk split the silence. A magnificent white bird swept across the room, circled back, and landed atop the television, facing toward the back. It squatted and shat a greenish, viscid glob that slid down the blinking election map of the United States, roughly following the course of the Mississippi. The creature turned, lowered his fluffy head and cocked one eye at my host. I never knew a beaked face could express such sympathy.

"You do understand, don't you, Dirksen?" my host said. "Good boy. I couldn't get through this without you."

I recognize my host now: Senator Harrison Westerly, head of the MOC or Mines Oversight Committee. Dirksen, the bird, had achieved almost as much fame as his owner. He was a bare-eyed cockatoo. With his white pompadour and wrinkled eye rings, he did, indeed, bear a strong resemblance to his namesake, the late Senator Everett Dirksen, a Republican far more moderate than Harrison Westerly.

Dirksen, the bird, had a bad reputation for biting anyone who was not the senator. Three of his victims had sued Westerly but, fortunately, all of them were low-level staffers who agreed on a modest settlement. Dirksen seemed to know better than to bite someone important, like a donor or a lobbyist. Still, numerous efforts had been made to ban the bird from the Rayburn Building, but Westerly had overcome them all. He had owned Dirksen for nearly 30 years, and he would not be separated from his bird.

Westerly stretched out his arm. Dirksen flew over and landed. He lowered his head and closed his eyes. Knotty fingers gently ruffled the bird's feathers, then Dirksen pushed his head into the cupped hand and made a noise somewhere between the purr of a cat and the coo of a pigeon.

"A tragic night," Westerly said to the bird, "and it's all the Mines' fault. Bunch of amateurs, getting caught like they did with their pants down, taking the administration with them, poisoning the party's chances. We would be celebrating tonight, if not for them. Now instead of celebrating ..." He choked, pulled a handkerchief from his pocket, and ran it across his eyes. It came away damp.

A black void and a hollow rush indicate the passage of time. When the view opens up again, I'm in the same place, the same vessel.

The senator's office had been decorated for Christmas with live pine bows, white candles, and red ribbons. A patch of pale gray winter sky showed at the window.

Senator Westerly turned to his bird, and Dirksen cocked his head. "Time for your training session." Westerly's efforts to train the cockatoo were a running joke on the Hill. He had spent years trying to teach Dirksen to quote his namesake and say, "A billion here, a billion there, and pretty soon you're talking about real money." Unfortunately, cockatoos are not as linguistically gifted as African Greys. Dirksen only got as far as, "Biwyon here, biwyon there, and pretty bird. Pretty, pretty, pretty bird."

"Let's practice," Westerly said. "Can you say the one about guns? Come on, guns ..."

"Guns kiw peepee," Dirksen responded.

"No," Westerly said. "Guns *don't* kill people. *People* kill people. Try it again. It's important that you get it right."

"Guns kiw peepee."

"No, Dirksen. Listen to Daddy. Guns *don't* kill people. *People* kill people."

"Guns kiw peepee." Dirksen added an earsplitting squawk for emphasis.

"Do you want the nut? Listen. Guns don't kill people. People kill people. Pee-pul, not pee-pee."

"Guns kiw peepee," Dirksen said.

The secretary's voice came over the intercom. "Senator, Dashiell Aspling is here to see you."

"Send him in." Westerly searched in his pocket and found a pine nut. Dirksen flapped and lunged to get it. "Be a good birdie," the senator whispered. "Daddy has a big bill he needs to pay."

"Biwyon here, biwyon there, and pretty bird! Pretty, pretty, pretty bird!" Dirksen screamed.

Aspling entered. He was a slight figure with a head like a light bulb. Like many men these days, he had decided that a shaved head had more dignity than a bald spot and fringe. It was a bad choice for him because it emphasized his prominent ears and protuberant eyes. He resembled a particularly ugly Chihuahua.

"Hello, Senator."

"Dashiell, good to see you." Westerly moved forward with hand extended, but the handshake was aborted when Dirksen took off and flew at Aspling's head. His talons grazed the shiny pate; then the bird banked and landed on the American flag in the corner. He clung to the field of blue stars, squawking.

Westerly let forth a wheezing laugh as Aspling crouched with his hands protecting his head. "Oh, he won't hurt you. He just likes to buzz people to see them jump. Have a seat. Relax. He usually only does it once."

Aspling rubbed his head and then examined his fingers. "Blood," he said.

"Oh, it's just a scratch." The senator dismissed it with a wave. "Buck up. If you want to get that job you're lusting after, you can't be afraid of a little blood or a little bird. Dirksen, come to Daddy." The bird squawked and swooped down from the flag to land on the senator's arm. Westerly ruffled the feathers on Dirksen's head, then crossed the room and held the bird out to Dashiell. "Here, you try. Go ahead. Scratch his head."

Dashiell swallowed, and his protuberant eyes widened, but he reached out with a hand that shook only slightly. He touched Dirksen, and the bird closed his eyes and cooed. Dashiell smiled in surprise as he ran a finger back and forth over Dirksen's pompadour. "He likes me."

"Cockatoos are the great lovers of the bird world." The Senator let Dashiell give the bird a good scratch, and then he placed Dirksen on his desktop gym and gave him another pine nut.

Dashiell planted his narrow ass in a leather wingback, cleared his throat, and got to business. "You have a tough primary coming up next year, Senator. First time you've had a viable opponent in years. And he's heir to the Keating Oil fortune. Deep pockets. Deep."

A phlegmy growl rose in Westerly's throat. "Glib son of a bitch with a family wholesome enough to rot your teeth. The other day he had the gall to call me 'the five-times-divorced senator.' But I'll still bury him."

Dashiel tilted his head. "That's not a sure thing." An oily glimmer came into his eyes, and his voice grew seductive. "But it could be. I can funnel you all the money you need through a couple of 501-cs."

The senator sucked loudly on his dentures. "Forget

the 501-Cs. I just want the money delivered into an off-shore account."

Aspling's tongue shot over his upper lip. "Are you sure? If you want the money for your re-election, it's cleaner to—"

"What I want the money for is none of your business. Do you have the amount we discussed?"

"Yes," Dashiell said, "But first, why do you think you can still deliver me the job I want given the political sea change? Surely the new president will ignore any recommendation you make."

Westerly fished a nail clipper out of his pocket and went to work on a ragged thumbnail. "I'm working on a deal with the new president's transition team."

Dashiell's face popped to full Chihuahua alert. "How can you work with them? I thought this country was way too polarized for cooperation."

"We're still capable of cooperation, but no one can know about it. In this instance, I can cut a deal because I have something they want badly."

Dashiell's eyes went wide. "What?" he asked.

Westerly raised a finger in the air and waited until Aspling focused on it. The senator said in a stage whisper, "The ability to turn two votes their way on their big banking reform bill."

Dashiell's face registered shock. "How could you vote for that piece of—"

"I won't vote for it, but I can strong-arm two guys in purple states to do the dirty work for me," the senator said. "We can repeal that piece of shit later when our numbers are stronger after midterms. You're a clever man to have never revealed your party affiliation publicly. I told them you were a private industry wizard, who would step in and reform the failing institution that allowed the Stadium Attack to happen. They're willing to take you to get their bill passed, as well as to get an easy confirmation under their belts in the first hundred days."

A smile spread over Dashiell's face.

The senator's finger waved again. "Don't measure the office for curtains yet. There's one more thing I need from you."

"I'm giving you a shit ton of money, what else is there?"

Westerly reached into his pocket and pulled out a business card. "I need you to hire this company on a Mines contract. I'll give you the details later." He glanced down at the bright yellow card before he passed it to Aspling.

The would-be BOM read it out loud. "Kreative Industrial Sunlight Solutions." He shrugged and appeared relieved. "Sure, no problem."

10

An Unbelievably Short Meeting

Virgil pulls his chair so close I have to shift my knees to avoid touching his. He removes a toothpick from his shirt pocket, retracts his upper lip, and begins to probe between a chipped canine and a stained incisor. I look away in disgust.

"For God's sake, Virgil, you're dead. Why do you need to pick your teeth?"

"I don't, Shelby. It's just one more way to make you want to run screaming from the room. The polygraph doesn't work unless the subject wants to run screaming from the room. Unless the room and the experience itself become worse than the truth." He engages in his sickening heeping, snorting laugh. "Did you know that the most successful polygraphers are flatulent?" Virgil shifts to one buttock and farts, releasing a miasma of sewer and sulfur. All the while he continues to talk. "Where were we? Ah, yes. Senator Westerly and his fool of a BOM nominee. So, Shelby, during those long weeks when Dashiell Aspling was going through the confirmation process—which turned out not to be as smooth as Westerly promised—

what were you doing?"

"My job," I say.

Virgil is so close I can study the red, branching vessels in his eyes. His breath smells like road kill in the sun, a scent that mixes badly with the recent fart. "Really?" he says. "You were doing your job?"

"Halfway," I admit. I start to ramble. "I thought I was a short-timer. I guess I wanted to leave all the problems for the next BOWM to solve. I thought the new BOM would fire me first thing." I can feel a whine rising in my voice, despite my attempts to suppress it. "I was angry because I hadn't been the BOWM that long. It was the job I had always wanted. I ... didn't expect things to happen the way they did. Tragedy got in the way. I still had great things I wanted to do, but I had fallen into a sort of ... funk."

Virgil interrupts. "By 'funk,' you mean alcoholic stupor?"

I look over Virgil's shoulder and consider the sad sack staring back at me in the mirror. The bird spatter hovers over his head like Pigpen's dust cloud. I try to make a convincing argument. "Even drunk I'm smarter than ninety-nine percent of the population. I still functioned... more or less."

Virgil raises his naked brows. "Less, Shelby, especially in those last few months. Brick appointed you because he remembered the brilliant, high-minded Shelby, who gave a shit about his work. Then he realized what you'd become. By that time, he was too caught up with his own problems to do anything about it. Greyson didn't have to fire you because it was so easy to push you to the side. You didn't even question it."

"Question what? What questions should I have asked?"

Virgil hitches up the left corner of his mouth in an ugly smirk. "Here's one. Why did Greyson hold such short morning staff meetings?"

"Why would I question that? It was a blessing. The man ran a meeting efficiently. It was his one saving grace."

"So Greyson didn't love the sound of his own voice?"

"Of course, he did."

"Maybe he didn't like how his voice sounded in the BOM's office," Virgil says. "It's so quiet in there with the thick carpeting and wood panels. Quieter than anywhere else in HQ. Maybe he was reluctant to disturb the silence with that big voice of his."

I begin to feel acutely uncomfortable. "Of course, he wasn't. I imagine he loved the sound of his voice in that room. They all do."

"Yes, Shelby, they do. They love the sound of their own voice so much that they confuse it with truth itself. So why did Greyson hold such short meetings?"

"I don't know."

Virgil stands up. "I have to go talk to management."

The polygraph room disappears.

I know where I am immediately, and it is the last skull I would ever want to experience from the inside. It smells like freshly dry-cleaned wool, cigar smoke, and cat piss. There was always something feline about Greyson with his predatory gold eyes. He was sitting in the BOM's chair.

I have a view across an expansive mahogany desk decorated with "feelies," rat-sized wood sculptures made to fit in the hand. The feelies were rounded, abstract, slightly suggestive, custom-fit to Greyson's enormous paws.

He rubbed them, squeezed them, bobbled them, sniffed them, and occasionally threw them against a wall at high velocity. When the BOBM visited a foreign station, it was customary for the local service to offer a gift. The station would hint that a feelie in a rare native wood—preferably one high on the Janka hardness scale—would be the most appropriate offering. Greyson's eyes rolled over a collection that included Australian Buloke, Palo Santo, and Patagonian Rosewood.

Greyson picked up a feelie in a dark wood that might have been Ebony. He tossed it high and snatched it out of the air. A small movement caught his eye. He focused on the brass pendulum of an elaborate anniversary clock near his elbow. It was seven fifty-nine a.m. or one minute before the start of the morning staff meeting.

At precisely eight o'clock, Daphne ushered us into the office. There was no love lost between Greyson and Daphne, but he had kept her on as secretary because she was popular in the building. Since Brick's death, Daphne had been treated more gently than his actual widow, Alberta. Greyson would have been criticized for dumping her. The lingering look he gave her as she exited suggested that he didn't trust her.

Meanwhile, we settled in. Vince Novak, the Acting BOBM, was there, too. I looked terrible, even worse than I did at Brick's last happy hour. My face was the color of bologna left out in the rain. It was painfully clear that my mind was elsewhere.

Where? I wish I could remember.

I wonder why Virgil chose to send me back to this particular meeting. Greyson gave a quick rundown of the progress of Aspling's confirmation hearings, an operation in Africa, and the repaving of the blue and red parking lots. He wrapped this meeting up in less than fifteen minutes. I watch the relief wash over my face, and then the Horsemen left the room, with me taking up the rear.

Greyson scratched a thumbnail up and down the side of a feelie as he allowed enough time to pass for me to exit the front office, and then he hurled the thing across the room. It slammed into the door with a sound like a shot. A minute later Arthur and Slinky returned.

"I wish you would just fire the guy so we wouldn't have to go through this charade," Slinky said as he settled back down on the couch.

Greyson picked up another feelie and began to rotate it in his palm. "So you think we should have a new, more alert BOWM? No, Shelby is the perfect man for this situation. You've got to learn to think things through." Greyson focused on Arthur. "Have you come up with a device?"

Arthur took off his glasses and examined them for smudges. "I've got my best man on it. Al Dufresne. He said he could get it done by Friday. We don't have a cleared avian vet, but we have a general vet who thinks he can handle the surgery. We should be able to get it done while Westerly is fact-finding in Switzerland next week."

"Excellent," Greyson said.

I don't feel the heat, but the face in the mirror blushes. "Did they do that every day?" I ask Virgil.

"Yes, they did, Shelby. You didn't suspect a thing, did you? Not until it all came out in the Welcome Wagon briefing."

Even without a real body, I feel unwell, unmoored. Little by little, my image of myself is crumbling—a second death. Coming so soon after the first, it's hard to take. I had never dreamed I was so deluded. I thought of myself as pragmatic, down-to-earth, and clear-sighted. I prided myself that—unlike the other Horsemen—I saw with eyes unclouded by overweening arrogance. But I didn't have a clue.

Virgil clasps his hands behind his head and leans back on two legs of his chair. "So, to summarize, the BOM supposedly drowned himself in the Potomac, but you were too out of it question the story the other Horsemen told the police and the press. While you sipped bourbon at your desk, Greyson and the others were doing things that could get the Mines into even more trouble than a fabricated intelligence report. Meanwhile, a disastrously unqualified insurance-company executive was nominated for the position of BOM."

I pounced on this last point. "Well, it's not like I could do anything about that. In my position, I couldn't go to the new president and say, 'we don't want that idiot.' You have to do your job with the idiot they give you. It's always been like that."

"Right," Virgil says. "Aspling was finally confirmed in early April, but because Brick's body still hadn't turned up, the president added the word 'acting' out of respect for Brick's widow. So Dashiell became the A-BOM."

"As if Alberta deserved any respect, she was—"

Virgil interrupts. "Now, Shelby, this is all about *your* sins. Other people's sins are completely irrelevant. Why is that so hard for your type to understand? Try to focus, please. Let's jump ahead a few months to Dashiell's first day on the job.

11

The A-bom

I find myself in a brightly-lit, highly-polished skull that smells like expensive cologne. Dashiell made a point of telling me the brand one day when he saw me sniffing. I was sniffing for alcohol on myself, but I didn't correct him. I didn't make any attempt to remember the brand either because all of my brain cells were busy with the names of world leaders, political factions, terrorists, and obscure capitals. I already begrudged the few cells I had to devote to remembering Dashiell's name, much less the name of whatever crap he dabbed behind his ears or wherever the hell he dabbed it.

I remember being stunned that Dashiell was confirmed. It took a rare configuration of stars to make it happen. A public demanding fresh blood at the head of the Mines, Westerly's plotting, and the president's need for Westerly's votes all conspired to present the Mines with this dunce. Dashiell's lack of qualifications concerned the new POTUS. So, to ensure continuity, he decreed that the current Horsemen remain in place until Dashiell was oriented to his new surroundings. So I kept my job. More to the point, Greyson kept his job. Greyson, who wanted to be BOM so bad he drooled at the thought, would remain on the seventh floor in pouncing distance of Dashiell. Everyone in the Mines knew that was bad news for the new A-BOM, everyone but the A-BOM himself. He was caught up in his own silly games.

Dashiell was inspecting his new office. Workers had come the week before his arrival to redecorate. Incredibly, interior decoration was his first priority. His eyes lingered over the pretentious new furnishings: a gleaming glass and steel coffee table, Lucite chairs, and brilliant white carpeting. He turned and glanced up at a framed Escher print, *Hand with Reflecting Sphere*. The skewed, anthropocentric perspective of the lithograph perfectly illustrated Dashiell's worldview.

Despite effort and expense, the renovations were a failure. The gleaming additions clashed with the Stygian aura of the Mines. An almost audible note of discord hung in the air.

Dashiell knew it. Small tsking and growling noises rose from in his throat as his eyes lit on the dark wood paneling of the room. He had tried to have it ripped out in favor of pale cyan, mineral composite sculptural wall panels in a crystal pattern. This plan ran afoul of MFAH-PC. Dashiell couldn't believe MFAHPC had the power to stand in the way of the BOM, but he underestimated it. The Fine Arts Committee was full of retired sharpers who knew a thing about power and influence themselves. They had the vice president himself call Dashiell to tell him to stand down on the most extreme renovations. Thus, they handed the new A-BOM a humiliating defeat and made sure everyone in the Mines knew about it before Dashiell even set foot in the door.

"Philistines," Dashiell muttered. He glanced at his reflection in the mirrored base of a lamp and adjusted his tie. "Philistines," he said again as his eyes turned to the dark mahogany desk. The MFAHPC made him keep that, too.

Daphne's voice came over the intercom. "The Horsemen are here." Dashiell had planned to bring in his own drop-dead-gorgeous secretary from private industry, but she had failed the polygraph, so he had reluctantly kept Daphne, too.

From the minimalist discomfort of Dashiell's skull, I watch myself and the other Horsemen as we hovered in the doorway. The things I didn't notice at the time! Greyson's paw clenching and unclenching. Slinky's skin quivering, his hook beating a silent tune against the leg of his trousers. Arthur's icy eyes pinning their victim. Me, I cupped my hand over my mouth, checking my breath for the smell of alcohol.

Dashiell paced, watching us from the corner of his eye. He was playing a power game. Finally, he made a curt gesture towards the seating area and said, "Sit, please."

He noted the sour looks we gave the new chairs. The only piece of upholstered furniture left in the room was Dashiell's new white leather desk chair. Everything else was Lucite. We sat gingerly. I wondered what my ass looked like through the Lucite. Dashiell chuckled to himself.

He didn't sit. We would soon learn that he liked to conduct meetings as if lecturing to a crowded hall. His gestures were expansive, his voice loud, and his stance manly. Never mind that he was a spidery, ridiculous little man. He cleared his throat, waiting until all eyes focused on his face.

"A spy agency is the same as an insurance company at its core," he intoned. "What works for one will work for the other."

Greyson snorted, but quickly covered it with a cough.

The A-BOM indicated a framed Time magazine cover on the wall. The headline was "America's Most Awesome Actuary" and the image was a silver coin with Dashiell's profile.

"Circumspectual was on the ropes when they hired me to turn it around. The trend lines were down. Morale was in the basement. Shareholders were screaming. Auditors were circling. But I brought the moribund giant back to financial health. I restored the company's morale and our clients' trust."

Dashiell took a crystal paperweight from the table. He held it up to the light, and then handed it to Greyson. "Take a close look and tell me what you see."

Greyson rolled cube in his hand, studying the embedded, laser-cut image. "Don Quixote?" he said.

"Percival," Dashiell snapped. "It's Percival." He snatched the paperweight from Greyson and handed it to me.

"Shelby, what do you see?"

He watched my doughy face as I examined the paperweight. He saw the recognition dawn as I focused on the eyes under the raised visor. They were wide-set and protuberant with that odd mix of arrogance and alarm. "It's you," I said.

"Exactly. My subordinates at Circumspectual had it made for me out of gratitude because I completed the impossible mission and saved the kingdom." Dashiell rested his fists on his hips, thrust out his pelvis, and stood wide-legged. "And I will save this kingdom, too. I intend to employ my unique genius for discipline, motivational campaigns, and pure, mathematical precision to this pitifully haphazard institution. The Mines is on the brink, its rocks ready to slide, its walls to implode from the fast accumulating weight of failure. Something has to be done, and I am the man to do it." Dashiell went back to his desk to punch the intercom. "Miss O'Shea, bring in the display."

"Her name isn't O'Shea, it's Sheehan," Slinky said through clenched teeth—he was still seething over the redecoration. "Daphne Sheehan. She survived the embassy bombing in Beirut and drove through a pile of burning trash to escape a mob in Mogadishu. At least learn her name."

Daphne entered, struggling with the door and a large easel. Slinky jumped up to help her. They set the easel up in front of the seating area.

"Thank you, Miss ..." Dashiell hesitated. "Thank you, Daphne, that's all I need now." When she had left, Dashiell stepped up to the easel, which held several posters. The first was simple: the words "MORE EXCELLENCE!!!" in gold on a black background. We would soon learn that Dashiell loved all caps and multiple exclamation points. He tapped the poster with the knuckle of his index finger. "More excellence is the key. We'll start with a series of motivational campaigns aimed at that goal. He took the first poster and let it fall to the floor. On the second poster, the words "IF IT'S NOT COUNTABLE IT DOESN'T COUNT!!!" screamed across a landscape of kidney beans stretching into infinity.

"Metrics," Dashiell said. "If we want to make this organization work, we need to measure everything, count everything. I'll elaborate on how I intend to do that later. For now, we'll move on to the next campaign." Dashiell let the beans fall to the floor, revealing a poster wallpapered with eyes of all ages, colors, and races. The title was "MORE VIGILANCE!!!"

"An image with impact," Dashiell said, "an image that will send miners back to their desks with a renewed sense of urgency."

Dashiell tossed "MORE VIGILANCE" to the floor to reveal a poster depicting dramatic burst of sun rays breaking through a cloud. The words "ILLUMINATE THE MINES!!!" were emblazoned across the top in neon yellow letters.

"Do you remember Goethe's last words?" Dashiell said. "More light. That's what I'm going to bring to the Mines."

"That's the last fucking thing the Mines needs," Greyson muttered. Arthur tapped his arm and gave him a micro-frown of warning.

"But that's *exactly* what the Mines needs," Dashiell said. His thin body trembled with enthusiasm. "In fact, I've just thought of a new poster. I'm going to improve on Goethe's words and say, 'More *and Better* Light.' We have a severe morale problem here. It's one of the things Congress has charged me with fixing. Our employees are down and no wonder. They spend long hours in windowless cubicles. In the winter, they often arrive before the sun comes up and leave after it sets. They're SAD. SAD as in Seasonal Affective Disorder. So what's the solution? Have them work less? Of course, not. We need more work, not less. What we can do, however, is replace the sun, replace every light in the Mines with a full spectrum equivalent. We will raise morale and reduce eyestrain so that our employees can work even longer."

Slinky blinked at the poster with an exaggerated squinching of the eyes. A muscle at the corner of his mouth quivered. "That will cost a fortune," he said, "money better spent overhauling the HVAC system. The people on the fourth floor of the New Shafts Building are complaining that their coffee freezes if they leave it too near the window. I think heat would improve their morale more than light."

"No," Dashiell said firmly, "light. The Illuminating the Mines Initiative, or IMI, will pay for itself. I've hired a contractor who is giving us a very good price." Dashiell uncovered a poster with a gold sunburst logo and the words "Kreative Industrial Sunlight Solutions."

Slinky gripped the arms of his chair and leaned forward as if to pounce on Dashiell. Arthur's hand shot out and grabbed his arm. Slinky sat back, but he couldn't suppress the anger in his voice. "You can't do that. Contracts go through the Smithery. They have to be competed. Federal regulations."

"Sorry," Dashiell said. "Done deal."

Uncountable and Unaccountable things

I have no time to consider my growing unease about Kreative Industrial Sunlight Solutions. After an instant of darkness and a hollow rushing sound, I find myself back in Dashiell's skull. I can tell that at least a couple of months have passed since my last visit. A pair of oversized flat-screen computer monitors sits on his desk. They didn't arrive until May.

Dashiell's favorite colors, cyan and gray, blinked through the display of bar graphs, pie charts, and scatter diagrams. This was the Dashiellboard. For weeks, drones throughout the Mines had labored over it, guided by meticulously groomed, conservatively dressed young consultants from ManagoTech Research. The process was grueling: one hundred thirty-seven Power Point presentations, twenty-four runnings of the Dashiellboard Metrics Training Module, twelve management offsites, seven town meetings, forty-two font changes, and special metrics teams set up in every office. ManagoTech Research invoices settled on the desks of government contract officers like Magnolia petals after a frost. At last, the database was online and populated with three months worth of data.

"It's all here, everything I need for fingertip control of the Mines," Dashiell said out loud, speaking to himself. He was alone in the office. His voice choked with awe. He pressed a button on a remote control, and one of the bar charts expanded to fill both screens. The words "White Mines Monthly Intelligence Production" glowed in a cyan Krungthep bold font. The bars stood for output of words printed with ink on paper or flashed in pixels across a screen. The A-BOM reached toward the pulsing bar to the far right, the one labeled "May." "What the hell?" he said. The May bar was shorter than the one labeled "April." "How hard can it be to generate words?" Dashiell jabbed the intercom button and spat out the words "Get me Shelby" with a shower of saliva that spotted his flat screen.

He reached into his top drawer for an antibacterial wipe. By the time I arrived breathless from jogging the length of the tunnel between my office and the A-BOM's, Dashiell had wiped screen, phone, desktop, and fingers, and deposited the used wipe in the trash can. When I entered the room, he was seated. The tips of his lemon-scented fingers pressed together in a prim steeple.

"Yes sir," I said with a deferential nod.

Dashiell focused on my tie, specifically on a coffee stain the size of a nickel right in the center of that tie. I never noticed that sort of thing, and I was unaware that other people did. I guess my wife was right all those years.

Dashiell raised one hand, cocked his thumb, and leveled the index finger of his right hand at the screen as if he were about to "shoot" it with a "gun." As I approached, Dashiell withdrew his "weapon," and his fingers returned to their righteous steeple.

"How do you explain this?" he asked me.

My rubbery features contorted with effort as I tried to come up with a suitable answer to the A-BOM's stupid question, an answer composed in such a way as to not let on that it was a stupid question.

"Shelby?" the A-BOM said sharply. "I asked you why the May bar is smaller than the April bar when production should be increasing, not shrinking."

"Yes, thank you. Intelligence production ... " I paused. I considered whether I needed to explain the term to this outsider, whom the president saw fit to plop atop the Mines like a maraschino cherry atop an onion soup. I began again. "Aggregating all of our intelligence production into a single bar on a chart is somewhat misleading. Intelligence production, as you well know, includes a broad range of things: short articles for the President's Intelligence Update, situation updates, memoranda in response to policymaker inquiries, periodic reports, long research reports, briefings ... a wide range. Wide. Does a thirty-eight-word PIU count the same as a half-page SitUp? Or a two-page Mempol or a ten-page PerRep, or a twenty-page ResRep, or an hour-long briefing—"

"Cut the gibberish, Shelby, and explain why production in your shaft has plummeted."

"I wouldn't describe a two-percent reduction as 'plummeting.' 'Sliding' would be a more accurate—"

"You don't want me to lose my patience."

I nodded. "In April, as you well remember, we had a coup in Central America, an embassy bombing in Pakistan, and an outbreak of civil war—"

"Cut to the point."

I so wanted to snap back, to lift this yappy Chihuahua by his outsized ears until he wet himself, but I was a good bureaucrat schooled the fine arts of genuflection, sycophancy, and palaver. I made my voice calm, soothing, reasonable.

"All of these events demanded a steady flow of short intelligence reports on a twenty-four-seven basis. By May, however, the events had cooled down, allowing us to return to normal operation. A lot of our alchemists were out of the office. The others returned to longer-term projects—"

"Why were your alchemists out of the office?" Dashiell said.

"They were attending the Dashiellboard Metrics Awareness Course," I said, careful not to look Dashiell in the eye. It had infuriated me to have to send so many people away for a week of training. To make it less of a waste, I had arranged for a team from Medical to provide CPR training at the same time. Maybe that would at least save a life some day.

"Don't try to shift the blame to me," Dashiell said. "How do you think this is going to look to Congress?" He removed his Excaliber letter opener from its faux stone holder and brandished it at the pitifully inadequate "May" bar, pulsing weakly in cyan-shadowed embarrassment. "My feet are to the fire. They're out of patience with the Mines. 'Reform it or abolish it,' is the mantra. Get with the program. This place is going to be run like a business. Zero percent intelligence failures. Zero percent. Nada. Zilch. That means more vigilance. More vigilance every month, including vigilance as measured by number of words of analysis delivered to the busy policymaker."

The intercom blinked, and Daphne said, "Sir, your ten o'clock is here. Madeline James, Chief of the Alternative Alchemy Unit."

Through Dashiell's eyes, I see myself frown. I remember being severely annoyed that Maddie was going over my head to the A-BOM. Sure, I had ignored her, but she shouldn't be going over my head.

"What is this about?" Dashiell said. "I'm in the middle of something important."

"It's about an impending terrorist threat."

"Tell her to consult a terrorism expert."

Another pause, then Daphne said slowly, "She *is* a terrorism expert. A senior bomb dissector. Remember, she was the one in charge of the canary crew before the Stadium Attack?" Her words elicited no response. "The one who testified before the committee?" Daphne's voice took on an edge of annoyance. "The one who got the Mines into trouble by uncovering the faked report on Iran's involvement in the attack." Another pause and the intercom picked up a faint sob. "You remember, don't you, that's why Brick killed himself? And why you're here?"

"Oh right, hold on a second." Dashiell turned to me, "After you take care of the bar chart issue, I want you to handle this alternative woman's problem."

"I'll take care of it," I said.

Dashiell spoke into the intercom, "Tell her the BOWM will deal with it."

I was about to make my exit, when Dashiell said, "Wait. How old are you?"

"Sixty-four."

"You're about five foot six. Right? How much do you weigh?"

"Two twenty."

"Let's say two forty. Family history of heart disease? Diabetes? Cancer?"

"Yes, yes, and yes." I answered with an air of tired tolerance. I no longer cared what Dashiell asked me or why.

"Smoke? Drink?"

"Not any more and yes."

"Heavy drinker?"

"Moderate."

Dashiell's eyes focused on the broken blood vessels in my nose. "Let's say heavy." He made a few quick calculations on his notepad. "Those issues combined with a high-stress lifestyle and beltway commuting, and you should have been dead a year ago. I'd better make a list of possible BOWM candidates. That's all."

So, he was only a year off.

Back in the polygraph room, Virgil flips his used toothpick toward the trashcan. "So, Shelby, how did you deal with the bar chart?" He burps, and I smell sulfur.

I straighten my back. "I told my executive assistant, Lyle the Idiot, to massage the figures until the May bar was bigger than April. Are you going to call that a sin?"

"No, Shelby, I'm not. The DashiellBoard was as useful to the Mines as an Etch-A-Sketch. And did you follow up with Maddie?"

I slump. "Not that day, no."

"Nor that week," Virgil says. "I'm not surprised. However, I have other issues to raise with you. But first, I have to talk to management."

Virgil leaves me alone. I grip the arms of the chair, but it's of no use. Soon my image in the mirror fades.

13

My Own Business

How could I fall apart any further? I've been crushed by concrete and the revelation of an afterlife. Everything that meant anything to me is gone. You would think I would be immune to shock by now, but the smell of Thelma's perfume devastates me. I'm not good at analyzing emotions, but I pick a few identifiable feelings out of the psychic assault: guilt, affection, and embarrassment. The embarrassment of a man who accidentally walks into a ladies' room. *I shouldn't be in a woman's skull, suppose she goes to the bathroom?*

Thelma was driving her minivan, tapping an elaborately manicured nail on the wheel as she threaded her way through Northern Virginia traffic. Rain spattered on the windshield, and the traffic slowed to a crawl. She glanced in the rearview mirror, catching the eye of her youngest son, twelve-year-old Martin. He had the fixed stare and stiff posture of a kid in big trouble. I've been on the wrong end of Thelma's scalding lectures more than once, and I feel a rush of empathy.

Her words came slowly; each one drenched in a mother's disappointment and humiliation. "No son of mine has ever been thrown off the bus before. What did you do?"

Aw, come on, I think. *Give him a break. Every kid gets thrown off the bus at least once.*

As she waited for her son's reply, Thelma adjusted the mirror so she could check her makeup. She spied a clump of mascara clinging to the end of a lash. She snagged it with the edge of a tissue, then adjusted the mirror so she could see Martin's face. "You'd better tell me what you did because you know I'll find out. I always do."

"I sprayed …" Martin's voice squeaked and broke. He swallowed and started again, rushing to get the words out. "I sprayed Maxx on a girl."

The creeping traffic came to a full halt, which allowed Thelma to turn and face her son. "You did what?"

"I sprayed Maxx on a girl." Martin's lip trembled, but he didn't offer excuses. He knew better. "I'm sorry. I'll never do that again. I promise."

"Is that what I've been smelling? I thought it was the new carpet cleaner. Where did you get perfume?"

"It's not perfume. That's for women. It's body spray for men."

"How did you get it?

"I bought it with my allowance."

Thelma stretched a hand over the seat. "Give it."

Martin relinquished the bottle without a fight, and Thelma tucked it into her purse.

"I'll throw this away when I get to work." The traffic began to move again, and Thelma turned back around to focus on the road. "You're too young to smell like a … like someone who makes their living on street corners," she said. "Where did you get the idea to buy it?"

No response from Martin. She tried to catch his eye

in the rearview, but he had slumped too far down in the seat.

"Sit up straight. You don't have to answer me, I know exactly where you got the idea. *Trevor.*" She pronounced the name with a venom suitable to more famous malefactors, like Hitler, Stalin, and Pol Pot. "Trevor, Kyle, and that boy with the terrible acne. You're running with the wrong crowd, and that scares me, Martin. You got a B minus in math on the last report card. Where did that come from? I'm going to have to get you into St. Mary's next year, instead of waiting until high school. I'll just have to work more overtime so we can afford it."

"Mom, I don't want to—"

"You don't get to say what you want. I won't hear another word out of you."

Thelma was a devoted parishioner of a Baptist church, but she put all of her boys into a private Catholic school as soon as they hit high-school age. She believed in discipline, and public school teachers couldn't hold a candle to nuns in that regard. The nuns were delighted to have Thelma's sons in their school. The Madison boys were not only excellent students—and nice children—they saved St. Mary's from an embarrassing lack of diversity. They were prominently featured on the cover of the school brochure every year, smiling in carefully arranged candid shots with other students. Thelma had told me how she negotiated for their scholarships. "I said, 'Who are you going to put on your brochure if I can't afford your tuition? All you have is Kevin Fukumoto, and he's only half Japanese.' That got me another ten percent."

Even with the scholarships, it was a stretch for Thelma to afford the school, but she was determined because she believed her sons' lives were at stake. She came to D.C.

from a small town, and her early years there coincided with a time of rampant gun violence, when young African American boys were the most frequent victims. She and her family had since moved to the suburbs, but the fear never left her.

Thelma spoke quickly, sucking her breath in the pauses. "I'm going to be late for work because I have to drive you to school. I need to get in there to look after Shelby. He's not capable of looking after himself anymore. If I'm not there, he'll drink his breakfast, and I'm not talking about coffee. He's got the same problem your uncle Mike has. You remember, we talked about that. Shelby will stumble into the morning staff meeting smelling just like Uncle Mike. There are two dangerous times in a male's life, your age and whatever age Shelby is. Honestly, I can't keep up with the two of you."

I send a silent apology to Martin, whose minor sins had gotten tangled in my larger ones in Thelma's mind.

Desperation crept into her voice. "If he's not careful, he's going to lose his job. Then what happens to me? The next BOWM will bring his own secretary, and I don't know of another opening on the seventh floor. Almost twenty years I've been with Shelby. I picked him out in my first month on the job. I had a friend who said, 'What you do is get yourself a rabbit. Find someone who's moving up and make yourself indispensable to him.' That's what I did. I picked out the smartest, nicest man in the office, and we got all the way to the seventh floor. Then, overnight, he goes down the drain. I know he has good reason, but he doesn't have the *right,* the right to mess up all the lives around him. Next thing you know, I'll be back down on the lower floors where they never shampoo the carpets and where I can't get regular overtime. Then maybe you'll all be back in public school getting into trouble, ruining your future." Thelma swiped a hand across her face, and it came away wet.

The thought that I was responsible for Thelma's tears, that she viewed me as a threat to her family, leaves me feeling more flattened than when I was hit by the concrete.

Virgil's hideous face reappears inches from my own. His bloodshot eyes peer into mine. He points an accusatory finger at my face, then slowly brings it closer until it touches my nose, and I go cross-eyed. "It never occurred to you that your drinking affected anyone else, did it? You thought it was your own business. Yes or no, Shelby, did you think your drinking was your own business?"

"Yes," I said.

"Yes or no, did you tell Thelma, Esther, and anyone else who raised the subject that your drinking was your own business?"

"Yes." I swallow and try not to gag from Virgil's rank breath.

"How many times did you use that phrase 'my drinking is my own business.' Was it more than a dozen times?"

"I don't know how many times. Do you think I counted? I don't think it was that many."

"Was it less than a dozen times, Shelby?"

"Yes."

"The machine detects prevarication."

I recognize this technique, it's the same one polygraph examiners use on subjects who have admitted to trying illegal drugs. I know because I smoked a little marijuana two summers before I entered underground. I admitted that to the polygraph examiner, but he wouldn't accept such a vague confession. He wanted to know *exactly* how many times I had smoked marijuana. The problem was I didn't know exactly how many times. Who counts? I smoked it all that summer. We went back and forth for over an hour as I tried to tally up every incidence of use, every blurry evening in a friend's dorm room, every stray toke at a party. *This can't go on forever*, I told myself as the day wore on. I was right, of course. Back then, it couldn't go on forever. We eventually came up with a figure of somewhere between thirty-five and forty incidents of drug use. That day ended, and they hired me anyway. But now? I think of the small print on the sign above the door: "*There is No Close of Business.*" It could go on forever, for all eternity.

The numbers rise, but Virgil won't let me jump ahead and admit to saying "my drinking was my own business" a million times.

"Come on, Shelby, don't cheat. I'm looking for a real number. I'm going to get one if we have to sit here for all eternity."

Hours pass. Or do they? My eyes scan the walls of the room, and I realize that something is missing, the one thing that should be in every room in every government office building: a plain round clock.

"Where's the clock? Why is there no clock?"

"Because there is no time, Shelby. No close of business. No end in sight." As always when delivering bad news, Virgil grins like a big, stupid dog. "Shelby, stop getting distracted. Yes or no. Did you say 'my drinking is my own business' more than 315 times?"

"No."

"The machine detects prevarication."

"Yes."

"Better. Did you say 'my drinking is my own business' more than 320 times?"

And on it goes. It goes on and on and on.

Finally, we arrive at a figure of more than 620 but less than 630. I have no idea whether this is correct or just where Virgil got bored and decided to stop.

"Okay, enough of that," he says without irony. "Let's return to that morning and put you back in your own head."

Because Thelma was late and not watching over me like a hawk, I had decided to conduct some research. Research into the degree to which I could be intoxicated and still do my job. Research into the effects of alcohol, stress, and lack of exercise on male mortality. My research tool in this instance was three fingers of Four Roses bourbon poured into a lead crystal glass engraved with the Mines seal. I had bought it at the Company Store. It amused me. Taking a drunken dive into irresponsibility after a lifetime of Midwestern uprightness was strangely exhilarating.

Thelma burst into my office without knocking, still wearing her raincoat and carrying her purse. She caught me as I tried to slip my glass into my lower right-hand drawer, which I kept empty for that very purpose.

"I knew it!" she said. "Ten minutes until the morning staff meeting and you're drinking like a fish. Like a fish."

I don't know what Thelma had against fish, but her biggest scold was that I drank like one. "Don't you ever knock?" I asked with as much indignation as I could manage. "And you're late."

"Don't you try to turn this around and make it about me." She used the same voice with me that she used with her twelve-year-old. She would have never done that in the early years. There was a time when Thelma was in awe of my intelligence. How did it happen that the higher I climbed up the ladder, the less she respected me?

Now she looked at me like I was cat crap on a freshly laundered sheet. "One thing I've learned in my years inside the beltway is that you can never underestimate how stupid a smart man can be." She approached my desk, put her hands on it and leaned forward, sniffing. "You smell like the gutter," she said.

"This is thirty-dollar-a-bottle bourbon. Gutters don't smell like this." I can't believe I made such a stupid remark. The alcohol must have damaged my judgment.

Thelma leaned closer, eyes burning with Baptist passion. She was a formidable woman, nearly six feet tall with regal bearing and remarkable bone structure. She could have been a model. People told her that all the time when she was younger, and she would always say, "Models do drugs and eat lettuce. I'm not interested." She was still a beautiful woman who took pains with her appearance. Her hair was elaborately coiffed, her clothes stylish, her heels high, her makeup perfect. She was the sort of woman who would have intimidated a man even if she weren't so damned morally upright.

"Don't you use that tone with me." Her eyes bored into to me. "I will not let you destroy your career and mine with it." She reached into her purse. I remember thinking, for an irrational moment, that she was going to pull a gun on me.

It was worse than a gun.

Thelma pulled out a plastic bottle and sprayed me liberally with the most noxious substance I had ever encountered. My hands came up to shield my face. "What is that? Mace?" I started to cough.

"Maxx." Thelma recapped the can and returned it to her purse. "I know it stinks, but it will disguise the liquor smell. It will keep you from getting fired, at least this morning."

Virgil's smirking face reappears. I don't give him time to open his mouth. I reach out, grab his shirt and pull him closer until our faces almost touch.

"Did she survive?" I ask. "You have to tell me, did she survive?"

Virgil's shirt suddenly becomes so hot it burns my hand. I let go. Virgil leans back on his chair, still smoldering. Smoldering and smirking.

"No," he says, "I don't have to tell you."

14

The Four Horsemen

I'm back in my own skull, where it smells like a rutting moose drinking Koolade.

I was walking along the seventh-floor tunnel, staring at my feet shuffling along the gray-flecked tiles. The sound of fast-clacking heels made me look up. A small irritant approached rapidly, arms pumping. It's Maddie James, head of the as-yet-unstaffed Alternative Analysis Unit forced down the Mines' throat by the Stadium Attack Commission. She raised her hand and made a motion like signaling a taxi. "Shelby," she yelled. "I have to talk to you about a threat."

"Not now, I'm on the way to the BOM's morning meeting."

"'Not now' is always your answer. I have to talk to you now." She yelled this from twenty feet away.

"Shh," I said. "This is the seventh floor."

"God forbid the leadership might hear about a threat." Maddie was in my face now. She was more animated than she had been at the Stadium Attack exhibit. This was the old Maddie: an odd mixture of delicate bone structure, grace, and terrier-like determination, which manifested in emphatic mannerisms and a rapid stride just short of race walking. Having warned and not been listened to before the last two major terrorist attacks, she'd developed a self-righteous attitude I found galling. Everything about her said, "I was right, and you were wrong." And everything about her—her rising intonation, her pointing finger, her insistence on standing too close while talking—got on my nerves. I heaved a sigh, adopted a wide-legged stance, and prepared for an onslaught of irritation.

"You've given me this briefing, Maddie, and I wasn't impressed. You have no hard data, just a stray intercept here, a codeword there, and your feelings. And you tried to go over my head to the A-BOM!"

"I'm in the BOM career service now. You're not in my chain of command."

"No, but you get your budget from the White Mines kitty."

"And when am I going to get enough money to hire staff?" she asked.

"We'll talk about it later," I said. "I have to go."

She actually tried to block me, throwing her undersized body in my path, but I gritted my teeth, pushed past her, and continued down the tunnel.

"Close your eyes, Shelby!" she yelled after me. "We all know the bombs won't go off if you close your eyes!"

Ten more steps and I made it to my destination, the only door in the Mines—other than the restroom doors—with no cipher or combination lock. I pondered the deeper meaning of this as I pushed it open. A dirty chuckle came from behind. I turned to see Greyson Earl. How could such a big man sneak up on me like that?

"Morning, Shel. Hope you've come equipped with

your high waders because before this meeting is over, we'll be up to our balls in manure."

"Then you know what the meeting is about?" I said.

"Of course. All of Dashiell's meetings are the same." He paused and sniffed. "Good God, Shel, where have you been this morning? Trolling for tender meat at the middle school?"

I ignored this.

When Greyson and I entered, we found the outer office empty. Before we could shut the door, the SCUDO appeared. He walked over to a wooden podium with a small brass light attached against the gloom. Dashiell had not been able to persuade the MFAHPC to allow him to redecorate this room.

"Good morning, sirs." The SCUDO scratched a notation in the visitor log. He gestured with the pen toward a couch and two chairs. "Please have a seat. We're still waiting for the other two gentlemen."

"Gentlemen! Ha ha, that's a good one," Greyson said.

While I leaned back into the flag blue upholstery of my chair, Greyson leaned forward, legs planted wide, elbows resting on his knees. He did not so much sit as crouch. His huge knuckles drummed a nameless tune on the coffee table while his eyes scanned the shadowy corners of the room. This room was too dark, even for me.

"Why do they make it so dark in here?" I asked. I hated the hushed, pretentious outer office. Its paneling reflected no light, and it's deep carpeting and plush upholstery swallowed sound like a lake swallows a pebble.

"Never heard of psychological warfare?" Greyson spoke just above a whisper, as befitted the space. "This room is calculated to make you uncomfortable. Of course, they can't make VIP guests uncomfortable in any obvious way. You can't put the head of some foreign intelligence service in a concrete room with strobe lights and rats. You have to be subtle. Make it look like you're doing everything possible to make him comfortable, while simultaneously unnerving him." Greyson paused in his finger drumming, then beat a flourish. "It unnerves people to walk into this office and find it empty. You know the SCUDO has to be watching you from another room. He appears, then disappears, leaving you to wait alone, knowing you're still watched." Greyson's cat eyes darted from one end of the room to the other. "You look around for security cameras, but it's hard to see anything in these dark corners. When you get back to your office, try to draw a blueprint of this room. You'll find you can't remember how it's laid out. Dark, confusing little nooks and crannies. Reminds me of a funeral parlor. Can you picture a casket by that wall? A spray of lilies draped over the podium? The corpse of a late BOM? And the furniture. Tell me, Shel, are you comfortable in that chair?"

"No, it's like brocade-covered steel wool."

"But a lovely chair, isn't it?" Greyson laughed. "And it's lower than most so that when the A-BOM comes in, you'll have to hoist yourself out of there like a hog out of a wallow. The hog, of course, has the advantage of not having to maintain his dignity during the process."

"You really think this is all part of a deliberate design?"

"No, I don't think they're that smart. It was a happy accident. Dashiell was such an idiot to try to change it." Greyson drummed another flourish. He glanced at his massive and expensive watch as the door opened to admit the missing Horsemen.

Slinky sat on the couch as far away from Greyson as

possible while Arthur lowered his slender body into a corner chair. "What reeks?"

"Shelby," Greyson said.

"Of course," Arthur said. "Anyone know what this conclave is about?"

"Some meaningless piece of idiocy, if past meetings are any indicator," Greyson said.

"Have we ever had a more clueless BOM?" Slinky asked.

"Maybe it's time to clue him in. He's been here for months now." Arthur said. "I can't remember ever waiting so long for the Welcome Wagon Briefing. The shit could hit the fan at any minute. He'll be even madder if he's blindsided."

I groaned and said a silent prayer that my fellow Horsemen would not choose today for the Welcome Wagon Briefing. It was a tradition in the Mines when a new BOM took office. The briefing was an orientation, combined with a hazing and a glove test—only that makes it sound much more pleasant than it really was. This was when the horsemen lay bare the "Toxic Turds," or dirty secrets that any new BOM must know. Usually, it was a dirty secret about to go public in a bad way, perhaps an undisclosed prison or a nasty sex scandal. The briefing traditionally came within the new BOM's first few weeks on the job, but the Horsemen kept finding excuses to delay this one.

The bourbon gurgled in my stomach. My mind felt soft and shaky. I patted my pockets and pulled out a notebook with a florescent red Top Secret sticker on the front. The only way I could keep from drifting off and drooling during these meetings was to take meticulous notes.

"You're not going to take notes during this meeting?"

Greyson said. "That is such a bad idea. How many times to I have to tell you alchemists not to take fucking notes at every fucking meeting?"

I shrugged. "I rip the pages out after the meeting and burnbag them. Taking notes helps me focus."

"Focus, fuck us," Greyson muttered.

"He's going to wonder why we waited this long to tell him." Slinky pulled a fresh pencil from an interior jacket pocket and bit into it. Along with his nervous tics, he had an addiction to chewing pencils. The tenser the meeting, the harder Slinky chewed.

"Slinky is smarter than you are," Greyson said to me. "It's far better to eat your pencils than to write with them in this place."

"How do we explain why we waited so long?" Slinky said. "We can't exactly say that we waited because we didn't trust him."

"We still don't trust him," Arthur said.

"True enough." Greyson leaned back and rested a huge wing-tip on the coffee table. "True enough, but he has to be told. The turds are ripening. The LI and the OLI are highly unstable. We could have a rockslide at any moment. Think how unpleasant it would be for us if the A-BOM found out about any of this from his morning newspaper."

I had no idea what the LI and the OLI were, but it wasn't the time to ask.

The hall door opened, and an elderly security escort poked in his head. The green Mines tag around his neck indicated that he was a contractor. Retired miners frequently took advantage of the lucrative contracts available to those leaving the Mines with their security clearances intact.

"Excuse me," he said.

The SCUDO appeared again. "Yes?"

"The workmen are here to replace the lights. Make it nice and bright in here."

"What a stupid idea," Greyson muttered.

Another door opened, and Daphne appeared. She ignored the escort and looked at us warily as if to judge whether or not we were planning to detonate any bombs at this meeting.

"Come in. He's ready."

"I assure you, my dear, he is not," Greyson said.

I made a move to rise, but lost my balance and fell back into the brocade-covered steel wool of my seat. Greyson lent me a hand, and I succeeded in standing on the second try.

"Bourbon before lunch is a bad idea," Greyson whispered as we filed into the BOM's office.

Another blink, and I am back in the polygraph room with Virgil.

"Such a fun group of boys," Virgil says. "I bet you miss them, Shelby."

"Like I miss hemorrhoids."

Virgil reaches for the polygraph machine but changes his mind. "I could ask you more questions now, but I think I'll wait until the end of Welcome Wagon briefing."

I groan. "Don't tell me I have to sit through the damn thing again? That would be torture. Have I really done anything bad enough to deserve that?"

Virgil shakes his obscene head. "Shelby, you are such a whiner. Tell you what, to give you a break, I'll put you in

Dashiell's skull."

"Oh, God, no. That would be so much worse."

"Bye, Shelby. Have a blast. Before you go, I must remind you. *Pay attention* this time."

The Welcome-Wagon Briefing

Dashiell waved us toward the seating area. "I'm sure you're wondering why I've called this meeting." He favored the hackneyed opening.

Greyson's grin stretched wide across his craggy face. "You want to announce a new initiative to improve efficiency and accountability at the Mines."

"How did you know that?" The A-BOM's voice was accusatory, filled with dark suspicions about the BOBM, who had perhaps bugged his office or recruited his secretary. Dashiell focused on Greyson's huge teeth as the grin grew brighter and larger.

"Merely an educated guess," Greyson said.

I could hear the effort in Dashiell's voice as he tried to sound firm and confident. "To get to the subject at hand: raising efficiency and accountability. As you are well aware, step one in this effort was the creation of the Dashiellboard." The A-BOM made a sweeping gesture toward his double computer monitors, which were turned so that we could view the flashing displays from our Lucite chairs.

"The purpose of the Dashiellboard is to give the BOM fingertip control of the Mines." Dashiell reached under his jacket, unholstered a remote from a leather case attached to his belt, and fired it at the screen. It brought each chart to the foreground as he named it.

"White Mines: Monthly Intelligence Production. Black Mines: Monthly Grouper Recruitment. Paper Mines: Monthly 357 Tasking Forms Completed. Smithery: Monthly Audio Penetration and Concealment Device Production. Does anyone see a problem here?"

We saw nothing but problems with the Dashiellboard, but we didn't respond. Instead, we affected a pleasantly blank and studied attentiveness.

"It's the word that appears in every title," Dashiell said.

"Monthly?" I volunteered.

Dashiell pointed at me. "Give that man a cigar. Monthly! Yes! Exactly! What good is fingertip control of the Mines, when progress is only measured on a monthly basis? One might have to wait twenty-nine or thirty days to spot a problem."

"So, I take it you would like the statistics on a weekly basis?" Slinky said. The corner of his mouth began to twitch, and he covered it by biting down on a pencil.

"No, weekly isn't good enough. I need statistics on a continuous basis. When you ride a horse, you want to feel the muscles of the beast between your thighs." Dashiell slapped his thigh. "You want to feel the blood pumping through its veins."

"Would you like us to design a mountable computer?" Arthur's thin lips and pale ears pinkened with satisfaction at his own wit.

Dashiell ignored him. "Continuous statistics are what

we need to turn the Mines into a well-lubricated machine. Furthermore, we have to expand our collection of information. The data need more granularity." He said that word "granularity" with an emphasis that suggested it was about to become his latest buzzword. Sure enough, Dashiell reached behind his desk and pulled out a glossy poster depicting a beach, shot from ground level. A hand in the foreground sifted sand. The depressingly predictable caption was "MORE GRANULARITY!!!"

Arthur made an involuntary scoffing noise, then covered it by taking off his glasses, folding them, unfolding them, frowning deeply at the spotless lenses. Dashiell's eyes focused on the small designer logo near the hinge. He was probably calculating the exact cost of those eyeglasses. Arthur returned them to his nose, and the platinum flecks in his eyes glinted. "Producing these continuous statistics," he said, "would be time-consuming, and given the reduction in support staff—"

"I've thought of that," Dashiell interjected. "We simply have Managotech expand the electronic portal. Then the alchemists, sharpers, smithies, drones, what have you, enter each piece of production as it is completed, along with some additional information that would amplify the utility of the statistics. Provide the granularity we need. No problem." Dashiell snapped his fingers.

We could have enumerated a host of problems: problems of accuracy, cost of more training, worker bee resentment over yet one more pesky bureaucratic task, the nightmarish error loops and horrendous bugs that infest any huge electronic database with thousands of users. Moreover, each of us could have come up with a hundred better uses for the funds that would be required to create the portal, test it, and train personnel. But experience had taught us that it was useless to argue with Dashiell. He was a mover and a shaker, just as a bull in a china shop is a mover and a shaker.

Greyson rested his elbows on his knees and drummed his walnut-sized knuckles on the coffee table. Slinky gnawed on a pencil, and his left eye twitched. Arthur took off his glasses and blinked. My jowls quivered as I gnawed the inside of my cheek and scribbled in my notebook. Dashiell couldn't see what I was writing, but I remember it: *Time to open the seventh seal.* Greyson cleared his throat and glanced at each of us in turn. Dashiell caught the silent exchange of subtle nods and, like a dumb animal sensing an earthquake, involuntarily shuddered.

Greyson cleared his throat. "As unquestionably vital as your adorable data points are to the running of the Mines, we have a Little Issue we must discuss. We actually call it the LI."

"LI?" Dashiell said.

"For Little Issue," Greyson said. "It originally cropped up at the Ear and then turned into something a bit more broad-reaching than we had anticipated." He noticed Dashiell's blank look and added, "The Ear is the National Audio Collection Agency, as you well know."

"Of course, I knew that. What little issue?" Dashiell asked sharply. "And when did it crop up?"

Greyson offered a sly, joyless smile. "Where to begin? Starting dates are always so arbitrary. Did it begin with this phone call or that minor incident? Impossible to say. The chronology is fuzzy. Very fuzzy. First, do you mind if I stand?" Greyson unfolded his lean, large-boned body from his chair. "I spin a tale so much better on my feet. Here, take my seat, Dashiell because this is a long story."

Dashiell started to protest, but something in

Greyson's expression paralyzed his vocal chords. Greyson loomed over him, guided him to a Lucite chair, and gently pushed him into it.

"Let me get you another coffee, sir," Greyson stepped over to the dining cart. "I believe you take one packet of sugar?"

Dashiell's eyes focused on the muscles of Greyson's back, as they rippled under the dark, pin-striped wool. The BOBM turned back around and set the cup and saucer on the table in front of his boss. He slipped his right hand into his pants pocket, then turned to face the A-BOM.

"Let me begin with the short intercept," Greyson said. "One Sunday morning the Ear intercepted a satellite telephone exchange. On one end was an unidentified individual who has been in contact with an Islamic radical, possibly in the UK."

"An imam," Dashiell said. He liked to use the new words he'd learned.

"No, they're not all imams," Greyson said. "The call came from the United States, less than two miles away from where we sit, to be even more precise. From Senator Harrison Westerly's McClean McMansion, to be completely accurate. Very foolish of him to call from there, by the way, but legislators are not known for their sensitivity to communications security. The phone call consisted of eleven words. The first six were spoken by a male voice we have identified as that of Senator Westerly. He said, 'How much will the screamers cost?'" The next five words, "Get off the fucking line," were spoken by the unidentified individual. End of conversation.

"How do you *know* it was the senator on the phone," Dashiell asked.

"Our voice identification techniques are extremely

accurate," Arthur said.

"Well, of course, he had a wrong number," Dashiell said. "It happens. Besides, what he said seems innocuous. Screamers? He could have been talking about anything."

Greyson raised one spiky brow. "We believe 'screamers' is a codeword for a new type of bomb. The radical in question is probably a man codenamed "the Shaker," who appears to be an engineer of some sort."

"What kind of bomb?" Dashiell asked.

Arthur shrugged. "Actually, we don't even know if it's a bomb per se. All we've managed to collect on it is that it's something we won't expect. Something loud, so we assume it's a bomb rather than a chemical or biological attack."

"That's all you have? I'm hearing a lot of uncertainty here, a lot of equivocation. Why don't we have any more information?" Dashiell made a move to stand, but Greyson clapped a ham-sized hand on the BOM's slender shoulder.

"Information on terrorist threats is always extremely fragmentary," Greyson said.

Dashiell raised his hands. "Stop right there. You don't have enough information. We certainly don't arrest every American who uses the word 'dance' over the phone, even though it's the codeword for a terrorist attack. I think you should be very cautious in even implying that a member of Congress would in any way be involve himself in something of this nature."

"Of course, sir," Greyson said with a slight bow and the exaggerated politeness he accorded BOMs and idiots. "We were well aware that such a situation should be handled with the utmost sensitivity and discretion. We even took the unusual precaution of having those intercepts deleted from the system."

I looked up in surprise. "You did what? You mean my bomb dissectors haven't seen them?"

"It's all right, Shelby, *my* people have seen them," Greyson said.

Spots of red showed in my pale face as I swallowed the insult. "How did you get the Ear to delete them?" I asked.

"Peach," Greyson said.

"Peach? Fruit?" Dashiell tilted his head like a clueless puppy.

"No," Greyson said. "Peach. Alberta. Alberta Bennet-Mason."

"The BOM's widow?" Dashiell asked.

"Yes," Arthur said, "the grieving widow." He couldn't keep the sarcasm out of his voice.

Greyson explained. "She was in the Black Mines for years. She got a law degree and became the Mines' Inspector General—but when Brick became BOM she moved to the deputy spot at the Ear, just to avoid any appearance of impropriety. Can't have a wife serving as the husband's Inspector General, can we? We hate the appearance of impropriety—it's worse than actual impropriety—which is why we have to be so careful how we handle this situation."

Dashiell spread his arms in a prayer-like gesture. "Handle? Why must it be handled at all? We have no real evidence of anything. Are you going to blame him based on a few words? Westerly is a US senator. It's not our job to determine his guilt or innocence. If the MOC found out we were monitoring the phone calls of its chairman, they'd slice our budget to ribbons. The matter must be dropped." Dashiell brought his fist down on the coffee table, but lightly, for it was glass-topped and expensive. "I demand that you cease any efforts to 'handle' anything."

"Well, sir. It's a little late for that," Greyson said. "Given that the intercept might indicate a terrorist attack, we felt that it was necessary to ... look into the situation more closely. Here we had two choices." Greyson held up two fingers. Dashiell's vision blurred as he tried to focus on them. "The first was to go the one hundred percent straight and narrow route. Letter of the law and all of that. The law says that we must report any suspected criminal activity to the Internal Investigative Organ."

"No," Dashiell managed to whisper, "Not the Organ." Dashiell wasn't good at keeping government agencies and their functions straight, but he knew the Organ and the Mines were bitter rivals. It went back to the days when an early Director of the Organ wore a dress and pearls on his off hours. The Boss of Mines found out about it and on the occasion of his birthday, sent the man a size XXL pink silk bustier embellished with Belgian lace and Swarovski crystals. What galled the Director was that the bustier was too pretty to throw away. Relations between the two agencies had been bitter ever since.

Greyson continued. "Exactly, sir. I can see that you completely understand what a disaster it would have been if we had brought in the Organ. First, the Organ hates us. Second, it leaks like a sieve. Third, given that Senator Westerly was coming down hard on the Mines at the time, it would have looked as if we cooked up the information in a clumsy effort to smear his name. Fourth, we would have lost the opportunity to uncover a possible terrorist plot. Other reasons come to mind, but those four are enough in themselves to argue against the straight and narrow. So that left us with no choice but to investigate this situation on our own, despite the inappropriateness—"

"Illegality," I said.

"Illegality, if you insist, of having the Mines"—here Greyson resorted to air quotes—"'spy' on a US senator. While the senator was on a fact-finding tour of Switzerland, we sent in an audio team. This is where the smithies dropped the ball, so I'll let you tell the story, Arthur." Greyson turned to the Boss of the Smithery.

Arthur recrossed his legs and cleared his throat. His ears turned bright pink. "Um, yes. We assigned the problem to our leading audio specialist—absolutely brilliant man—Albert Dufresne. He was the one who has successfully planted devices in both the Iranian—"

"This is not a recitation of your successes, Arthur," Greyson said.

"Of course, that would take too long." Arthur narrowed his eyes at Greyson and continued. "The most critical decision in any audio operation is where to place the listening device. Westerly's home is huge, 15,322 square feet, not counting the semi-detached sauna. We planted various devices in his bedroom, study, his bathrooms, and the sauna, of course, but we wanted another device that would follow him around. As you all know, the senator was quite fond of his parrot and took him everywhere. Even showered with him. The bird was a bare-eyed cockatoo or *cacatua sanquinea normantoni.*"

"*Normantoni,*" Greyson repeated thoughtfully.

"*Normantoni,*" Slinky echoed.

"Dirksen," Dashiell said.

"Excuse me, sir?" Arthur said.

"The cockatoo's name is Dirksen."

Arthur shifted in his chair and recrossed his legs. "Um, yes, the cockatoo's name was Dirksen. Unfortunately, he didn't survive the operation to implant the listening device."

"You killed Dirksen?" Dashiell said.

"We didn't kill him intentionally. I assure you that every effort was made to save his life. We had a superb veterinarian, but the bird went into shock. These things happen." Arthur raised his hands and shrugged.

"What did you do then?" Dashiell said.

"We disguised the tiny incision as neatly as we could and replaced him in his cage," Arthur said. "We took some bits of shredded coconut fiber from one of his toys and stuffed them down his beak to make it look like he choked to death. The housekeeper found him the next morning and immediately called the senator, who took the next flight back from Geneva. Regrettably, the senator didn't believe that his bird was stupid enough to choke himself. He had a necropsy performed."

"Oh my God." Dashiell cradled his head in his hands. Through his fingers, I see his thin knees trembling under the gray wool of his trousers.

"The necropsy revealed that there had been, so to speak, foul play. Fowl play." Arthur waited for Dashiell to laugh at his pun, but the A-BOM didn't lift his head. "You know it's important to keep a sense of humor in this business." Arthur frowned and continued. "Unfortunately, we had failed to completely remove the listening device from the dead bird."

"Oh my God." Dashiell's right knee jerked.

"So the senator went directly to Hunter Johnson." Arthur paused, and then added, "Director of the Internal Investigative Organ," in case Dashiell didn't know.

"Oh ... my ... God." Dashiell slid down in his chair.

Arthur continued. "Hunter immediately suspected

the Mines. He called me up and asked if it was our work. Of course, I denied it. He didn't get enough out of the bird to prove anything. I told him that we had a defector report indicating that the Iranian service was targeting Senator Westerly." Arthur forced a laugh, "Ha ha when in doubt, blame the Iranians."

"Isn't that how the Mines got in trouble last time?" Dashiell's voice shrank to a whisper. "That fake report implicating the Iranians—"

"... In the Stadium Attack. Right," Arthur said. "Excellent point, sir. Actually, it turned out to be problematic this time, as well. Hunter asked to see the report. So we had to fabricate it."

"Oh my God." Dashiell slid down further in his chair until his knees butted up against the coffee table and he had an eye-level view across its glass surface. The laser-cut Percival Aspling stared back at him. Dashiell must have envied him his armor and sword.

"Hunter didn't believe the report was real, but he couldn't prove otherwise. He also had other suspicions about the Mines relating to ..." Here Arthur glanced at Greyson, who shrugged and nodded in the affirmative. Arthur took a deep breath. "Relating to the murder of your predecessor, Brick Mason."

Dashiell struggled to sit up in the slippery chair. "Murder? You told me he was missing. You told the whole world that he was missing, that he probably committed suicide, drowned himself in the Potomac."

Greyson cut in. "We wanted you to get comfortable in your new position before we briefed you on this Other Little Issue. The OLI, we call it."

"OLI?" Dashiell said.

"Other Little Issue," Arthur said with a trace of impatience.

Dashiell tried to argue with Greyson. "But he can't have been murdered because you found a suicide note."

"I haven't forgotten the note, sir. It was genuine," Greyson said. "We found the weapon, too, an old Russian Tokarev "TT" pistol, registration number 102774."

I looked up sharply because I recognized the number and knew who owned that pistol.

"I thought you said Brick drowned in the Potomac?" Dashiell said. "There was security footage of him walking to the river."

"We never said he drowned," Greyson said. "We never even said that he died on—or in—the Potomac. And that was Huey on the security footage. It was enough to divert the Organ and keep them down by the river, instead of up here in his office, at least until we tidied it up a bit."

"Tidied it up?"

"There was blood and brain matter."

"He shot himself in this office?" Dashiell was aghast.

"He was shot in this office, but we don't believe he shot himself."

"You found a suicide note," Dashiell said.

"Yes, I will allow that we found a suicide note. We found a weapon. We found blood." Here Greyson paused and finally said, "But we found no body."

"I don't understand. What did he do with his body?"

Dashiell clearly wasn't thinking straight, so Greyson began to speak more slowly. "Um, yes. That's the point. He couldn't do anything with his body if he killed himself. So someone else must have killed him. We can piece together a few facts. From the blood and traces of hair, we can surmise that after he was shot, his head fell forward onto his desk."

Dashiell twisted around to look at the desk. "My desk?"

"Yes, but don't worry, we went over it twice with Murphy's Oil Soap and then used a whole can of furniture polish. "We found a trail of blood indicating that someone dragged the body across the room and stuffed it down the burn chute."

"What burn chute?" Dashiell whispered.

"There used to be a burn chute in here, but we paneled over it after the tragedy." Greyson pointed to a nearby spot on the wall. Slinky's team had done such a good job of matching the new paneling to the old that you would never guess anything had been changed. Dashiell didn't look in the direction that Greyson pointed. Instead, his wide eyes remain fixed on the index finger. Greyson slowly moved his hand right, then left as if conducting an eye exam. Dashiell continued to focus on the finger. Greyson let his hand fall and continued.

"Naturally, when we saw that, we assumed we would find the corpse in the basement in a pile of burn bags. You would think, wouldn't you? Well, no body. Then we thought perhaps that the body had lodged in the chute. So we lowered a camera down. But again, no body." Greyson shrugged. "Damnedest thing. We thought the smell of decomposition would eventually give him away, but evidently the murderer somehow managed to get the body out of the building past the SCUDOs." Shelby gravely turned to Slinky, who was in charge of the SCUDOs. "I'm afraid it doesn't say much for grounds security."

Slinky gave him a scalding look.

A thin note of panic rose in Dashiell's voice. "The old BOM died on my desk? He bled on my carpet?"

Slinky leaned forward. Logistics was his bailiwick.

"We installed new carpet. We always keep a few rolls of carpeting on hand, just in case."

"In case what?" Dashiell asked.

"In case of this sort of thing." Slinky waved a gnawed pencil toward the crime scene. "We had the carpet in by three o'clock the next morning. Stainmaster Saxony. Patriot blue with gold flecks. We put down Prestige Delux padding. Bonded urethane cushion. Anti-bacterial. Moisture and mildew resistant, which is important because there was no time to make sure the area dried properly, although we had about twenty fans in here." The corner of Slinky's mouth twitched wildly. "We used Enzyme Eraser on the area. Same stuff I use at home when my dog wets the carpet. Enzyme action takes care of all sorts of bodily fluids—there was some urine, too, I believe. Great stuff. I mean the Enzyme Eraser, not the urine." Slinky laughed. "Leaves everything smelling nice and orangey." He waved a hand dismissively at the floor. "Then, of course, you had to go replace my Saxony with this bleached wool crap. Mark my words, you will regret natural fibers when the bacteria start to grow."

I placed a hand on Slinky's arm. "I think that's enough."

Slinky sat back. "Everyone expects the physical plant to be perfect, but no one ever wants to hear what goes into making it that way. Yet you people can yammer nonstop about some podunk country no one's ever heard of—"

"Slinky," Greyson warned.

"Isn't it illegal to destroy evidence?" Dashiell asked.

Greyson assumed a look of offended innocence. "But we didn't destroy a thing. We carefully preserved the old carpet. It's stretched out in the basement. We're going over every fiber."

"But you cleaned and polished the desk," Dashiell said.

"Only after examining and photographing it thoroughly."

"Why didn't you just give me a new desk and put this one in the basement with the rug."

"Tradition is very important here, Sir. That has always been the BOM's desk."

Dashiell scratched at his ear as if he had a bug in it. "It was obstruction of justice. You broke the law."

"This is Mines territory," Greyson said. "We have our own laws."

"But why didn't you let the police investigate?" Dashiell said.

Greyson rolled his eyes at the hopeless naiveté of the question. "It would have been the Organ, not the police, and the Organ will not stick its nose into the Mines while I breathe. No. The murderer was one of ours, and we'll take care of him our way."

"You haven't caught him yet?"

"We're working on it. We're tracking down the owner of the pistol."

Dashiell once again covered his face with his hands. A long silence ensued. "So, we have a murderer loose in the Mines," he finally said.

"Well, that's not our worst problem." Greyson's tone was dismissive.

"It's not?" Dashiell said.

Greyson spoke. "We believe that the Organ has laid a Molothrus in the Mines."

"A mole?" Dashiell asked.

"No, we don't use the term 'mole' anymore. It got to be a cliché. We now use 'Molothrus,'" Greyson pronounced the word again, slowly. "Mo-lo-thrus. It's the genus of the common cowbird. A cowbird lays its eggs in another bird's nest. When the chick hatches, it pushes the other chicks out of the nest. Then the Molothrus is raised by its adoptive parents."

"That's terrible. Do the other chicks die?" Dashiell was distraught. He was beginning to lose the ability to distinguish between large problems and small problems.

"I'm not an ornithologist, but I assume the chicks are toast," Greyson said. "To get back to the real problems, we have some audio of Hunter Johnson referring to a Molothrus in the Mines—"

"We're bugging the Director of the Organ?" Dashiell was aghast.

Greyson shrugged. "Self-defense."

"But aren't we all on the same side?"

"No," Greyson snapped, "but I'll explain all that to you some other day. To get back to the Molothrus, we know he or she became active shortly after Brick's murder. We're now combing through the records of everyone who entered underground at that time: new miners, transfers, contractors, what have you. Of course, there's always the chance that it's a long-time employee who became disgruntled."

"So you're investigating all the disgruntled employees?" Dashiell asked.

The horsemen exchanged another of those looks. Greyson cleared his throat. "That would take rather a long time."

"And the murderer?" Dashiell asked.

Greyson waved off the question. "Yeah, yeah, we're looking for the murderer, too, but the Molothrus—"

"But the murderer is your top priority, right?"

Dashiell said.

"Let me see if I can explain this." Greyson adopted a tone of parental patience. "Even if the murderer strikes again, he's just killing an *individual*. All indications are that he's a deliberate, one-shot type of guy, not one of those semi-automatic, bullet-spraying wackos. The Molothrus could kill the Mines as an *institution*. We're already on thin ice for faking intelligence after the Stadium Attack. So we've set up a special Molothrus Task Force."

"But, the individual the murderer kills might be me." Dashiell's voice broke like an adolescent's. "He kills BOMs. He's someone with access. It could be the SCUDO sitting in the outer office. It could be my secretary. It could be one of you!" Dashiell looked at us with panicky eyes. Greyson had the barely-contained raw energy of a psychopath. Arthur had a frighteningly bloodless intelligence and no visible eyelashes. Slinky's twitching could have be mortal guilt. Shelby ... I looked like I was about to fall asleep or fall off my chair. No, I was the one Horseman who didn't concern Dashiell.

The A-BOM pulled his legs up into his chair and hugged his knees, rocking back and forth gently. As the Horsemen looked on, Dashiell turned his head and pressed his mouth against his shoulder. He opened his lips and nipped the fine wool of his suit jacket. We shifted in our chairs and our eyes rolled toward the ceiling, as the soft sound of suckling grew audible in the quiet office. The A-BOM was nursing on his jacket.

"Well," Greyson said, "Perhaps we should let you absorb what we've told you thus far, and we'll save the rest for another day."

Dashiell's response was muffled by damp wool.

"We'll give you some time to think about what we've

told you." Greyson rose.

Slinky and Arthur were out of their chairs quickly. It took me somewhat longer. I knocked my shin against the coffee table and once again required Greyson's steadying hand. In a moment, we were gone, and Dashiell was alone in the office. He sucked harder on his jacket as his eyes wandered about the room. They fixed on the Dashiell-board, flashing and winking in cyan and gray.

"Fingertip control of the Mines," Dashiell said. First he laughed, then he began to cry.

"Welcome back, Shelby." Virgil gives me a distinctly unwelcoming smile. "That was an interesting meeting, wasn't it? And you took such excellent notes, which was a good thing since you were hearing a lot of that information for the first time. How did you feel about that?"

"Confused," I said. "I knew that a lot of it—especially the part about Brick—was lies, but I didn't know how much."

"Now it's time for some questions." Virgil leans over and turns on the machine. "First, did you hear anything at that meeting that you should have followed up on?"

"Yes," I admit.

"Was it that report from the Ear, Shelby? The one that disappeared?"

"Yes."

"Did you follow up, Shelby?"

"No."

Virgil flips the machine off. "Time for some longer answers. Why would you not follow up on that?"

"How could I? The Ear disappeared that report. Alberta did it herself. What was I supposed to do? Call her up and ask for it? She not only wouldn't tell me anything, she *couldn't* tell me anything. Since the Ear doesn't officially disappear reports, she would have been forced to deny it. What would I do then? Call up POTUS and tell on the Ear? Government agencies don't tattle on each other. No, I was between a rock and a hard place."

"Those are all excellent excuses, Shelby," Virgil says, "but you're still dead." He slaps his knee and laughs with a high-pitched "heep, heep, heep" followed by a wet snort. "Tell me, was there anything thing else, any small detail, you didn't notice the first time you sat through the meeting? Anything that struck you as odd?"

I remember how Greyson bent over the Caterico cart. "I had never seen Greyson serve coffee to anyone." I ran the scene over again in my mind. "He stood so that Dashiell's view was blocked when he poured, even though that meant standing at the corner of the cart and reaching over some plates. Then he turned and set the coffee down and put his hand in his pocket." Suddenly I knew exactly what Greyson had done. "He put the empty sugar packet in his pocket because something was in that sugar. Greyson was drugging Dashiell with something, something that increased paranoia and anxiety."

"Bingo," Virgil said. "Now, I think we've spent enough time with the powerful men in your life for now. Let's go visit the powerful women."

16

Spiritual Blubber

I smell a heady mix of toner fluid, perfume and rose potpourri. I'm in Thelma's head again, a place that feels warm and safe in sharp contrast to everywhere else I've been.

Her fingernail, embellished with tiger stripes this week, tapped a slow rhythm on the potpourri bowl. She raised her eyes to the desk across the room and watched my executive assistant, Lyle Voth, shuffling papers. He made more noise than necessary, ostentatiously straightening piles, loudly stapling, and for some reason humming the Marseillaise. The tune called up a resemblance I had never noted before. Add a mustache, widen the forehead, and reduce the size of the chin, and Lyle could have been Inspector Clouseau.

Thelma stopped tapping and grabbed her purse. "Lyle, thank you for covering the phones for me, even though I don't know why you're suddenly being so nice when you never were before."

"Don't look a gift horse in the mouth," Lyle said.

Thelma studied Lyle again. He pretended not to notice and went back to his stapling. "Gift snake is more like it," she said under her breath as she exited the suite. She threw one last glance over her shoulder to see Lyle looking toward my office door. She hesitated, then headed out.

It was quiet except for the hollow sound of Thelma's heels striking the floor. Despite those high heels, her walk was rapid and purposeful—even more so than usual. The doors of the seventh-floor tunnel flew past. She took the elevator to the ground floor. Once out of the building, she sprinted to her van. A few moments later she was out on Route 123, maneuvering the van around the slower traffic like it was a sports car. She pulled into a parking garage, stepped on the gas, and beat out an SUV for an empty space. She took the elevator up to the Cafe Bombay. It was a favorite destination for Mines employees because the buffet made a speedy lunch possible. But why would Thelma come here alone? Usually, she went out only when the whole office was going out to celebrate a retirement or promotion.

"I'm meeting someone," she said to the hostess. She scanned the black-lacquered tables until her eyes lit on a sweet-faced, white-haired lady with beryl eyes. Esther waved and flashed a lovely smile.

Hell. An alliance between a man's wife and his secretary is an unnatural thing, a fearsome thing, an assault on his privacy. It shouldn't be allowed.

Thelma hurried over. They hugged and exchanged a few pleasantries before heading off to the buffet. They were familiar enough with the offerings that they could go straight for the butter chicken without peeking into all of the copper chafing dishes.

Returning to the table, they watched the waiter pour their spiced tea. They each took a sip, then Thelma put her cup down and said, "We have to take action on Shelby."

Esther's squeezed her lips together until they turned white under their pink gloss. "I know, but what are we going to do? Kidnap him and send him to rehab?"

"I have a plan," Thelma said.

Esther's eyes widened behind their silver bifocals. "I can't imagine anything that would work."

"Have you heard of Antabuse?"

"Yes. It's a medicine that makes you sick if you drink. But it wouldn't work for Shelby. First, he wouldn't take it, and second, he's not in good enough health to take it safely. He has high blood pressure and a heart murmur."

Thelma speared a papadum with her fork and swirled it in tamarind sauce. She glanced around at tables crowded with diners, many of them Mines personnel. She spoke softly. "Suppose I told you that there's another drug that makes you sick as a dog if you drink. It doesn't have long-term side effects. You don't have to take it regularly. You actually put it right in the alcohol, and the person doesn't even have to know it's there. It doesn't leave a trace in the system. You couldn't find it even if you pumped his stomach and tested the contents."

Esther whispered, "I've never heard of such a thing."

"It's not out there for use by the general public if you know what I mean." Thelma scooted her chair to be closer to Esther. She lowered her voice even more. "It was developed for operations as a safe way to put someone out of commission for a few hours. I have a friend who's a smithy. I met him in the mid-career course years ago. He dresses badly, but he's a nice man and a genius, which you would never guess from looking at him or listening to him. I was telling him my troubles with Shelby, and he told me about it."

Esther brought her fingers to her lips as she considered this information. "You're sure it's safe?"

"I'm sure. You remember when President Beldon puked on the Japanese Prime Minister? Well, that was because he picked up the wrong drink. He was just fine a few hours later."

"Why would the Mines try to make anyone sick at that banquet?" Esther asked.

"I don't remember." Thelma fluttered her fingers in a gesture of dismissal. "There's always some long, drawn out reason that never makes sense. But the point is that it's safe even for a president. Besides, it's got to be safer than letting Shelby drink himself to death or do something really stupid and lose his job. I think that slimy executive assistant of his, Lyle Voth, is looking for evidence to get Shelby in trouble, maybe even get him fired. Lyle's up to something sneaky."

Esther's face went pale. "I can't imagine what would happen if Shelby were suddenly home all day long. Lord forgive me, but he's gotten so grumpy in the evenings I can barely tolerate him."

"I know what you mean." Thelma returned to her usual speaking voice. "He's not exactly a ray of sunshine during the day either. But he's done so much for me over the years, getting me promotions and overtime and performance awards. Helping out when Ray lost his job. He's kept me supplied with garden vegetables every summer. Lots of things. It's just this past year that he's disappeared underneath ..." Thelma tapped her fingernail on the edge of her saucer as she tried to come up with a word. "Underneath a ton of spiritual blubber," she finally said.

"That's exactly it," Esther said. "Spiritual blubber. It's made up of all the lies he tells himself."

Thelma lowered her head and her voice. "He can't afford to be so out of it in his job. I know it hasn't been that long since he ... lost his mother, but—"

"You know it's not that," Esther said. "His mother's death is the excuse he likes to use because he won't talk about what's really wrong. Shelby spouts off this garbage about recognizing his own mortality, but you know what the problem really is."

Thelma reached out and squeezed Esther's hand. "Edward." It wasn't a question.

"Of course," Esther said in a thick voice. "Shelby won't even say his name, won't say anything about him, won't visit. That's what makes me so angry. He's still Edward's father, but he claims he can't bear to visit his own son? It was me Edward tried to kill, not Shelby." Esther took a microscopic bite of food.

Thelma's eyes briefly flitted to Esther's neck. A pretty blue scarf covered the scar where Edward had taken a butcher knife to his mother's throat as she sat at her sewing machine. Thelma lowered her voice. "He didn't know what he was doing. It was the disease."

"I know. The disease and the voices. You can't imagine the shock. Edward was always so smart, so strong, so confident. So perfect I could hardly believe it. All those years of trying to get pregnant, and I finally produced this one, perfect boy. For sixteen years, he was the center of his father's existence. Shelby talked about him all the time then. I bet he talked your ear off, didn't he?"

"Yes," Thelma said. "We both talked about our boys."

"He doesn't talk about Edward anymore, does he?"

"No, and I try not to mention my sons in front of him because I don't want to make him unhappy, but I forget all the time."

"You should be able to talk about your sons," Esther said. "A mother should never feel bad about that." She sipped her tea, put the cup down, and swiped her lips with her napkin, leaving a vivid streak of pink and turmeric yellow on the white linen. "Schizophrenia. Shelby won't say that word, either." Esther returned her napkin to her lap. "Edward, our son, is schizophrenic." She spoke so loudly that people at other tables looked up and then quickly looked away. Esther lowered her voice. "It's a relief to say it. If I said that to Shelby, he would take a swan dive into the nearest bottle and never come out."

Back in the polygraph room, the man in the mirror truly looks dead. His face is white and frozen. His lower lip trembles.

"Shelby," Virgil says, "Let's talk about—"

"No!" I shout. "No, I will not talk about it with you. I will not." I pull the sensor off my finger and rip at the wire across my chest. I will leave this room if I have to walk out and fall straight into the maw of Hell. The fire might be a relief. I try to stand with the lower wire still around my middle.

Virgil holds up his hands. "Stop. Fine. We won't talk about it. Settle down."

In the mirror, I see a foolish old man, half standing, half crouched. A curling black wire circles his ample hips. His mouth gapes. He falls back into the chair and jams his fists into his eyes, even though tears are no longer an option.

17

102774

Virgil has sent me away again. I'm relieved until I realize where I am. It's damp inside this skull and smells like mold and cabbage. Something cold and unforgiving seeps into my spirit and makes me want to howl like a wolf on the frozen steppes. I know who this is by the funk of hopelessness.

An elegant, elderly hand reached for a bottle of vodka and poured half a glass. He raised it. "To lies, stirring, noble, gorgeous lies that lift us up, nurture us, then set us down in Hell." He leaned forward and touched his glass to that of a pale, overweight, and unhealthy-looking man—me.

"To lies," I repeated after a moment of hesitation. I took a sip. I was sitting in a beige chair on a beige carpet in front of beige walls. "Why are we toasting lies?"

"They made me what I am today," he said.

I'm in the head of William Sibley. His pseudo, chosen for him by computer, was AXEL P. Hardacre. If anyone had asked if he had ever committed a murder, he would have said "yes" and left it at that. Lamplight. That was the codename of the dead man, William's grouper, which is Mines jargon for foreign asset. William chose the codename himself, with Diogenes in mind, back when he believed in all the beautiful lies.

"The pause," William said, "that's what haunts me."

It was the night after the Welcome Wagon briefing, and I had come to ask about the pistol, registration number 102774. It was the one thing I did follow up on. I remember thinking how sterile William's condo was. Most ex-sharpers collect souvenirs from their time overseas, but William's quarters were devoid of the Palekh boxes, Matryoshka dolls, lacquered trays, and other colorful tchotchkes one would expect an ex-Soviet hand to own. William didn't need souvenirs to remember.

"The pause?" I prompted when the silence stretched too long.

William started and came back to himself. "The pause after he had kneeled on the floor, touching his knee to a white chalk line. The pause between the moment they pressed the pistol to the back of his head and the instant it went off. The muzzle rested in the lower left quadrant of the occipital bone." William pressed a finger to the back of his close-cropped gray head. "Imagine that pause between the first touch of steel and the shot. They were in the basement of the Lubyanka. I've never been there, of course, but I can smell it. You know that uniquely Soviet smell: cheap synthetic cloth, those vile Russian cigarettes, sweat, that cloying, cabbagy stink. Add to that the smell of rodents, dried blood, perhaps disinfectant." William studied the palm of his hand. "After the pistol was fired, an official recorded its registration number in the record of the execution. Bureaucracies love worthless numbers."

"How did you find out the number? How did you get

that pistol?" I asked.

William rubbed a finger around the rim of his glass again and again as if putting himself into a trance. "I consulted with several high-profile defectors. They told me whom to approach, how much money to offer. Fortunately, I had a hefty savings account thanks to hardship pay and no family to support." William expelled a bitter laugh. "First I got a copy of the official account of the execution. It included the registration number of the pistol: 102774. I found out the pistol itself was sitting in a glass case in the KGB's museum—they have one, just like we do. Probably have their own version of the MFAHPC. I paid a much larger sum to the night janitor to steal the pistol for me. He replaced it with a weapon of the same vintage that I provided. I doubt if anyone ever noticed. The metalsmith I hired did a rather good job of altering and aging the serial number."

"How did the real pistol wind up in Brick's office?" I asked.

"I hosted a small get-together of my old sharper friends last summer. Brick was there. At the end of the night, 102774 was gone. Lord only knows why Brick chose to take my pistol. I doubt he deliberately planned to throw suspicion on me. More likely he was aiming for irony."

"They're going to figure out that it's your pistol," I said.

"They've already figured it out." William lifted his thin shoulders in a world-weary shrug. "They're surveilling me. Doing a damn clumsy job of it, too. I think they must be using the latest crop of baby sharpers. I'm trying to make it easy for them—professional courtesy, you know. I'm careful not to make any sudden, unsignaled turns; I don't look over my shoulder; I slow down for yellow lights, so they won't have to run the red. I don't want a traffic accident on my conscience too."

"Have you thought of going to Greyson and explaining how Brick got the gun?"

"What use has Greyson got for the truth? It's irrelevant to him. Besides, Greyson is only watching me out of curiosity. He won't do anything to contradict the story they told the press. If that story were to fall apart, however ..." William took a sip of vodka and raised his eyes to the ceiling.

"They would need a scapegoat," I said.

"I'll cross that bridge when I come to it," William said. "Cross that bridge ..."

I waited for him to continue, but from the expression in his eyes, his thoughts had strayed far from Greyson and his machinations. When William spoke again, he was in the distant past. "I remember walking over a frozen bridge in Leningrad in the dead of winter. I was about to fly back to HQ for an awards ceremony." His voice grew bitter, self-mocking. "I was getting an award for 'the outstanding quantity and quality of information' I had attained from Lamplight. I think I may have even been composing my acceptance speech in my head. I was watching the traffic roll past—such antiquated vehicles. I looked around at the lousy, crumbling apartment blocks. I compared what I saw to the strength and vigor of the United States. A revelation came to me: the Soviet Union would not stand another twenty years. I felt like I was walking a foot above the pavement. I saw the end of the empire then, years before the alchemists suspected.

"What was it, three, six more steps after that when I saw the mark on the bridge railing? It was an open chalk triangle, a signal that Lamplight was in trouble. It was his last communication. Pride before a fall. Lightness before the dark. Hubris before humiliation ...

"How ironic that now, like Lamplight, I am under surveillance in my own country. Sure, I was used to being followed in Leningrad. I could always feel it, a heaviness. It's different to feel it in your own country. What was it that I was fighting for all those years? Freedom? The American dream? Camelot versus the Evil Empire? Good versus evil?"

I tapped on the side of my glass, uncomfortable with his implication and impatient to return to the point of my visit. "How did you discover that it was your pistol found in Brick's office?"

"Daphne. She's an old friend. She's going to try to get 102774 back for me. I swore an oath a long time ago to look at it every day."

"Maybe it's time to forgive yourself," I said softly.

"I'll forgive myself when I'm dead." William stared into his vodka, watching the green bar-shaped reflection of the library lamp on its surface. Finally, he said, "You're right. Maybe it's time."

When I return to the polygraph room, Virgil stares at me intently. "You didn't pick up on it," he says. "He was telling you he was going to commit suicide, and you didn't pick up on it. You excused yourself and left right after that."

"I got lost in the pause," I say. "I thought he was saying it was time to forgive himself, not that it was time he was dead. I suppose I was in a hurry to get out of that oppressive room."

"I suppose," Virgil says. "For a long time William didn't understand how he was responsible for Lamplight's execution. Then he remembered a figure hovering at the edge of his vision as he hurried to a meeting with his star grouper. It was just a flash sighting quickly pushed out of his mind. If he had been paying attention, he would have identified the surveillance and aborted the meeting. He should never have met with Lamplight at all. They should have done everything through dead drops, but the two were drawn to each other. Dour kindred spirits. William should have left a signal for Lamplight telling him to end all communications, but he was impatient for more information. Impatience, Shelby, it's America's great sin; impatience, short memory, historical ignorance. So be patient. You won't get your answers all at once."

18

Tainted Bottles

I close my eyes for a second to formulate a response to Virgil's words. I should know by now that debate is useless, but it's such a habit. Some stubborn part of me still thinks there's a way to win. It would be better for me to be quiet, but I think of a point I can make. I open my mouth, my eyes, but Virgil is gone. In his place, I see a single white feather leaning in a cracked coffee mug on a metal desk. Nearby a dusty nameplate reads "Al Dufresne."

"Morning, Dirksen. I'm sorry. I told them it was a bad idea."

I am in the head of a man who spoke softly and sadly. A fascinating place, like Willy Wonka's chocolate factory rising up in the middle of a bayou.

Al leaned back in his chair and stared down into a mug of coffee that rested on a silver belt buckle in the shape of an alligator. A long, gray-blond beard snaked down the front of a plaid shirt.

Al started as a heavy grocery bag, the old paper kind, landed on his desk.

"Your stuff is ready." An extraordinarily thin man with thick glasses leaned over and whispered, "Five bottles: two Four Roses, one Jose Cuervo, one Jack Daniels, and one Smirnoff. All in the requested sizes and sealed like new from the distillery." The man slipped two small vials with droppers out of an interior pocket of his jacket. "These are for the open bottles in his desk and at home. Add two drops per liter, no more or it could get messy. I won't ask what this is for."

"Thank you, you're a prince," Al whispered.

"You made me that tracking device for my kid, so we're even." With that, the man was gone.

Al peered into the bag, then pulled an old Washington Post from the pile under his desk. He separated it into sections, crumpled them, and stuffed them between the bottles. "Don't need no clinking," he muttered. Officially, alcohol was forbidden in the Mines. Everyone from the BOM down to the summer interns ignored the rule, but Al wasn't going to take any chances. He pulled a plaid jacket from a hook in his cubicle. A moth flew out. He put on the jacket and picked up the bag.

Al left the vault. As the door closed, I catch a quick look at the sign next to it: OSTMO—AUTHORIZED PERSONNEL ONLY. The acronym stood for Office of Special Technical Methods and Operations. It was the home of Arthur's best techies. Al Dufresne was the man who made the listening device they implanted in Senator Harrison Westerly's bird.

And here he was with a bag full of bottles that exactly matched the ones I owned at the time.

Al took the elevator to the seventh floor and walked to my office. Thelma was delighted to see him and even more delighted to see the brown paper bag. She gave him a big hug, right in the middle of the executive suite. A sudden close-up view of Thelma's silk-clad bosom suggests that Al was a man of short stature.

Lyle Voth eyed Al with suspicion. "What's in the bag?" he asked.

"A gator," Al said, "for Thelma's boys. They've been asking for a real Cajun gator."

"You're lying." Lyle tipped his head and peered down his beaky nose.

"Go ahead, stick your hand in the bag." Al started toward him with the bag, and Lyle pushed his chair back.

"I have a meeting downstairs." Lyle grabbed a pen and notepad. "I don't have time for this. If that is an alligator in that bag, it's illegal, and it's a salmonella risk, not to mention against Mines regulations."

"We are all animals," Al growled, "and I guarantee I'm more dangerous than this gator." He made a quick movement that caused the bag to rustle, and Lyle practically leaped out the door.

Thelma and Al allowed a brief pause after the door closed before they burst into laughter.

"Makes me wish I had a baby gator to put in his file drawer." Al's eyes scanned the cherrywood furniture and patriot blue carpeting and came to rest on a framed print of Renoir's *Luncheon of the Boating Party*. "Quite a place you have here, down to the fancy pictures."

Thelma followed his gaze. "That one used to be in the inner office when Sharon Pendergast was Boss of White Mines, but Shelby didn't like it, so I put it above my desk. I like the little dog and the colors, even though everybody in the picture is drunk as a skunk. Look how red their faces are."

"I'd rather have dogs playing poker." Al rustled his

bag. "Speaking of drunk skunks, have you worked things out with his wife?"

"Yes. Poor Esther, she has the patience of a saint. She gave me an extra set of keys to his car. All I have to do is put the bag in the trunk under an old blanket he keeps in there. She'll get it out when he gets home and switch out his bottles. He has them hidden all over their house, like Esther wouldn't notice a bottle of bourbon behind the sheets in the linen closet."

Al took the vials from his shirt pocket. "This is for the open bottles. Add two drops of this per liter. Two. No more. One vial for you. One for the Mrs."

"Great. Hold on. Shelby is in the A-BOM's office. Let me do this right now because I know he'll take a drink as soon as he gets back. Watch the door for me and yell if he comes."

Thelma took a vial and one bottle of bourbon into my office. Al stationed himself at the open vault door where he could see down the tunnel.

I am in Thelma's skull again. I peer out through her lovely, almond eyes and see her manicured hands inside the lower left-hand drawer of my desk. How did she know where I hid the key to that drawer?

She laughed as she removed the gym shorts that covered my stash. "Like Shelby would ever wear these." She unscrewed the cap of a half full bottle and carefully added two drops from the vial. She started to replace the cap and then whispered, "A couple more for good measure, just to make sure it works." She added more drops. Thelma replaced the bottle in the drawer exactly as she found it:

with the label facing north. Then she switched out the un-opened bottle with the one Al had given her and replaced the gym shorts in their original position. She emerged from the office holding my untainted bottle. She handed it to Al. "Here, you take this one. You know I don't ap-prove, but since you're going to drink anyway, you might as well take this for all your trouble."

"*Merci beaucoup.*" Al slipped the bottle into his bag, turned to leave, and collided with Maddie James as she burst through the door. He almost dropped the bag but recovered himself in time. "Excuse me, ma'am," he said, even though the collision was clearly Maddie's fault.

As Al escaped with his bottles, Maddie threw herself in front of Thelma. "You have got to get me on Shelby's schedule ASAP."

"He told me not to put you on his schedule," Thelma said.

Just then, a retired contract escort stuck his head in the door. "Excuse me, the workmen are here to change the lights. You need to put away any classified items."

"Can you give me a couple of minutes?" Thelma said.

Maddie leaned close to Thelma and whispered, "This is about a terrorist threat. I believe something is going to happen soon. Can you ignore me in good conscience?"

Thelma looked into Maddie's brown eyes and saw desperation. She sat down at her desk and pulled up my electronic calendar. "Is two o'clock okay?"

Virgil shakes his head. "You made Thelma cancel that meeting, didn't you, Shelby? Why didn't you take her more seriously? It might have saved your life."

"Was that the threat that killed me? Of course, it was. I ... well ... you don't know Maddie. She always had her tail on fire about one threat or another."

"But she was right about the stadium attack, wasn't she?"

"Yes," I admit.

"And she was right about the strikes, wasn't she?"

"Yes, but she was wrong about twenty other things," I point out. "At least twenty. And we can't keep the alert level at red or orange constantly. Do you know how much alert level orange costs the taxpayer? As soon as the alert level goes up, everybody is yelling at us to lower it because the expense is eating them alive."

"But you could have given her some staff."

"I suppose," I say reluctantly, "but she would have used it to make trouble for the Mines."

"Wasn't the attack trouble?" Virgil asks. "Listen to yourself, Shelby, you're arguing the case for ignoring the warnings about the attack that killed you. Your ass is dead, flatter than a pancake, and you're still trying to cover it. Do you see the irony in that?"

"All I see is irony."

19

The Mourner

I smell Werther's candy, sour breath, and something vaguely poultry in nature. A curious room comes into view. The high Palladian windows, elaborate woodwork, and sumptuous furniture speak of wealth. The dust, bird droppings, missing chunks of wood, and scattered bits of dried fruit, seed hulls, and white down suggest something altogether stranger.

Weak eyes scanned the room and came to rest on a single white feather stuck to a well-gnawed volume of the Louisiana civil code. Senator Westerly sobbed.

A knock sounded on the door.

"Go away!" Westerly howled.

The door opened a crack to reveal a weathered strip of cheek and a brown eye wide with apprehension. "Sir, your wife told me to clean the room. She said you can't put it off any longer."

"I don't care what Alice said."

A slow blink. "Alice was your second wife, sir. It was Adele told me to clean the room. She said it's not healthy to let them bird poops sit around. It's been weeks now."

Westerly rose from his desk and crossed the room quite rapidly for his age. He pushed the door shut and locked it. "No," he yelled. "You will not clean this room. It's a shrine to Dirksen. These are his last poops. You won't touch them."

"Yes, sir." The maid's steps receded down the hallway.

Westerly returned to his desk. He picked up the phone and dialed a number. The answering "hello" was gruff, challenging.

"Gordy?" Westerly said.

"I told you not to call."

"I need to talk to you immediately."

"We shouldn't meet anymore."

"I need to. It's my money you're using."

There was a long pause on the other end of the line. Finally, Gordy said, "Fine. Tomorrow three o'clock. You know where."

The line went dead.

And my view went black. A hollow rushing sound ...

The senator again. His vision is blurrier than ever. Along with the usual Westerly odors, I smell stale grease.

He swiped at the top of a gray Formica table with a paper napkin, crumpled it, and pulled two more napkins from a metal dispenser. He carefully spread them out so that he could rest his arms on the table without soiling his cuffs. A waitress came to the booth to offer a bright laminated menu, but the senator waved it away. "I don't eat in places like this."

She opened her mouth to speak, thought better of it, and retreated with a barely perceptible eye roll.

Westerly scanned the eatery—he was the only customer—then focused on the cracked green vinyl of the opposite bench cushion. He started and blinked when a man abruptly slid into the seat.

"This is bullshit," Gordy said.

He was a tough man with an incongruous tendency toward dandyism. Despite the obvious effort he put into his appearance, he never looked quite right. Expensive suit jackets pulled too tight over his muscular frame. His starched white shirts didn't fit properly. All the product he added to his curly dark hair turned it greasy.

Gordy had always made me uncomfortable with his fake, back-slapping friendliness, but today he was scowling and angry.

"We should not be meeting anymore. Everything's in place. The ball is rolling. The only purpose this meeting can serve is to screw it up. You want that?"

The senator sat back and sucked his teeth. Finally, he said, "Remember who you're talking to. Remember who obtained the funds."

Gordy started to answer but stopped when the waitress approached with her menus. He, too, waved them away. "Coffee, burger, fries," he said. She left, and he turned back to the senator. "I don't care who you are," he whispered. "My only concern is success. We won't pull this thing off if you don't learn to follow instructions. I told you not to try to contact me while I was in Manchester and what did you do?"

"Look, you've already scolded me for that. It's old news," the senator said.

"Why did you ask for this meeting?"

Westerly lowered his voice to a whisper. "I need reassurance. I need to make sure they're punished. All of them. Their screw-ups cost us the Iran operation and the White House. Then they murdered Dirksen." A sob rose in the old man's throat. "They can't get away with that."

Gordy looked closely at Westerly's face. He swallowed and spoke in a slow, soothing voice. "Of course, they won't get away with it. We've talked about this before. Everything will go off as planned, but only if we are careful."

"Oh and another thing," the senator said. "We have to change the date."

"What the fuck?" Gordy said too loudly. He sat back and closed his eyes, probably counting to ten. He opened them again. You don't know what's involved here."

"I want them to do it on Dirksen's hatch day," Westerly said. "I can't get through that day without a distraction. It's only a couple of weeks earlier than the original date and it would mean so much to me."

"We can't go any earlier for two reasons," Gordy said. "One, our friends won't go for it, and two, now that I know Brick Mason was murdered, I need the time to find out who did it."

"You still think it wasn't suicide?" the senator asked.

"It wasn't. I've got a very good source on the seventh floor who knows the details of the coverup, but not who the murderer was. Not yet. He's still working on it. I'll put some heat on him, but we've got to give him enough time to get more evidence. My guess is it's one of the horsemen. If they survive this attack, I want to make sure that they'll have even worse in store. Proving one of those barons guilty of murder is like a wet dream. I can't imagine anything better." A sly look came over Gordy's face. "You know it was probably the same guy responsible for offing your bird."

Senator Westerly looked up sharply. "You think so?"

"Makes sense, doesn't it? In both cases, has to be somebody high level."

The senator thought a minute. "What do you mean 'survive the attack?' You promised me you would call in a bomb threat first. Remember, we just want to destroy the buildings, not the people. I am a Christian, after all. That will be enough to spell the end of the Minds as we know it. If they can't manage to stop an attack on their own compound, Congress is certain to break them up and farm out their functions to other agencies. You haven't forgotten your promise, have you?"

"Of course, not," Gordy said. He reddened. The waitress came with his lunch. As she poured his coffee, he made a visible effort to get control of the expression on his face. The waitress left. Gordy upended a bottle of ketchup over his fries and slapped his palm viciously on the bottom of the bottle until a few dollops came out. He set the bottle down, replaced the cap, and dragged a fry through the sauce. The red drained from his face as he chewed. Now and then he threw a furtive glance at Westerly, likely calculating the best strategy for dealing with this man who was so powerful and yet so disturbed. Gordy took a big gulp of coffee and set the cup down. "Sure," he said. "Anything you want."

I barely notice Virgil's reappearance. He leans back on two legs of his chair, arms crossed over his chest, and allows me to absorb what I've just witnessed. Then he leans forward, and the two elevated legs of his chair hit the floor with an amplified bang. "Pretty amazing alliance wasn't it?" Virgil says. "An elderly senator with a crumbling brain, an agent of the Organ with a grudge against the Mines, and a shadowy figure in Manchester. Let's see what you were doing while Gordy and Westerly were plotting."

20

In Memory of Harvey Barton

Back in my own skull, it smells like bourbon, orange Tums, and vomit.

I headed down the BOM tunnel, where the portraits of former BOMs hung in stiff array. My destination was Medical, which might offer something stronger than Tums for my stomach. I thought I had a touch of the flu. I never suspected Esther and Thelma. I was so wrapped up in my gastric distress that I didn't notice Greyson until it was too late to avoid him. The man had been a real ass lately, calling daily and sometimes twice-daily meetings on the LI and the OLI. I was convinced that the purpose of these meetings was not to inform the A-BOM but to unhinge him.

Greyson was standing before the portrait of Harvey Barton, who had served only weeks as BOM before he was found curled beneath his desk in a fetal position, whimpering and sucking on a Tootsie Pop. He left the building in cloth restraints a couple of weeks after his Welcome Wagon Briefing.

That spooky Cheshire grin broke across Greyson's

face as he hailed me and nodded toward the pale, startled face of Harvey Barton. "He was an outsider, too."

I stopped reluctantly. "I forget," I said, "Where'd he come from?"

"Diplomatic Service," Greyson said with the same dismissive tone he might have used to say "Girl Scout Troop 37" or "kindergarten."

I considered the poor bastard in the painting. His smile was a hair away from a grimace. He sat ramrod straight in his chair. "What an unnatural pose," I said.

"Well," Greyson said, "this thing was painted in the mental institution. He was strapped into that chair."

I examined the portrait more closely and saw something odd clutched in the man's fist. "What is that in his hand? Is that—"

"Tootsie Pop," Greyson said, and his grin seemed to stretch beyond the borders of his face.

A suspicion rose in my mind. I looked sharply at Greyson. "What drove him over the edge?"

"No one ever figured it out," Greyson said with a look of mock innocence. Then, after a pause. "Do you remember who was BOBM at the time?"

"Your father," I said as I watched pride suffuse Greyson's face. Then a surge of nausea almost bent me double. "I have to go," I said and hurried off.

"Special meeting in Dashiell's office at seven o'clock sharp tomorrow morning," Greyson called after me.

Darkness. A hollow rush. A sudden view of the rising sun boring a hole through the window and into my skull. I was sitting at my desk in the executive suite. I didn't have the strength to get up and close the blinds. I looked down at my fingers as they struggled with the impenetrable foil packaging enclosing an antacid tablet. My insides were in revolt.

Nasty time for Greyson to call a special meeting. I wanted to go home and go back to bed. Failing that, I wanted to chew my antacids and dig into that new assessment on emerging political movements in sub-Saharan Africa. But instead, I was obliged to straighten my tie, loosen my belt to give some relief to my bloated stomach, and hoist myself out of my chair. I checked my pocket for my trusty notebook and opened it to see how many blank pages were left. Only three, not nearly enough for this meeting. I took a fresh one from the stash in my drawer. I slapped a red Top Secret sticker on the front, and I was as ready as I could make myself for the upcoming ordeal.

Daphne waved us into the inner office. I settled into the chair nearest the BOM's nickel-rimmed Lucite trash can, just in case. I thought perhaps if I said nothing and merely observed, focusing on my notes and barely breathing, I could get through the meeting without outing my breakfast. Greyson conducted the proceeding. Dashiell no longer made an effort to appear in control. I noticed that he had stopped shaving his head. Light brown hairs had collected around the genuinely bald dome like girl scouts around a campfire. I peered more closely and saw a pale fuzz invading the A-BOM's chin. The man was losing it. He sat rigid in his chair as if strapped in. His eyes had a wide and pleading look. I knew what they were saying: "Don't tell me anything else, please."

The Dashiellboard was dark.

"Good morning, gentlemen. Shall we begin?" Greyson's tone was cheerful, almost chirpy, even though he had nothing pleasant to impart.

"Wait a minute," Dashiell said. "I should go to the men's room." He got up and made his way unsteadily to the office's private bathroom and shut the door.

Greyson quickly rose and went to the BOM's desk. He pushed the blotter aside and spread his handkerchief over the bare mahogany surface.

"What are you doing?" Arthur whispered.

"Shh, I have an idea." Greyson took a pewter globe paperweight and thwacked it down on the handkerchief. He thwacked it again, near the first strike. Then he replaced everything as he found it and sat back down, ignoring the questioning looks of the other Horsemen.

Dashiell returned from the bathroom just as Daphne's voice came over the intercom. "The refreshments have arrived."

Slinky got up to open the door. Daphne pushed in a cart with heavy, cream-colored ceramic cups and saucers, napkins, two carafes of coffee—regular and decaf—and a pyramid of powdered jelly donuts on a tray.

"Shall I pour the coffee?" Daphne's voice was cool and clipped, her eyes tired. Blue shadows showed through her makeup. Grief had taken its toll.

"No, sweetheart, we'll take care of it," Greyson said. The condescending "sweetheart" was a deliberate effort to annoy Daphne, who had never made a secret of her disdain for the man who cuckolded Brick Mason.

If she had been a cat, she would have clawed his nose bloody, but as a senior secretary at the Mines, all she could do was narrow her eyes. "Fine," she said and exited. Daphne—who could enter and exit as quietly as a mouse—slammed the door. Dashiell jumped. I worried that his bulging eyes would pop out and roll across the room.

Greyson chuckled and turned to the A-BOM. He assumed the obsequious smirk of a *maître d' hôtel*. "Coffee, sir? Decaf? You look a bit jittery. Perhaps we should send for some nice chamomile tea."

Dashiell grew defensive. He straightened his shoulders and said, "I'm not jittery. Give me regular. Strong. Black."

"A manly brew for the A-BOM." Greyson's voice flirted with open mockery. He positioned himself between the BOM and the cart, poured the cup, added sugar, and handed it to his boss, who took it with two trembling hands. Some of the scalding liquid sloshed into the saucer and spilled over the edge, onto the fly of Dashiell's trousers. He elected to ignore the incident or perhaps he wasn't aware of it.

"Donut, sir?" Greyson asked.

"Please," Dashiell said too brightly.

Greyson used tongs to select the largest of the pastries. He placed it on a plate and set it down on the coffee table in front of Dashiell. He served coffee to Slinky. Arthur declined refreshment, as did I. The very smell of the coffee was making me nauseous. I hated Greyson for stretching out the preliminaries. Why didn't he state his business and get on with it?

But that wasn't Greyson's style.

Only the A-BOM took a donut. The rest of were wise enough to know that dark suits and powdered sugar are an unfortunate combination. The A-BOM came to this realization too late. The donut was a veritable sugar bomb.

The slightest touch set off a cloud of sweet powder. Dashiell picked up the plate, bent over it, gently lifted the donut, and took a cautious bite, which triggered a magmatic eruption of raspberry jelly. He recoiled from the blood-red wound, still smoking with white sugar.

Greyson handed Dashiell a small Mines-logo napkin, which proved pitifully inadequate to the task. As Dashiell wiped at his jellied fingers, Greyson said, "Have we ever told you the story of Vaughn Sutter Wayne and the donut?"

I groaned. I meant it to be an inward groan, but it broke out in a hound-like growl. The rest of the Horsemen turned to stare at me.

"My stomach," I said.

"Perhaps you should appease it with a donut," Greyson suggested.

I glared at him, then lowered my eyes to my notebook and scribbled, *The BOBM can stick his donut.*

"The press didn't pick up on the donut," Greyson said to Dashiell. "Only a few people in this building know the story. As one of his successors, you should know it, too."

"Oh yes," Slinky said. "It's actually rather amusing, but for the tragedy of it."

Amusing, but for the tragedy of it, I wrote and underlined it twice. I added, *New motto for the Mines?*

Dashiell still wiped at his fingers and face, only managing to smear the mess. The Horsemen would eat this little Chihuahua alive. They covered him with sugar to make him go down easier. I glanced around at their faces and saw a gleeful rapaciousness. Even Slinky, the most decent of the other Horsemen, hated Dashiell. He never forgave him for ripping up that new patriot blue carpeting.

"*A-BOM toast,*" I wrote in my notebook, "*Greyson men-*

tally redecorating office in colors of his alma mater. Bastard thinks he's going to be next BOM."

"The newspaper stories said he had a stroke at his desk," Greyson said, "but we didn't tell the reporters about the donut."

"He was eating a jelly donut," Slinky said.

"Raspberry," Arthur added. "A raspberry-jelly-filled powdered donut. What a coincidence! Just like the one you're eating now."

"Those were his favorite," Greyson said. "Baked right here in our own executive dining room. They're good, aren't they?"

Dashiell didn't answer. He continued to smear jelly over his fingers with the tiny napkin.

"Here," Greyson said, "Let me give you a clean one." He leaned forward with the napkin, and, for a moment, I feared that he would dab at the A-BOM's besmeared chin like a mother. Instead, he merely handed it to Dashiell.

"He had a stroke and fell forward into the donut," Greyson said. "His nose landed dead center."

"They found powdered sugar in his lungs," Arthur said, "which suggests that he wasn't dead before he hit the donut. He actually died in the donut."

"I thought you said he died before his head hit my desk," Dashiell said.

"Well, he actually died in the donut," Slinky said.

Dashiell began to cough sugar, and Greyson clapped him on the back and continued to spin out his tale. "The Horsemen cleaned him up before the ambulance arrived. For the sake of his dignity, you know. I've been told it took forever to gouge all of the sugar and jelly out of that honker of a nose. And how's this for irony? You know who wielded the Q-Tip? Brick Mason himself. He was the Executive Assistant to the BOBM at the time. Couldn't trust the job to just any low-level drone. Had to be kept a secret for the sake of Vaughn's dignity."

"Dignity," Slinky repeated solemnly.

"Dignity," Arthur said. "We would do the same for you any day of the week." He reached over and clapped Dashiell on the back, which sent him into a fit of coughing that sprayed sugar across the coffee table.

"Let me show you something interesting," Greyson said. He got up and went to the BOM's desk and lifted the blotter. "Come look."

Dashiell rose from his chair and approached the desk with caution.

Greyson pointed to the two dents he had made earlier. "That," he said, "is where Vaughn's head hit and that is where Brick's head hit. That's one of the reasons we couldn't have you replace this desk. It's a piece of Mines history."

Dashiell's mouth fell open as he stared at the dents.

"By the way, speaking of dead BOMs," Greyson said, "I had Medical Assessments do a psychological profile of Brick's murderer."

I made an effort to straighten up in my chair. "Medical Assessments is my unit."

"Oh, you don't mind, do you, Shelby?" Greyson said with an air of innocent surprise.

What he had done was a major breach of Mines etiquette, but I said nothing out loud because calling out a colleague in front of the A-BOM would be an even worse breach. Besides, a certain lower-tract instability was beginning to make rash action, such as moving or talking or breathing, inadvisable.

"I must admit the psychological profile is a bit ... disturbing," Greyson said. It was a masterly use of the ellipsis. "Stuffing the body down the burn shaft, according to Medical Assessments, indicated what is known as a 'morbid-slash-psychotic sense of humor.'"

I made a move to protest, but a sudden liquid shift in my lower intestine stopped me, silent but open-mouthed.

Greyson raised his eyebrows. "You have something to add, Shelby?"

"No." The word came out soft and squeezed.

Greyson gently led Dashiell back to his Lucite chair. "Morbid-slash-psychotic sense of humor. Deadly irony. He laughed when it was done. That's what they do: laugh while jerking off. That's why we can be sure that he'll strike again. Nothing else will bring him any ... satisfaction ... now." Greyson smiled and sat back in his chair. If he had grown fur, he would've looked exactly like a cat. That avid, unapologetic attitude toward killing. Shaking his hand, one would not have been surprised to feel claws. I tried to concentrate on this psychological assessment of Greyson to take my mind off the pressure building in my gut. To take my mind off the A-BOM's private bathroom. Even the Horsemen—Dashiell would've said *especially* the Horsemen—were not allowed to use it. I would have to break that rule as soon as my stomach cramp eased up enough for me to move.

"He stood right by the burn chute and got it off," Greyson said. "We found a few dribbles of semen on the carpet."

That was a lie. I was sure that no such evidence was found. I tried to catch Arthur's eye, but the Boss of Smithery stared straight ahead with an inhumanly placid look on his face. Then I realized that he had fallen asleep. Slinky nudged him with his foot, and he awoke with a snort.

"As to why we didn't find the body at the base of the chute, my guess is that he decided to have some more fun with it. Probably took it home and dressed it in drag á la a certain former Director of the Organ," Greyson said.

"Perhaps he cut it up, wrapped it, and stored it in his freezer," Arthur said, "with the parts appropriately labeled: BOM hocks, BOM shank, BOM brisket."

Slinky slapped his thigh and added, "BOM loin, BOM flank, BOM rump roast."

"BOM chops, BOM rib, leg o' BOM," Arthur said.

"Don't forget BOM oysters!" Greyson's eyes gleamed, and the Horsemen, except for me, burst into raucous laughter. They were in dangerously high spirits.

I lowered my head and directed a sidewise glance at Dashiell. The A-BOM's mouth gaped. Drool pooled between the pouty lower lip and the cosmetically whitened bottom teeth. His eyes dilated and fixed on the donut.

"You think we're tasteless, don't you, Dashiell?" Greyson asked.

Dashiell was in no condition to respond to even the simplest query.

"The thing is, to understand a morbid-slash-psychotic sense of humor, one must learn to laugh at morbid things, to think like the perpetrator. You have to insert yourself into that sick, sick mind and think, 'what could I do to the BOM's body?' Perhaps he's thawing it and eating it for dinner every night."

"Or breakfast every morning," Arthur said. "BOM-elets."

"Or, if he's southern, fried BOMiny," Slinky said. He twirled his chewed pencil between his fingers.

"Don't forget BOMbalaya," Arthur said.

"Cheer up, Dashiell," Greyson said. "If he's eating the

body, it will probably keep him appeased for months. Arthur, how long do you think the average man could feed on two sides of BOM?"

"Well," Arthur said, "I would say it would depend on portion size. I mean, whether he's eating plain BOM steaks every night or just stir-frying a small amount of diced BOM with vegetables and eating it over rice. In the latter case, it could drag on for some time. Moreover, he would be a much healthier murderer. Especially if he's using brown rice."

I'm going to shit myself, I thought.

"What do you think he's doing with the bones?" Slinky asked.

"Oh, they're probably gnawed and buried in his yard. He has a dog," Greyson said. "We found red hairs on the carpeting. We thought they might belong to Daphne, but they were the wrong color and texture. Testing revealed that they came from an Irish setter. Of course, Brick didn't have a dog."

Complete fiction. I clenched my teeth and tightened all of my muscles, but most especially the sphincter.

Dashiell suddenly shook his head. He sat up, and an angry frown brought some life to his pale face. "This doesn't sound right. None of it sounds right."

I sent him silent instruction: *Fight back.*

"I want to see all of this in writing," the A-BOM said, "And all four of you sign it."

"In the Mines, we don't set this sort of thing down on paper," Greyson said.

"I'll bet you don't. Well, I don't care how you've always done things. Now you will do them my way." For a moment, Dashiell sounded like his old self, but then he pushed it too far. He leaned forward and banged his fist on the table to emphasize his point. But a powdered, raspberry jelly donut—one bite missing—came between fist and table. Scarlet jelly squirted out in Pollack-like arcs, and a thick cloud of powder rose over the scene. Dashiell lowered his sugared lashes and looked down to see his fist embedded in the wounded, bleeding donut.

I had time for only one urgent thought, *Bathroom*. I tried to rise, but all the matter between mouth and anus had liquified and expanded. The pressure could not be contained. I exploded, gushing from the mouth, spewing from the other end.

Arthur woke up from a mini-nap and started yelling, "Oh my God" over and over again.

Only Greyson was quick enough to avoid collateral damage. He sprang from his chair and went to the door. He opened it and said, with exaggerated nonchalance, "Oh, Daphne, sweetheart, could you come in here for a sec? And bring some cheesecloth and cleaner."

Too Much

Virgil's rheumy eyes shimmer with mirth. "Your face!" he says. "Look at your face!"

I refuse to look in the mirror because I don't need any more shocks, even slight ones. I need a drink, a nap, a break. Ten minutes outside this room would be a godsend. Godsend? Bad choice of words. Who is behind that mirror? It's time for Virgil to quit dicking around and give me some answers.

"Ever heard of the word '*schadenfreude*?'" I ask. "Any alchemists ever teach you that word?"

"*All* of them tried to teach me that word."

"You're just torturing me," I said.

My interrogator gets up from his chair and leans over me. He is close. His foul breath is closer. "Speaking of torture, let's turn the machine on, Shelby. Remember, answer the questions yes or no."

"Yes or ... what was the second option, Virgil?" I say.

"Very funny. First question: were you and the other Horsemen torturing Dashiell Aspling?"

"They were. I wasn't."

"Shelby, I repeat: Were you and the Horsemen torturing Dashiell? Yes or no."

"No."

The styluses swing wildly back and forth across the paper.

"The machine detects prevarication. Come on. You were in the room with them. You didn't stop them."

"I couldn't stop them."

"Yes or no, Shelby. Were you and the other Horsemen torturing Dashiell Aspling?"

"I should have to answer only for myself."

"In an ideal world that might be true." Virgil gestures at our cramped cell. "Tell me, Shelby, does this look like an ideal world?" He heeps and snorts. "While we're on the subject of torture, let's go back a few years to when the Mines was waterboarding detainees. Did you protest that, Shelby? Yes or no?"

"No," I said. "I didn't speak up. It wasn't my place. It wouldn't have done any good. I didn't really think about it too much." I catch sight of my gaping mouth in the mirror. I never even thought of this as something to be counted among my sins. I try a weak defense. "They weren't exactly nice people, you know. They were terrorists."

Virgil cackles. "This is rich. Now you're the one in an undisclosed location. No one knows you're here. No one can help you. You are completely at my mercy, and I can do whatever I want. If you don't cooperate, I can send you to my Egyptian counterpart, and he will make this look like a picnic."

"You don't mean—"

"Exactly. Post-mortem rendition." Virgil glows with satisfaction, and that is not a figure of speech, the man is emitting an actual, sickly-yellow glow. "But I would hate to cede the fun to a foreigner. Let's see, what else could I do to send you over the edge?"

"What edge?" I ask. "What does 'over the edge' mean now that I'm dead?"

Virgil pushes his face closer until our noses almost touch until his breath wraps around me like a cloak dipped in a cesspool. I look into his pupils and see a tunnel and, at the end, an inferno. I hear the roar. I smell the sulfur. I gasp and avert my head.

"I ask the questions. Do you understand?" Virgil says.

"Yes," I answer meekly.

"I can't torture you physically with water or electric shock or what have you. So how does one torture an alchemist, a lover of reason and order, an opinionated ass?" Virgil sits down in his chair and adopts the pose of Rodin's *Thinker*, with elbow on forearm, chin on hand.

At least he's not naked, I think.

Virgil laughs, stands, and begins to disrobe. I quickly shut my eyes. "You mean my thoughts are no longer private?" A long pause. I'm tempted to open my eyes, but I don't. I experience the most profound quiet I've ever known. I cannot even hear the sound of my heart beating because, of course, the damn thing has stopped.

Virgil's voice finally comes in a whisper. "The illogical. The inexplicable. The intangible. The proof that you were wrong about everything. That is what torments an alchemist."

"You mean it's not enough that I have to go back and watch terrorist devices put into place while the living Shelby ignores it?"

"No," Virgil says, "that's not nearly enough."

※

I find myself in an unfamiliar skull, one that is round, smooth, and full of soft light. It smells of something spicy, flowery, and familiar. It smells like India in here, the good parts without the open sewers. A feeling of peace comes over me. Can Virgil be giving me a break?

My host's eyes were cast downward, barely open. I can't figure out who this is or what he's looking at. My first impression is that it is a life-size version of one of Greyson's feelies—big rounded swellings and protuberances sculpted of some dark, exotic wood. But then the picture resolves itself into a wooden bowl cupped in plump hands resting atop thighs dressed only in a sort of loincloth. A belly protrudes into the picture.

No. This has to be a joke. I am not in the skull of the Buddha.

His right hand reached out to pluck a blue grape hyacinth. He raised his eyes further, to a sidewalk that disappeared into a stand of trees; then he lowered them again to the hyacinth and English ivy tickling his legs. I recognize the view. He was sitting at the base of the Berlin Wall, or rather a graffiti-splattered fragment of that demolished wall, flown from Germany and reassembled on the south side of the Old Shafts Building. It occupied a raised island in the middle of the walk leading from the south parking lot to the southeast entrance of the building.

The Buddha closed his eyes. Through his ears, I hear the hum of traffic out on the parkway, the shuffling feet of miners walking past, the trill of a towhee advising him to drink his tea. He looked up again as two young men came into view. They were laughing over a sheet of paper and didn't notice the Buddha. As they neared, a gust of wind tore the sheet away and sent it swooping into the air. They let it go and hurried toward the building.

The wind died, and the paper came to rest near the Buddha's feet. He picked it up and studied the glossy image of beans, a landscape of nothing but beans stretching off into eternity. A bold font declared, "IF IT'S NOT COUNTABLE IT DOESN'T COUNT!!!" His thick fingers traced the letters once, then again. What did he make of Dashiell's silly slogan? Perhaps he thought it was a *kung-an*, a tool to help one reach awakening. What is the sound of a single hand clapping? That's a kung-an. The Buddha laid the shiny paper on the ground, nestling it in the grape hyacinth. He breathed in their scent.

Miners flowed around the Gautama Buddha. From the angle of the sun, they were late arrivals: those who had morning medical appointments or who slept in after working late the night before or who were caught in one of the area's interminable traffic jams. Some didn't notice him at all, for the slow, grim commute had eaten away their peripheral vision. Others saw him, but their brains evidently dismissed the sight so quickly it didn't register in their conscious minds. One very young woman paused, mumbled, "I can so not deal with the Buddha this morning," and trudged on.

For a while, the path was empty. At last my old sharper friend, William Sibley, emerged from the shadows into the sunshine. His gait was stiff and slow, but he held his body rigidly erect. He was thin, meticulously groomed, and dressed all in gray. He was not as watchful as he once was because he had turned inward on himself. Even so, he noticed more than the others did.

Twenty feet away from the wall, William stopped. He wasn't halted by the sight of the Buddha, but rather by a squirrel, known in the Mines as "the shakedown squirrel." He pestered pedestrians, running at their feet demanding handouts with raucous squirrel obscenities. Others had hurried by or tried to shoo him with hisses and gestures, but William stopped and reached into his pocket. He brought out a few cold French fries wrapped in a brown government-grade recycled napkin. He leaned over and offered them to the squirrel with a clucking noise. The creature snatched one and ran up a tree, fussing loudly. The man rewrapped the rest of the fries and returned them to his pocket. He straightened, reassumed his pained dignity, and continued on his way. As William came abreast of the wall, the Buddha stretched out his hand, his begging bowl cradled in the smooth palm.

The old sharper stopped and studied the Buddha. His face registered no surprise, for nothing more could surprise him. Wordlessly, he reached into his pocket again, retrieved the crumpled napkin, and shook the last of the cold fries into the Buddha's age-smoothed wooden bowl. He started to leave, then stopped, checked another pocket, and brought out a packet of ketchup. This, too, went into the Buddha's bowl. The sharper hesitated as if considering whether to ask the Buddha a question. He looked like a man who hungered for an answer. Then his mouth curved into the shadow of a smile. Was he afraid of answers or did he think he didn't deserve one? William started to move on, but then the Buddha said, "Borders are not real."

"What?" William turned back to stare at the Buddha.

"The illusion of separateness is the source of suffering," the Buddha said.

"Not guilt? Not remorse?" William took a step closer.

"The illusion of separateness. False borders."

William clutched his tie. "The Berlin Wall? The Iron Curtain?" he asked.

"They were never real," The Buddha said.

"Then I'm not real."

"Lamplight," the Buddha said.

William's eyes widened. "You know about him?"

"He stands in front of me," the Buddha said.

William swayed on his feet as if he were on board a ship. He backed away, raised his hand in a diffident wave, and continued on his way, head tilted to the side, thinking, thinking about the Buddha's words.

The Buddha took a long time to squeeze the last drop from the ketchup packet. He put the plastic into his mouth and sucked it.

Back in the polygraph room, I open my eyes to see Virgil standing naked in front of me. I quickly shut my eyes.

"That was an illusion you created," I say. "It makes no sense."

"And a dead polygraph examiner filling your brain with illusions? Does that make sense?"

"Nothing. Absolutely nothing makes sense. It's too much. The Buddha? What else have you got for me?" As soon as the words are out of my mouth, I regret them. But it's too late. The polygraph room is already fading.

When I open my eyes, I find myself in the basement tunnels of the Mines. From the hollow quietude, I guess that it's night. What's in store for me? Something else illogical, inexplicable, intangible?

But it's just the Buddha again. It's going to be a Buddha rerun. Okay, I can deal with that.

He sat on the floor next to the vending machines. Once again, I pass into his head and listen through his ears to footsteps. The feet were dragging from the sound of it. The Buddha watched the man as he passed by, evidently leaving after a long, frustrating day.

The Buddha's eyes turned to his own plump hand as it reached far under the vending machines. It came out with four quarters and two dimes. The Buddha hefted himself to his feet and fed the change into the slot. His wide thumb hit the "E" and "47" buttons. Peanut butter crackers. As he fished them out of the machine, his eyes wandered to poster affixed to the wall nearby. It was another one of Dashiell's brain farts. The words "MORE VIGILANCE!!!" screamed from a field of eyes—blue eyes, green eyes, brown eyes, bloodshot eyes … "And yet they are so unaware here," the Buddha said.

A noise far down the tunnel attracted his attention. The Buddha emitted a poignant and protracted sigh. Can discontent and enlightenment occupy the same Buddha? I would think not, yet the Buddha sighed.

Then I see what he was looking at: Virgil's latest nasty trick, a ghost. He approached from the South end of the Old Shafts Building, looking just like his portrait in the BOM tunnel. It was Vaughn Sutter Wayne, the legendary BOM who had a stroke and fell forward into a raspberry-filled powdered donut. I'd heard that he haunted the Mines, but I thought it was a joke.

The Buddha and Vaughn had apparently already met. Vaughn yelled, "Hey Buddha boy, figured out this shit hole yet?" He didn't wait for an answer. "Didn't use to be a shit hole back in the day." He arrived at the vending machines and assumed the stance of a lecturer.

The Buddha settled back to the floor. He looked down at his crackers and unwrapped them carefully.

"This place used to be a *real* spy agency." Vaughn paced. He led with his enormous gut, thrusting it forward like the base drum in a marching band. The soft white fringe around his pate glowed in the florescent light. His bulbous nose was also white, still covered with confectioners sugar, no matter how much he wiped at it. His arms ended abruptly in angry fists that took the occasional wild jab at the air. As he talked, Vaughn spat puffs of confectioners sugar.

"Do you know who the new A-BOM is? Fucking insurance company executive. Insurance! As if there were any guarantees in this business. Someone you would call for a wrecked car, not a wrecked agency," Vaughn said.

The Buddha slipped a cracker into his mouth.

"Damn MOC. That's Mines Oversight Committee, in case you Buddha boys don't know your acronyms. They're going to kill us, suck us dry."

The Buddha emitted an "mmm" as he sucked his cracker.

"Chihuahua. Dashiell Aspling is a fucking Chihuahua. The Horsemen are lucky he didn't piss on their shoes when they told him about Brick. Now, Brick, *he* was a decent BOM, at least until he got all wussy penitent. All BOMs should be ex-sharpers. The only ones who understand the business. You know I was a sharper, don't you?"

"Mmm," the Buddha said.

"France," Vaughn said. "Second World War. Parachute opening in the black of night. Broke both ankles landing in a vineyard in the Languedoc-Roussillon. Vines were Grenache. You know a pure Grenache can reach seventeen proof? But you Buddha boys are teetotalers, aren't you?

Never trusted teetotalers, not worth even trying to recruit them. Anyway, broke both ankles and still managed to haul in three groupers my first month. Drank a case of Grenache. Slept with all four of the vintner's daughters and his wife. That was back in the day when you didn't have to fill out a bunch of foreign contact forms to bone a local. I was a sharper's sharper."

The sucking grew louder.

"Brick was a decent sharper. Had an over-active conscience. Got hung up over fabricating a little report. Never knew he was such a wuss. The BOM has to give the president what he asks for. Why do you think they call us an intelligence service? We serve."

"Mmm," said the Buddha.

"What a fool to fuck up his own suicide." Vaughn's lopsided scowl, which never left his face, cut deeper and veered further to the right. "I suppose it's better than dying in a donut. I will never get over the ignominy." He blew a puff of sugar from his nostrils.

The Buddha watched the sparkling cloud settle down the front of Vaughn's pin-striped suit and onto the scarred tile floor. Vaughn took a linen handkerchief out of his pocket and swiped it back and forth over his frosted nose as a shoeshine boy might buff a wingtip. He couldn't get rid of the telltale sugar any more than Marley could slip his chain.

"Let it go," the Buddha said in a voice like worn silk. "Leave the Mines to the Living."

"The living are frigging idiots." The speed and fury of Vaughn's pacing increased. He huffed with the exertion, and with each ghostly breath, more sugar sifted down.

"Horsemen ought to know better. Screwed things up like a damn bunch of amateurs." Vaughn raised both fists to heaven and bellowed, "The Organ! The wretched Organ!" He squatted down next to the Buddha and in a slow, conspiratorial whisper said, "Did you know that the Organ has laid a Molothrus in the Mines?"

I wonder if the Buddha knew that the Organ was the Internal Investigative Organ or that Molothrus was the genus of the cowbird and, in Mines cant, a penetration agent. If he didn't believe in borders, how could he have understood the decades-old bureaucratic rivalry that led one government agency to spy on the other when they should have been on the same side?

"I know who the Molothrus is," Vaughn said. He waited, but the Buddha didn't ask. What was the advantage of a secret, if the other person didn't want to know it? "Well," he huffed, "I'm not going to tell some fat foreign national, so there." Vaughn strode off down the endless tunnels, where his footsteps no longer left behind an echo. I imagine that made him even more furious.

Just as I think that this interlude is about to end, I hear the sharp clack of heels. Another figure approached rapidly: Maddie James. She wore a black suit. She wore a lot of black. She was my personal raven, always hanging about my door cawing. She was talking to herself, gesturing, clearly angry. "That fucking idiot BOWM," I hear as she came closer. "Damn you, Shelby Wexler, you arrogant, blind dipstick. You may think that you can ignore me, but you won't be able to ignore what's coming. It will bite your ass so hard." She passed in front of the Buddha and her rant ended abruptly as the heel of her right shoe snapped. Maddie pitched and almost fell, but caught herself at the last moment. She stood, lopsided, rubbing her back and staring at her feet. She reached down and slipped off the broken shoe. With a fearsome cry of frustration, she lobbed it at the vending machine. Then she slipped off the other shoe and threw it after the first. Maddie continued down the hall in stocking feet, cursing me all the way.

The Buddha looked down at the worn black shoe that had landed in his lap. He picked it up and slowly turned it over and over as if to divine the meaning of the thing.

Manchester

hen I return to the polygraph room, I almost say, "What's next? A dancing bear, a leprechaun, and the ghost of Yorick?" But I quickly bite the words back, remembering some advice I received long ago: "Never use sarcasm with a polygraph examiner—they take everything literally." Then I remember that I don't have to speak out loud because Virgil can hear my thoughts. I steal a look at him. He is once again sitting in the manner of the Thinker, now stark naked. He leers at me and raises his brows twice, quickly. I look away.

"What can I do to you next?" Virgil asks. "I have to keep shaking you up or else your natural inertia will erase all the progress we've made. I've put you in the head of a bitter senator, an agent of the Organ gone bad, a clueless BOM, the Buddha…" Virgil's voice trails off as he sits in his Thinker pose thinking. "Aha! I know, you have yet to visit the head of the terrorist himself: Fahad."

I open my mouth to protest, knowing all the while it will be futile.

✳

Chiaroscuro. That's what it's like in this skull. Searing light and black shadow. Hot and cold simultaneously. It feels pressurized and smells like ozone.

Fahad was watching his own feet, shod in good dress shoes, tread across a stained concrete floor covered with scattered carpet remnants: turquoise shag, orange Saxony, bright green indoor/outdoor. From the cinderblock walls and pipes running across the ceiling, I guess that this was a basement room. He reached a concrete wall and turned to look at a squat, bearded man seated between a copy machine and a cat carrier.

"Odd sort of prayer rugs, Akil," Fahad said. He kicked at a cheap square of gray loop pile.

Akil pointed toward the corner. "The prayer rugs are stacked over there."

Fahad saw a cat, a copper-eyed blue British Shorthair, sitting on the pile of rugs.

Akil threw a pencil at the cat. "Get off, Whiskers, have some respect."

The cat didn't move, and Akil let him be. "The carpet remnants are for the men to sit on during lectures. My wife brings them home free from Carpet King. She's their salesman of the month."

"Extend my congratulations."

Akil laughed. "You sound so damned British, it's hard to trust you sometimes." Akil himself had an accent that sounded North African, perhaps Yemeni. "Of course, my wife has your accent, too. Not a trace of her birthplace in her voice."

"You trust your wife?" Fahad asked.

"I do, but I tell her nothing. She doesn't want to

know. She's happy that I allow her to work and don't insist that she wear traditional clothing, which would get in the way of her sales. The more western she sounds, looks, and acts, the better for me. It reduces suspicion."

"Good woman," Fahad said. He resumed pacing.

"Sit down," Akil said. "You're making me nervous. The most difficult parts of the operation are behind us. We shipped the packages. The money came through. You've shut down the factory, covered your tracks. They should finish up the installation of the screamers within a few weeks."

"Suppose one of the workmen notices something strange?"

"They won't. We gave specific instructions: hire men who have never worked with lighting before and train them. Terrorists with clean backgrounds who don't even know that they're terrorists. A couple of your own techies to supervise, to optimize the installation for the greatest effect. And no explosives. Nothing for the bomb-sniffing dogs to find. Pat yourself on the back. You're brilliant."

"We don't even know if the screamers will bring the buildings down," Fahad said. "The whole thing could fizzle."

"At the very least, we will have stunning visuals."

Fahad nodded. "I planned it that way." He sat down in front of the computer and opened a file with photographs of the Mines compound from the ground and the air. He pulled up a shot of the entrance to the Old Shafts Building. "There," he said, "that concrete portico balanced on columns that are wide at the top and narrow at the bottom. See the lights set into the underside? I custom-designed the screamers for that structure. They will quickly set up a harmonic vibration, the portico will twist and fall. That visual is important because this is the stock photo that the newscasters show when they're talking about the Mines." Fahad pulled up another photo, taken in the atrium of the New Shafts Building with its crisscrossing escalators. "This is the other area where I have asked the supervisors to pay special attention. All that glass will come down easily."

"Another great visual. We can count on the media to focus on whatever destruction there is and make it look as bad as possible. There will be heart attacks. They will be cut and bleeding from the broken glass. The bastards will piss themselves and shit themselves, and the smell of it will rise to the sky. It will be a victory. We can't say how big a victory, but it will be a victory."

"But I want more than just good visuals," Fahad said. "I want to bring the buildings down. Have I ever shown you the video of the Tacoma Narrows Bridge collapse?" Without waiting for an answer, Fahad pulled up black and white footage of a suspension bridge twisting in the wind. The bridge contorted and bucked ever more violently. He pointed at the screen, "Troops break pace when they come to a bridge because a rhythmic step can set up a harmonic vibration. Here the wind did it. Fahad tapped on the screen as the bridge went into a final violent twist and crumbled. That is what I want. Catastrophic failure of support elements. If I've chosen the right frequencies, the right rhythm for the screamers, it will happen."

Fahad stood up and looked around. His eyes settled on a particleboard bookcase stuffed with the works of al-Ktub, stacks of green brochures for the Manchester Cultural Learning Center, and well-thumbed paperback Korans. "You should get rid of all of this stuff."

"I want to keep the Center running for a couple more

weeks; then I will pass everything along to Ahmed. He'll be ready by then."

"What do we really know about these American men we're working with?" Fahad said.

Akil shrugged. "We know that one was kicked out of the Internal Investigative Organ, and the other is a politician with influence and access to a shitload of money."

"How can we trust a US politician and an agent of the Organ?"

"How can we trust you for that matter?" Akil said in a manner that was only half joking. "You've done rather well for yourself in British society—big technical degree, inventor, entrepreneur. You've even turned into a dandy with that mop of hair."

Fahad's hand rose to swipe back his hair. Akil's face assumed a look of alert interest. "Where did you lose the ear?"

"Sliced off by a bottle. My little brother and I were attacked by a group of skinheads trolling for a Paki. I only lost an ear. My brother was not as lucky." Fahad's voice thickened with bitterness. "They beat in the side of his head with a tire iron. Unfortunately, he lived. He still lives if you can call it that. Whenever I find my resolve weakening, I visit him. He was the wittiest, funniest boy I ever knew. Now all he can do is drool into his pillow and stare and see nothing."

"You do have credentials," Akil said. "Such things are excellent for recruiting. This whole city will explode one day, and that will be good for us."

"Why are we wasting time talking about my credentials? The Americans know when we're planning to strike. The sources of money should be kept apart from the operational details. That's an old and simple rule, and we broke it."

Akil leaned back, shrugged, and raised his palms in the air. They showed red, rubbery scars—probably from the careless handling of explosives. "On his insistence," he said. "We had no choice. No one else was stepping forward to give us anything after we quarreled with the Base. One successful operation, however, and the money will pour in. And what an operation. A strike on the Mines? Overnight we'll be transformed from a splinter to the backbone of global jihad."

"Or we'll all be betrayed and in jail being paraded around naked at the end of a leash."

"I don't think they do that anymore. The publicity was too bad last time."

Fahad stopped pacing and reached up to chin himself a dozen times on a pipe installed for the purpose. The physical exertion sent electric currents flashing through his brain. He finally dropped to the floor and lay on his back, breathing heavily.

"Something's wrong. I can feel it."

"Pray to Allah."

"It's Allah who tells me that something is wrong. These sponsors of ours know the day and time of the operation."

"Then change it," Akil said. "Move it up. We need nothing else from them. And afterward, we'll roll in the money like ... whatever rolls in money."

"Okay, we move it up, and then we go somewhere else for a while."

Akil stopped for a moment and listened. "Shh, my wife is coming."

Fahad got to his feet as Akil's wife came down the steps carefully in her heels and business suit. She was a younger and more attractive a wife than one would expect Akil to have. She smiled at Fahad. "Good to see you, but I don't know why you and Akil want to hang out in this smelly basement." She scanned the room. "Aha, there you are! Come on, Whiskers love."

The cat tried to make a run for it, but the woman lunged for him, managing to snag him before he could get past her up the stairs. She straightened her skirt and clamped him firmly under her arm.

"How does he know he has an appointment with the vet? He always knows. Open his carrier," she said to Akil. "I have to take him to get his anal glands expressed. He has another blockage. Do you smell him? It's bloody awful."

I find myself back in the polygraph room, where Virgil waits, stark naked. To say it is an ugly sight would be a gross understatement. To say it is a gross sight would be a gross understatement. Words fail me.

"Hi, Shelby, miss me?" Virgil pulls his foot onto his knee and begins to pare his toenails with a small clipper.

"I don't need to see this." I shut my eyes tight.

"You know your toenails keep growing after you're dead. It's not a myth."

"Could you please get dressed?"

"No. Look, Shelby, you gave me the idea. It's quite brilliant. If I had been allowed to do this while I was alive and working for the Mines, I could have wrung the truth out of people in a fraction of the time."

"No doubt," I say. "Just ask me whatever you're going to ask me." I feel cold even though I shouldn't be able to feel anything at all.

"That one spooked you, didn't it?" Virgil asks.

"Of course. I just spent time in the head of the man who killed me."

"No," Virgil says, "but you're in his head now."

He catches me again. As I say the words out loud, I know that they're true. "Oh my God, I committed suicide."

"Of course," Virgil says. "If you had moved your fat ass you could have escaped before the portico fell."

I think back to the attack, to those seconds looking up at the concrete rippling above my head. "I knew," I said in a whisper, "I knew it was my fault and I didn't want to survive."

Virgil nodded his approval. "Good choice. The MOC and the press would have slathered you with sauce and grilled you until your skin fell off the bone."

"But you're doing that now," I said.

"Right, bummer for you."

For a moment, I allow myself to wallow in self-pity, and then hope almost lifts me from my chair. "I don't think the screamers could bring down the Old Shafts Building. There's a big difference between a narrow sliver of bridge and a big solid building. Even if the screamers worked, it would take much longer to bring down the building than the awning. People could escape." I feel a smile breaking over my face.

"And the New Shafts Building?" Virgil asks.

I think of the indifferent construction of that building, how you could feel the floor vibrate when a cart rolled down a tunnel.

"Tell me, Shelby, how does one exit the New Shafts Building?"

"Through a tunnel of glass." My heart falls, but then

my brain reasons its way to hope again. "That building must have been built with safety glass, right? The type that shatters into a harmless crumble?"

"That was the plan," Virgil said, "but the Boss of Black Mines needed money for a big, expensive secret operation in some Middle Eastern country. Or maybe it was Africa. Or Pakistan. I can't remember. Anyway, Congress gave him a big fat thumbs down and took away his funding. So he cut a deal with the Boss of Paper Mines to divert the money from the construction of the New Shafts Building. So many corners were cut; I'm surprised the building didn't turn out round."

A Fast-Moving Virus

Virgil's features grow unnaturally rubbery and elastic. He leans back on two legs of his chair and makes fun-house faces at me as he watches my reaction. I would like to grab his nose and pull it out as far as possible and let it snap back. I imagine the rebound knocking him over backward.

"Where did we leave off with your story, Shelby?" Virgil says. "Oh, I remember you had just pooped your panties in the BOM's office."

"What need is there to revisit that humiliation?" I ask.

"I thought you'd like to see the aftermath from a different point of view."

Abruptly I find myself back in the clean, bright, well-organized expanse of Thelma's head. She was sitting at her desk, sorting the morning mail, and humming a happy tune when the phone rang.

"Thelma, it's Daphne. Shelby just got sick all over Dashiell's office. I'm afraid Greyson will make hay out of this. He'll use it as an excuse to have Medical look into Shelby's drinking."

"I'll be right there." Thelma hung up. "I knew it," she muttered. Thinking quickly, she reached into her top drawer and grabbed the vial Al had given her. When she arrived in the BOM's outer office, she found Greyson, Arthur, and Slinky standing around, finishing their coffee and laughing over the "success" of the meeting. They sucked in their guts when Thelma entered. The only thing they envied me was my beautiful secretary.

"I'm so worried about Shelby," Thelma said in her sweetest voice. "Could you gentlemen please move some of this furniture aside so the medical cart can get in here?"

They scrambled to comply, setting their coffee down on a side table. While they shoved a credenza out of the way, Thelma quickly backed up to the table, glanced over her shoulder, and slipped a few drops from the vial into each cup. When the nurse arrived, Thelma helped her get me into the cart and then watched me leave accompanied by a flashing red light, siren, and the strong smell of caca.

On the way back to the BOWM suite, Thelma stopped by the executive dining room and dosed two coffee pots that were about to go out among the linen-covered tables of senior officials. Upon reaching the suite, she added a few drops to Lyle Voth's latte while he was in the men's room.

Thelma phoned Esther to come pick me up. "Cover your car seat with plastic," she said, "and bring some air freshener and wet wipes. And don't worry, he'll be just fine."

Within the hour, it appeared that a fast-moving virus had swept the seventh floor of the Mines, and I was merely its first victim. Meanwhile, Thelma sat at her desk organizing her files and sipping at her untainted coffee. She went back to humming that same happy tune. She was probably imagining the Mines' senior-most officials pooping their innards out down in Medical.

I'm back in Thelma's head. A week had passed, according to her desk calendar.

"Are you losing weight?" Thelma asked as I arrived with a black coffee in one hand. Under the other arm, I carried the morning newspapers and a copy of the President's Intelligence Update, which I had picked up at the Operations Center. I already appeared transformed, although, frankly, the new Shelby was not a huge improvement on the old.

"Huh?" I grunted as I doddered past. I dumbly stopped before my office door. I was surprised to find it closed, although I always closed it before I left at night. I didn't have a free hand to open it. I looked plaintively at Thelma.

She ignored the look. "I said, 'Are you losing weight?'"

"Probably."

"Don't you weigh yourself?"

"No. Why would I do that?"

"To find out how much you weigh."

"I don't care."

"How can you not care about that?" Thelma was genuinely surprised. "I weigh myself twice a day. If I put on a half pound, then I skip my next meal and go down to the gym. If I didn't do that, I would creep up a size every few years. Before you know it, I'd be buying plus sizes, and they don't sell anything cute in a plus size. That's not going to happen."

"They sell the same kind of suits in every size," I said. At the time, it seemed to me a clever response.

Thelma lowered her eyes to focus on my baggy rear end. "Well, your buns aren't filling out that one, so you'd better get something smaller or start eating. What did you have for breakfast?"

"My breakfast is my business. Would you *please* open the door?" I made my voice irritable verging on rude. I was thinking that I had spoiled Thelma too much, that I was too generous and benevolent a boss, and now she was paying me back with disrespect. It was high time I put my foot down.

"I'll open the door when and if I feel like it." Thelma gave me a look that took about two inches off my already modest height. I lowered my eyes, but she wasn't going to let me off easily. "You look at me, Shelby, and answer my question. What did you eat?"

I changed tactics and decided to go for sympathy. "I still have a touch of that flu, I think. I need to sit down, so if you would please—"

Thelma rolled her eyes. "I said, 'What did you eat?'"

"Nothing."

"Well, I'm going to the dining room and get you some fruit and yogurt." Thelma got up from her chair.

"No. I'm not hungry. Would you just please open this door for me? My hands are full."

"Well, put something down. If you're going to ignore my good advice, I'm not going to wait on you hand and foot." Thelma sat back down and turned to her computer.

Lyle Voth, who had his head buried in his copy of the

PIU, watched from the corner of his eye, but didn't offer to open the door. Only in the Pentagon do executive assistants open doors for their bosses.

Thelma watched as I sighed deeply, set my coffee cup on a file cabinet, and opened my own damn office door. I remember what was running through my mind at the time. I was thinking about when I was young and in awe of senior officials. I used to scramble to do menial tasks for said officials. Now that I was old and senior, no one scrambled to do the same for me. They all had too damn much self-respect. Life was getting to be a piece of shit.

Thelma watched from the corner of her eye as I fell heavily into my chair. I had left my coffee on the file cabinet. She wasn't about to fetch it for me. I threw her a series of increasingly reproachful looks. Finally, I hoisted myself out of the chair and came out to get it.

At the time, I felt like a martyr and imagined that she was feeling bad about the inconvenience she'd caused for me. Now I hear a faint chuckle deep in her throat.

24

The Details

Now I'm in Esther's head. It has a no-nonsense church basement feel to it. In fact, that's where I met Esther, in the basement of her father's church preparing for a Christmas party. A local nursery had hired me to deliver poinsettias after school. That's the only reason I would ever set foot in Pure Grace Baptist Church, which had a reputation for being too fervent for the midwest. As I carried in foil wrapped pots, I noticed an exceptionally sweet-faced blond at the refreshments table arranging Maraschino cherries around a quivering ring of green jello. She wore cat-eye glasses on a chain and a red sweater with a Christmas tree brooch pinned above her nicely-rounded right breast. She smiled at me, showing a pair of deep dimples. I was hooked.

On this night, she was not smiling. She watched me carefully place a wastebasket by the bed in case of vomiting. She knew damn well what was making me sick but out loud she theorized that God was using sickness to send me a message.

"It's because he loves you, Shelby. He's saying, 'Put

that bottle down, and I'll raise you up and make you new and give you a second chance.'"

I pulled the covers up, belched, and gave my wife a mournful look. She was sitting up in bed with her Bible open, but she was watching me from the corner of her eye.

"I'm an agnostic, Esther, you know that." Actually, I was an atheist, but I always said "agnostic" to Esther because if I had said "atheist" she would have stopped making my favorite stringy pot roast altogether.

"I can't decide whether I do or don't believe in agnostics," Esther said. She turned a page of her Bible and carefully repositioned the black grosgrain bookmark with a silver letter 'E' dangling from one end and an 'S' from the other. These were the initials of her maiden name, Esther Sweetbriar.

Her father was a mechanic as well as a minister. He could lay hands on any engine, no matter how derelict, and bring it back to life. He bought broken down school buses, fixed them up, and sent them rolling across the countryside to gather the faithful to worship and partake of a potluck meal. Esther made the coffee and served up the food. Sometimes I thought I could still detect the aroma of creamed corn and lima beans on her flesh. It was not an aphrodisiac.

"No living human can definitively prove or disprove the existence of God," I told Esther, "much less the ridiculous details."

"What ridiculous details?" Esther snapped shut her Bible, took off her reading glasses, and laid them on the nightstand between her box of Kleenex and her glass of water. It was a remarkably precise and consistent act. As long as I'd known her, she'd kept a pink floral box of

Kleenex and a glass of water on her night table just so. She'd take off her glasses at night, after scanning a few verses, and put them on the stand between box and glass. She would lay the Bible right side up in the very center of the small drawer of the stand. It was the only object ever kept in that drawer. Esther didn't like to mix the sacred and profane. And I never knew her to lose track of her reading glasses—and she owned only one pair—whereas I bought mine by the dozen and seeded the house with them. Still, I never could find them when I needed them. I had to appeal to Esther, who would invariably locate a pair immediately and hand it over without a word and only the slightest smirk of superiority.

"What details?" Esther asked again.

I'm ashamed to say I scowled at her question and barked my answer. "The fictional details. These are stories people make up because they need stories. A child in a manger. Gold, Frankincense, and Myrrh. Buddha under a banyan tree. Mohammed ... doing whatever Mohammed did. All of these stories are jam pack full of detail presented as truth, but you know somebody made it up to give an illusion of authenticity to something fake."

"God is in the details."

"The devil is in the details."

"Those stories give real comfort."

"Not to me they don't," I snapped. "Then there are the picayune rules."

"Thou shalt not kill?"

"No, I don't mean that kind of thing." I kicked at the covers to give my feet more room. Esther always tucked everything in too tight, and it was killing my feet. "I mean the silly head coverings and red socks and uncomfortable collars. The fish on Fridays and the meat of cloven-hoofed creatures and the sacred cows. If there is a God, do you really think he cares how humans dress or what they eat? Or exactly what they say in church? Or what day they worship? If there is some supreme creator, I don't believe that he or she or whatever is anal retentive. I just don't." I took off my reading glasses and flung them toward the dresser on the other side of the room. They hit the dresser and landed on the carpet, and if they were ever to be picked up, it would have to be Esther to do it.

"What's the point?" I said rudely.

Esther was quiet for a long time. She stared down at her hands, folded atop the Bible that she received at her first Communion. Finally, she got up and went to pick up my glasses.

I remember hating her a little bit for that.

And she knew it. The knowledge pushed her to say more than she was planning to say. "The point is that you drink too much, and it sours you to everything on Earth and in Heaven."

"What I drink is my business."

"And who you are is my business because I have to live with you. Shelby, the fact is I don't like you when you drink. Not one bit. It makes you crabby and hard to bear. I have to walk around on eggshells, or you'll get mad and break something. You're scornful of the whole world, including yourself, and I can't stand scorn. I don't want to spend the rest of my days with someone who's in a sour, scornful mood all the time. Someone who refuses to talk about the child we brought into this world. I won't divorce you because I don't believe in that, but I'm going have an apartment built in the basement, and you're going to live down there. I've already made arrangements with a contractor. He starts tomorrow."

"What? Are you serious, Esther?" I squinted at her, trying to read her face, but without my glasses, it was a blur.

"Dead serious. Why do you think I read this Bible every night? I'm looking for the patience to put up with you. But I'm not finding it, Shelby. If I thought I could help you, maybe it would be different. But I've been reading up on drunks, and I think I'm what they call an enabler."

"Me? A drunk? Esther ... out of the blue ... " I was stunned, then angry. "Out of the blue! I thought you had gotten over menopause years ago, but this is ... capricious, unpredictable, out of the blue."

"Out of the blue! How can you possibly say this is out of the blue? Where have you been? Where do you go? I'll be talking to you, and then I look and see that you've checked out, zoned out, or whatever it is you do. The only time you speak to me is to complain."

"I haven't had much to drink lately," I said. "You know that. It's not like I'm an alcoholic deadbeat." I wanted to take the glass on the bedside table and throw it against the wall, but that would have proved Esther's point, and the thought made me even angrier.

"No, you're an alcoholic government employee. One who is crabbier than ever because now he can't drink without consequence to himself. When the consequences affect other people, you didn't care. You need to get it out of your system altogether."

"Don't tell me what I do and don't need to do."

"Well, I'll tell you this: I don't want you in this room again until you can be civil. Until the basement is finished, you can sleep in the guest room. Get out."

"What? You want me to get up now? I'm settled in."

"Out!" Esther yelled. Well, she wasn't quite yelling,

but she might as well have been. I took one look at her face and knew it was no use to argue.

I didn't sleep much that night. I hated change in any form. The guest bed was too hard. And my head pointed north, whereas it pointed south in my old room. And I could see the streetlight shining through the blinds.

On my way out the door that morning, I saw the contractor's van pull up. Esther pushed past me and ushered the man into the basement. Until that moment, I had thought she was making the whole thing up to scare me, but no, there the man was in the flesh. He and Esther had already worked out the blueprints and selected the materials. They spoke together as if they were well acquainted. The man taped a building permit to the front window.

"I would have asked your opinion on the remodeling," Esther said, "but you never notice your surroundings. And I want something nice that I can rent out when you die of cirrhosis of the liver."

Flit. I am once more in my own head, back in my office, feeling nauseous and thinking about Esther.

I wondered if I could risk a drink, but just then my stomach cramped and rumbled. I thought perhaps I should see a doctor. Then something surfaced, a persistent little perturbation that had been hovering just below the level of conscious thought. All this time I'd been sick, and Esther hadn't once nagged me to go to a doctor! This was unprecedented. At any other time, she would have nagged and nagged and then finally called the doctor herself to make an appointment. Then she would have enlisted Thelma's help to put it on my schedule. She would have driven to the Mines Visitors' Center on the day, called me from there, and pleaded until I came down and allowed her to drive me to the doctor. But this time, she hadn't said a word.

My hand shook as I dialed home. The phone rang half a dozen times before Esther finally picked up. Her "hello" sounded distant, impatient, harassed.

"Honey," I said tentatively, "it's me. I was wondering whether you thought perhaps I should see a doctor. You know, in light of the vomiting, diarrhea, and abdominal pain. And I think I'm beginning to get some pain and numbness in my left arm."

"If you think you need to call a doctor, then call a doctor. I don't have time to talk now. We're deciding where we need switches and light fixtures."

She hung up, and I listened to the dial tone for a full minute. I felt like the floor had opened underneath me, and I was hanging in space, unloved and vulnerable. Finally, I reached into my lower left-hand drawer. But I stopped before my hand touched the bottle. I shut the drawer and put my head down on my desk.

"Okay, Shelby." Virgil, still naked, gets up to adjust the machine. "I only have one question this time, but it's a doozy. It's going to make you feel like shit on a biscuit. Are you ready?"

"Get on with it."

"This concerns that episode with Esther that you just

witnessed again. The earlier one in your bedroom. Yes or no, Shelby, were you aware that it was your thirty-fifth wedding anniversary?"

What's left of my self-esteem crumples. "Oh, crap, I forgot."

"You were never good with women, Shelby. While we're on the subject, there was another woman who was ready to kill you. Would you like to spend some time with Maddie? Of course, that's only a rhetorical question. You don't have a choice."

25

Whiskers

This is my least favorite skull yet, and that includes the terrorist. This woman has a serious problem with tooth grinding. Being in Maddie James' skull is like being inside some machine that needs oiling. The discordant scraping and gnashing puts me on edge. Then there's the coffee breath.

She was in the process of cussing me out, not to my face, of course. She was sitting in her office talking to one of my bomb dissectors, Vivian Fields.

Maddie wanted to kill me. The conviction was in her voice. "I saw Shelby Wexler crossing the perimeter road this morning and it was all I could do to keep from running him over. It would probably be like hitting a deer though, it would ruin my car and he would limp away. I can't afford a repair right now."

"Oh, you don't mean that," Vivian said. I had always liked her. She was hard-working, pleasant, and mild-mannered in a profession that attracted argumentative, opinionated, and cranky personalities. She had kind eyes. She frequently rubbed at them as if she were tired. She wasn't the sort of person I would have ever promoted past MS-14, because she didn't have the fire in the belly, but she was the type I would put in a room when I needed compromise language. Yet she was Maddie's best friend. Maddie, who behaved like a wet cat with a burr up her tail. Maddie, who was still fantasizing about killing me.

Maddie reached into her drawer and picked a yellow gummy bear out of a bag. She stood it atop her desk. "I ought to get a bigger, heavier vehicle so that I could take advantage of opportunities like that. I could probably get away with it if I just said I stomped on the gas instead of the brake. It happens." Maddie took her stapler and ran it over the gummy bear. The little guy was pinned under the "vehicle." Maddie spoke in a high, silly voice that in no way resembled mine. "Help! Help! Get me out!" She reverted to her own voice. "No, Mr. Shelby, not until you approve my funding request."

Vivian giggled. "Shelby Wexler isn't the worst BOWM we've ever had," she said with equanimity. "He was popular when he was Chief of the Far East Asia Office."

"Well, he's worse than dead wood now. And he's done everything possible to keep me from doing my job. I have no budget. I'm supposed to be running a ten-person unit, and I'm lucky to have this stapler. He won't even let his alchemists talk to me."

Vivian held up a silk scarf. "I put this over my head when I came up here. I don't want to get caught fraternizing with the enemy. So what is this threat you wanted to talk about?"

"Are you familiar with the Shaker?"

Vivian's eyes searched the ceiling as she pulled data from her memory. "Some sort of engineer or technician. Reporting has put him at various times in the UK, Germany, and Iraq. He quarreled with the base. Apparently he had some far-fetched ideas, and they laughed at him. This was two years ago. I can't recall any reporting since then. Do you have something?"

"Bits." Maddie scanned the chaos of her desk. It was a welter of printed cables full of neon highlights in five colors. Evidently she used some sort color-coding system, although "system" seems too orderly a word to apply to anything related to Maddie. The cables weren't stacked into discernible piles. Everything was helter skelter. A strange thing happened to as she ran her eyes over the mess. Rather than a single point of focus, she focused on four or five points at once: fragments of text from various cables. The background blurred. Her mind drew connecting lines in the air.

"Here," Maddie said. Her finger fell onto one of those fragments. "This was an intercept picked up in early December from a former associate of the Shaker. He's talking to his cousin—not further identified. He says, 'I hear our English friend got a big shipment of honey from a new outside supplier.' Then the cousin says, 'Might as well pour it down the toilet.' Then they switch to another subject."

"What makes you think the 'English friend' is the Shaker? We're not even sure he's from the UK," Vivian said.

Maddie's hand fell on another piece of highlighted text. "I remembered this report from a couple of years ago. She picked it up and read, "'I tried to teach Abu Musab a few phrases, but his accent is atrocious. We should send him home to his nanny." Maddie put the cable down. "Abu Musab was one of the Shaker's aliases. Of course, there are other Abu Musabs, but I have the feeling that this is the same man. 'Nanny' suggests that he's British. Then there's this report." Maddie reached for a cable and read, "No one will give him anything anymore. He's crazy and he's finished, but he doesn't know it." She scanned the ceiling as she speculated. "So, he had lost his funding, but now he's apparently gotten money from a new source. An 'outside' supplier, which implies it's not from the Gulf. Which means we have a large new problem, one we should devote resources to, but try to convince Shelby Wexler of that. Oh, and then there's this." Maddie grabbed another cable. This is a conversation we believe to be between two newly recruited radicals in the UK. The first one says, 'They cleared out just like that.' The other says, 'Overnight. No warning. The only one left is Whiskers. He's moved in with a neighbor.'"

"Bad sign when they clear out like that," Vivian said.

"Imminent attack, is what it means," Maddie said.

"Not always, but I admit my stomach turned over when you read that. Let me see that cable."

Maddie handed it over. "Is anyone downstairs focusing on this?"

"Not that I know of. Everyone is caught up with threats from the Base. And unless you put these reports together—and we don't know for sure that they're connected—it doesn't look like much," Vivian said.

"There's not much because our focus is elsewhere. No one downstairs is sending out requirements to the Ear or the sharpers on this, and everyone ignores me when I send out requirements. I'm *persona non grata*. Just because there's not much doesn't mean we can ignore it. How much did we know about the mastermind behind the Strikes before they happened?"

"Nothing," Vivian said.

A dull, steady thump, thump, thump sounded from below. Maddie was kicking her desk. "Shelby Wexler was never a terrorism analyst. He was a political analyst. He has a different concept of how much proof you need before you raise an issue. He thinks I've lost my objectivity or my mind, but I've spent a couple of decades now living inside the traffic, feeling its rhythms. I can hear an awful music in it. I hear it now, with these reports. The crescendo is coming. I know it. I *know* it."

"Are you having the nightmares?"

"Of course. More vivid every night."

Vivian picked up the last report and scanned it. "I'm not familiar with any 'Whiskers.'"

Maddie's eyes fell on another cable. "I found one mention of a Whiskers. It's five years old. It refers to Whiskers writing an article in a Yemeni journal. I found the journal, found what looks like the article described. The name of the author is Sameer al Bazzi. I'm having some of it translated. I plowed through what I could with my crappy Arabic. He wrote religious justifications for the use of various types of weapons. He touches on every nasty weapon you can think of: chemical, biological, nuclear." Maddie reached for yet another cable. "Then I found Sameer al Bazzi mentioned in the traffic two years ago. It says he died in an automobile accident. So either this is the wrong Whiskers or a false report on al Bazzi's death. I've already spent hours on this guy, but I don't feel like I can drop it because of his interest in unconventional weapons."

"If you like I can come in on Saturday and work on Whiskers."

"No, Vivi, I don't want to take your family time for what is in all likelihood a dead end."

"Actually, I was looking for an excuse to be away from

home. Jeff finally agreed to clean the basement on Saturday. If I'm home, I'll end up doing most of the work, and the mess isn't mine. It's his and Josh's. A quiet day at work without managers, phones ringing, and taskers sounds delightful. Almost like a vacation."

"You're a doll, Vivi. If you take Whiskers, I can spend the day on the finance aspect. I don't even know where to start there. Perhaps it's a UK source?"

I return to the polygraph room to find Virgil in stitches, heeping and snorting until he almost chokes himself. "A few weeks before an attack and two of your most experienced bomb dissectors are spending time looking into the background of a cat."

"That's their stupidity," I say.

"And whose fault is it that they had nothing else to work with? Maddie wasted hours looking for a source of funding when you could have handed her the critical piece of the puzzle."

"Hand her information incriminating the Chairman of the MOC? That would have brought the wrath of God down on the Mines."

"And that would have been worse than the terrorist attack?" Virgil's hairless brows arched. "I could spend all day chuckling over the ironies, but I have a job to do. I think I'll send you back to Dashiell, to see what he was doing as the attack approached. It's hilarious."

26

The Third Thud

In an instant, I find myself back with Dashiell Aspling, the Acting Boss of Mines. His Chihuahua skull was in a quivering state of hyper-alertness. His eyes wandered aimlessly. Finally, they focused on the bare expanse of mahogany that stretched in front of him.

At the A-BOM's request, technicians from Managotech Resources had come in the night and removed the Dashiellboard—the news had already swept the seventh floor. Also missing from the desk were the bronze bull pen holder, the Excalibur letter opener, the crystal Percival paper weight, the pewter globe paperweight, photos of his latest platinum wife, and even the telephones and the blotter. Dashiell's eye briefly lit on these items now piled on the glass coffee table. Then he focused on the two inconspicuous dents that marred the surface of his desk.

I had seen Greyson make these dents himself with the globe paperweight. Then he told the A-BOM that the bullet-shattered skull of Brian "Brick" Mason had made one dent while the tuber-like nose of the dying Vaughn Sutter Wayne had left the other, a mere sixteen centimeters to the right of the first. I was sure Dashiell would see through such an obvious lie, but he stared at those dents until his vision blurred. He started, refocused, and put his index finger on the larger of the two dents.

"Thud," he said. He moved his finger to the second dent. "Thud." Dashiell allowed his head to sag forward until his nose touched the desk. He sat up straight again. He had marked the spot where his nose touched with his index finger. With his other hand, he reached into the top drawer and took out a pen. He moved his index finger and scratched an "X" where it had been.

"Thud," he said. "The third thud. I'll be the third thud."

Greyson and the other Horsemen had really done a number on Dashiell's mind. He had deteriorated to the point where he did little but sit through excruciating daily meetings with the Horsemen. Apparently it didn't occur to him that it was within his power to cancel these meetings, to reprimand all four Horsemen, even to resign from the Mines altogether and walk away. Something about this majestic expanse of executive mahogany held him in thrall. It stilled the wise interior voice that said, "Walk away while you still retain a vestige of your (insert appropriate noun here, i.e. sanity, soul, reputation, dignity, ethics, self-respect.)"

Daphne no longer used the office intercom because it startled her boss. She knocked softly, and when there was no response, she peeked in and whispered, "Dashiell?"

No response.

"Dashiell? Your seven thirty is here."

"What?"

"You have a meeting with Maddie James."

"Who?"

"The head of the Alternative Alchemy Unit."

"What's that?"

"You remember. She was here earlier talking about the terrorist threat. She claims she has new evidence this morning that an attack is imminent."

"Tell her to go away," Dashiell said. He heard a woman's voice in the background shout, "We could all get our asses blown off!"

"Would that make things worse?" Dashiell asked no one in particular. Then he shook his head and said, "Make her go away."

A half-hour later, Daphne again knocked softly at the door and opened it a crack.

"Dashiell, the Horsemen are here."

"Of course, they're here," Dashiell said with deathly resignation. "I don't suppose you could tell them to go away?"

"I could, but they wouldn't."

Indeed, Greyson was already pushing past her. He barreled into the room heedless of the hushed atmosphere that would put off a normal visitor.

"Good morning, Sir!" he boomed.

Dashiell recoiled. He focused on Greyson's huge teeth.

"Shall we get started?" Greyson was bursting with cheer and enthusiasm.

Dashiell didn't answer, but made his way unsteadily across the new, blood red carpet and lowered himself into a chair.

"I don't like the carpet," Dashiell said. "I hate it. Nobody brought me any swatches. I always get swatches."

"I don't like to burden the A-BOM with every little detail," Slinky said. "This was available, and we had to get that Berber out of here fast after Shelby's little incident.

Like I said, those natural fibers are a breeding ground for germs, and they hold onto smells like grim death."

"I hate red," Dashiell said.

"Well you didn't like the Patriot Blue either," Slinky said, a little sullen. "And the white was impractical. This is the US Government. Red, white, blue. Those are your choices unless you work on the lower floors, then you get gray, gray, or gray."

Daphne knocked on the door and rolled in a cart from the executive dining room. Apprehension showed on her face as she removed the heavy linen covering the spread and lifted the dome of the breakfast platter. But this morning there were no explosive raspberry jelly do-nuts covered in powdered sugar, but only an innocuous assortment of mini muffins.

"Thank you, Daphne, I'll pour the coffee," Greyson said.

Daphne cast a suspicious look at the BOBM as she withdrew.

"Coffee, Dash?" Greyson asked.

Dashiell shook his head vigorously.

"Muffin?" Greyson picked up the tray and offered it to the A-BOM. "I highly recommend the lemon poppy seed."

Dashiell shook his head again and shrank back into his chair. He no longer ate or drank anything in the company of the Horsemen.

"Are you sure you won't have a muffin?" Greyson moved the tray within inches of Dashiell's face. "The bran raisin are quite tasty, although we try to keep the high-fiber choices away from Shelby." He laughed and set the tray back on the table.

"Coffee for anyone else?"

All declined, and even Greyson didn't take a cup.

None of them had consumed any form of food or beverage in the A-BOM's office since the "fast-moving virus" incident. This cart would return to the executive dining room exactly as it left.

Greyson must have found another way to administer that paranoia-enhancing drug to Dashiell because the man was obviously still under the influence.

"All right, shall we begin then?" Greyson said. "Arthur, I understand that you've now completed a battery of tests on the carpet—that is the original patriot blue carpet that was in here at the time of Brick's murder. Why don't you give us a rundown of what the smithies came up with?"

Arthur nodded. "Certainly. My experts—and my Scientific Excellence Recruitment Initiative has attracted some of the best analytical chemists in the business—tested the fibers utilizing gas chromatography."

Greyson interrupted. "I beg you, Arthur, *do not* explain to us what that is."

"Very well. I'm sure you wouldn't understand it anyway, although it was considered a gut course at MIT." Arthur took off his glasses and gestured with them toward a spot behind Dashiell's desk. "The most productive fiber samples were collected from under your chair." Arthur gave Dashiell a smile as thin and pleasant as a paper cut. He reached into his jacket and removed a folded sheet of paper.

"I have a list of all the substances, both organic and inorganic, found on the carpet. To begin with the organic, naturally we found Brick's blood, skull fragments, and hair, as well as some of his urine and fecal matter. People don't seem to realize when they go to shoot themselves, that the bladder and bowels evacuate when the gun goes off. I say, if you can plan ahead enough to write a suicide note and load your weapon, then you ought to at least have the foresight to visit the men's room." Arthur gave Dashiell a significant look. "It's a courtesy to those who have to clean up after you. But, I'll get off my soapbox. We analyzed the urine and found nothing unusual, except that Brick was borderline diabetic, but that's hardly an issue now. I believe I've mentioned to you before that we found a few hairs from an Irish setter. We theorize that the murderer was a dog owner because Brick himself owned only cats. We found quite a bit of cat hair that Brick had evidently carried in on his trouser legs. We did DNA testing to match it to Brick's two Maine Coon cats, Sappho and Vanzetti."

"I believe you mean Sacco and Vanzetti," I said, pleased that I could condescend to Arthur for once.

"No," he said, "I don't make that sort of mistake. They were named Sappho and Vanzetti. Alberta named the female Sappho; then Brick named the male Vanzetti. To get back to the report, we found a few of Daphne's hairs, as one might expect. Brick apparently liked to pare his nails at his desk because nail filings were present, as well. Surprisingly, we found no semen. I always thought Brick would be the type to have porn on his computer."

"You mentioned earlier that there was semen from the murderer near the burn chute," I pointed out.

Arthur glared at me. "I meant *other* than that semen."

Greyson leaned forward. "So there was nothing pornographic on his computer?"

"No," Arthur said, "but we're going off-topic. To get back to the carpet, we also found coffee stains and a few spots of Tabasco. We know that Brick put Tabasco on everything, so that's no surprise. There was another extremely salty substance that had us stumped for weeks, but it turned out to be some sauce from the General Tso's chicken that they serve downstairs in the cafeteria. Daphne confirmed that the chicken was one of Brick's favorite entrées."

"So you have squat," Greyson said.

"We have a detailed and expert analysis," Arthur said.

Greyson grinned. "Like I said, squat. Well, I guess we'll just have to wait until the guy strikes again. Let me see what else is on the agenda today." He tapped his head. "Oh yes, there was another intercept from Senator Westerly."

I was dead sober and quite depressed. My jowls sagged a good inch lower than usual. But at this I sat up and appeared almost alert. "I didn't see that."

"Alberta had to suppress it, of course," Greyson said.

"But I should get to see it. My bomb dissectors should see it."

"I'm telling you about it now, Shelby. Calm yourself. Again, it was a short intercept from Senator Harrison Westerly's house. He should know better, but the rumor on the Hill is that his brain is softening like a month-old pear. Anyway, he dialed a cell phone, probably a throwaway, and said, 'Don't forget. We have to hit the sewer on Dirksen's birthday.' We're trying to find out now exactly what day the bird was born. He's about thirty years old, so it's not as easy as—"

"What sewer?" Dashiell asked.

"It's a codeword," Greyson said. "We think it means a federal agency."

"Either the Mines or the Organ. Possibly Capitol Hill, although I don't think a senator would target the Hill," I said. "We've never been able to pin it down."

Dashiell's eyes wandered the room. "They wouldn't dare target us, would they?"

I remember being surprised by the A-BOM's naivete. The sympathy that I felt for the man was fast being overtaken by impatience. "Oh, they've been targeting us for years. I could give you a list of the plots if you'd like."

"Yes," Greyson said, "the A-BOM should definitely have that list."

"Definitely," Arthur said. "Remember the Pizza with Pepperoni, Extra Cheese, and Ricin Plot?"

"That was a close one," Greyson said. "The Base managed to get an operative hired by Mama's Pizza in McLean. Employees frequently order from Mama's for office parties. On the occasion of the retirement of one of our White Mines office chiefs, 18 poison pizzas arrived at the front gate. Fortunately, the MS-9 employee who was sent to pick up the pizzas complained that the boxes were late and not even warm. He refused to accept them. The delivery boy-slash-operative lost his temper and started cussing out the MS-9 in Arabic and telling him that he and all of his friends were about to die a horrible death. Well, the MS-9 was an Arabist and answered him back in Arabic. The operative panicked and took off at a run for his car. A few SCUDOs tackled him, and that was the end of that plot."

"Oh, and then there was the Improvised Explosive Stairmaster Plot," Arthur said. "This was back when "Chip" Nestle was BOM. He always did thirty-five minutes on the Stairmaster in the Mines gym every morning at ten o'clock. I believe you're fond of the Stairmaster, too, aren't you? Anyway, the Base was able to infiltrate an operative into the company that services Mines athletic equipment. He implanted plastic explosives in the handholds of the Stairmaster and timed them to explode at 10:30 a.m. Unfortunately for the Base, one of the guys who used the Stairmaster earlier that day sweated so profusely, it deactivated the timer."

I tried to catch Dashiell's attention so I could roll my eyes at him, but he wouldn't look at me. The Pizza with Pepperoni, Extra Cheese, and Ricin Plot and the Improvised Explosive Stairmaster Plot were entirely fictional creations. The Horsemen were playing with the A-BOM- now. They could have told him about real plots against the Mines, but they were just having fun. I couldn't understand their malicious high spirits. The Mines was, after all, in serious trouble.

"By the way," I said to Greyson, "have you identified the Molothrus from the Organ yet?"

Greyson gave me a sour look. "We're working on it."

"Do we have a strategy should the cockatoo thing go public?" I asked.

"What cockatoo?" Dashiell said.

"Look, we've explained to you about the bird," Greyson said impatiently.

Dashiell had no further questions. He let the words float over his head as the Horsemen droned on about bombs and birds and budgetary constraints. Dashiell stared down at his tie, which featured an Escher print of birds turning into fish. He untucked the tie from his jacket and touched each bird with his index finger as if he were counting it. "Birds," he said. "You bug birds, don't you?"

The Horsemen ignored this and continued to talk about fictional threats.

Dashiell held the end of the tie up to his ear, listening for the telltale electronic buzz of a listening device. He removed the tie and looked around. His eyes fell on the coffee pot.

"That plane!" Dashiell pointed to the window. "That plane is about to fly into the building!"

The Horsemen turned, and Dashiell lunged for the cart and stuffed his tie into the coffee pot.

Flit. I am in the head of a white-coated employee of Caterico, the company contracted to run the executive dining room.

He came to retrieve the cart from the A-BOM's office. He pushed it down the hallway to the kitchen of the dining room, emptied the untouched mini-muffins into a black plastic garbage bag, and poured the cream down the sink. He removed the lid from the coffee carafe and dumped it into the sink as well. When a long, thin, thing uncoiled from the carafe, he dropped it and jumped back as if he'd seen a snake. But it was only a coffee-saturated silk tie. The worker picked it up gingerly and threw it into the garbage bag on top of the muffins. He washed his hands with hot water and anti-bacterial soap.

27

Red-Handed

I return to the polygraph room to find a naked Virgil squeezing a ripe boil that has appeared on his neck.

I shut my eyes before it bursts. "You have postmortem acne now?"

"My superpower is my ability to elicit revulsion. Don't knock it. It works. There. Done. You can open your eyes now."

I open them just as Virgil applies a final push, and the damn thing spews. I cover my eyes. "Aw, ugh, disgusting. You said you were done."

"I lied. Haven't you figured out by now that polygraph examiners lie? We lie to get at the truth."

"So the end justifies the means?"

Virgil ignores the question. "Enough fun. Let's get back to the subject. You've been quite the little skull hopper lately. Your own head must be spinning. That's the effect we're aiming for: total disorientation. We have to spin you faster and faster until all the lies go flying out."

I open my eyes. "And when do your lies go flying out?"

To my surprise, Virgil's face takes on a sad and wistful expression. It's the first genuine emotion he's shown. "My lies won't leave. That's why I'm still in this room. But you, you have a chance. See you later."

This skull is narrow, slimy, and smells like sweat working its way through a thick coating of deodorant. This man spent a lot of time looking out of the corner of his eye or staring down at his hands as they straightened papers and carefully aligned a stapler perpendicular to the broad edge of his desk.

Lyle Voth.

The stapler would have given it away even if he hadn't been humming the Marseillaise. Whenever Lyle left the suite, Thelma would get up and push the stapler crooked. She used the tip of a pen, so that when an infuriated Lyle dusted the thing for fingerprints, he found only his own.

Lyle was congenitally disgruntled, terminally snide, and steeped in disdain. In a vain attempt to cover all the fear and sourness at his center, he treated the rest of the world as if it were mildly amusing, like a bad pun or a fart joke. Despite the fact that no one liked him, Lyle had achieved a reasonably high rank. Instead of being grateful for this miracle, he believed he should have achieved a much higher rank, considering his extraordinary abilities. He was in awe of his own abilities. He once told me that in a perfect meritocracy, he would have risen to the top quickly and smoothly, like a fishing bob. I called him Bob for a week until he got so mad he almost burst into tears.

The Mines could never be accused of being a perfect meritocracy or a perfect anything. I'd sat in on Lyle's most recent career panel. The consensus was that he had peaked, that he would haunt the upper strata of the General Mining Schedule grades and never reach the senior executive ranks. One member of the panel remarked, "Promote him? He'll be lucky if someone doesn't drown him in a toilet." The final judgment on Lyle Voth had been passed.

I had innocently hired Lyle as my executive assistant because he came highly recommended by a well-respected office director. I should have known better. Sometimes a glowing recommendation is just a clever way to transfer a monkey from one back to another. Tag, you're it.

Lyle was useful in one respect: I could make him the object of my ill temper without guilt. Any flak I launched in his direction could only do him good. It was better than being short with Thelma, who didn't deserve it. Mostly, though, I ignored Lyle. I can't imagine why Virgil would even bother to send me into the skull of such a nonentity.

Lyle glanced at the clock. It was 7:15 in the evening. He watched as I emerged from my office with a marked-up draft of the President's Intelligence Update in my hand. I would drop it off with the PIU staff on my way out the building. "Good night," I said to Thelma and Lyle. "Don't work too long."

"I'm going now," Lyle said.

"Oh, look at the time." Thelma reached for her purse. "I'd better get home too."

Lyle followed me out the door, leaving Thelma to secure the vault. "Big evening planned?" he asked.

I didn't answer, just looked at him like he had two heads.

Fortunately, he turned into the men's room without any more irksome attempts at small talk. Once inside, he crouched down and looked under the stalls. No feet at this time of the evening, just layers of newsprint. This bathroom was one of the messiest in the building because of Thelma. Whenever a man left the executive suite with a newspaper under his arm, she would point her finger and say, "If you take that to the men's room, DO NOT bring it back."

Once reassured that he was alone, Lyle set his briefcase on the floor and paced back and forth in front of the urinals, now and then glancing at his watch or his reflection in the mirror. After about fifteen minutes, he picked up the briefcase and returned to the executive suite. He opened the vault and turned off the alarm system, but didn't bother to initial the sheet at the door.

Lyle didn't turn on the lights. He made his way to my office door by the dim light over the security panel. Once inside, he took a flashlight out of his briefcase. The beam crawled along the floor until it found the burn bag under my desk.

Lyle got down onto his knees. His thin hand plunged into the bag. He pulled out everything written on a 3 ½" x 5 ½"-inch page, all the notes I had taken in the BOM's office.

Greyson was right: I should never have taken those notes. Lyle was the Molothrus. I had handed this resentful little man the power to alter fates, destroy careers, and ruin reputations. He must have read my notes about the coverup of Brick's supposed murder, the bugging of Senator Westerly's home, and the fateful operation that killed Dirksen. God knows what else.

Fortunately, I had a guardian angel, and Lyle never saw her coming. The office light popped on, and Lyle looked up to see Thelma standing in the door, hands on hips. "Just what do you think you're doing, Lyle Voth?"

The sudden, sharp smell of urine suggests that Lyle

briefly lost control of his urethral sphincter muscle.

"What are *you* doing here?" he said, trying to fill his voice with righteous indignation.

"I'm Shelby's secretary. I belong here. I came back because I left one of Martin's school forms on my desk, and he needs it for tomorrow. I heard something rustling in here that sounded like a big rat. So I came in to check it out. And here you are, a big rat. I repeat: what are you doing?"

"Well, I am Shelby's executive assistant, and I belong here, too."

"Not going through his burn bag, you don't."

"I was just ... " Lyle fumbled for a plausible excuse and finally said, "looking for a copy of the Global Threat Testimony. I lost mine."

"That is so lame. An electronic copy of the Global Threat Testimony is in the office database and you know it. What are you doing here? And don't give me anymore lies because I can sniff them out a mile away."

Lyle looked into Thelma's keen eyes and quailed. He knew she was right. To Lyle, Thelma's ability to ferret out lies must have seemed supernatural, but flushing out a liar is merely a matter of acute observation and empathy. The ability to suppress one's ego and crawl into the mind of another. Thelma was a master at the skill, but for Lyle it would have been easier to spread his arms and fly.

After an excruciating minute under Thelma's gaze, Lyle finally came up with something else. "This is so embarrassing," he said, "but I was looking for the draft of my performance appraisal report. There's a job I was thinking of applying for, so this report will be important to me. You won't tell Shelby, will you?"

Thelma's eloquent eyes rolled upward, and her glossy

lips parted. She hesitated as she considered whether or not this sad excuse might be true. Lyle was the sort to do such a thing.

Then Lyle had a burst of inspiration. "Popcorn!" he said. "Isn't one of your sons selling popcorn for the school band?"

Thelma narrowed her eyes but said, "Martin is selling popcorn for the Boy Scouts, and Gerald is selling nut brittle for the school band."

"Is it too late to buy some?" Lyle managed to sound eager. "I love popcorn and nut brittle."

"I thought you said you didn't want any of what you call 'that overpriced junk.'"

"I changed my mind. Now that I think about it, it would be great to have some extra on hand for guests."

Thelma weighed her choices. These school sales had always been important to her because they allowed her sons to afford trips that would have otherwise been out of reach. I had bought boatloads of wares from her over the years, everything from chocolate bars to tulip bulbs. Thelma could continue to hold Lyle's feet to the fire, or she could sell enough popcorn and nut brittle to get Martin a marketing badge and Gerald a discount on the upcoming band trip to Virginia Beach. Her children came first. After a moment of hesitation, Thelma went to her desk and came back with two glossy brochures. She handed them to Lyle.

"Popcorn. There are five flavors: Campfire Chipotle, Cool Dude Ranch, Burnin' Hot Barbecue, Caramel Cruncheroo, and Rocky Road Runner, which has chocolate chunks and mini-marshmallows shaped like cartoon characters." Thelma gave Lyle a dazzling smile. "I'm guessing you'd like all five."

"Really, all five?" Lyle asked.

"You know you didn't initial when you entered the vault, and that's a security violation."

"I'll have all five."

Thelma's spokesmodel smile returned. "Excellent. There are five sizes: small, medium, large, jamboree jumbo, and ginormous. The ginormous comes in an attractive five-gallon woodland creatures decorator bucket. I'm guessing you'd like a ginormous bucket of each flavor."

Lyle's "yes" came out like the chirp of a bird.

"Now, for the nut brittle. There are five kinds: Peanutty Pete, Macadamia Madness, I Am the Walnut, All Almond, and Nutelicious Mix. You'll take all five?"

Chirp.

"The brittle comes in a half-pound Baby Bear Box, a pound Mama Bear Box, or the deluxe Daddy Bear Box, which has five pounds of brittle. Shall I put you down for a Big Daddy Box of each flavor?"

Lyle's answering chirp was almost inaudible. He was notorious in the office for being not only a cheap, but also a health nut. Now he had ordered several hundred dollars worth of junk food. He signed the check in a shaky hand. Thelma looked it over carefully before slipping it into her purse. She wagged her finger at Lyle.

"And don't you dare do something mean like stopping payment on this check, or I'll go straight to Shelby and tell him that you've been pawing around in his trash. And by the way, you are not going to have the opportunity to snoop around again because I'm going to have logistics put a lock on his door. And I'm going to throw this bag down the chute before I go home. Put everything back where you found it." Thelma hovered close over Lyle as he gathered all my notes and stuffed them back into the burn bag. She made him take off his jacket so she could go through the pockets. Then she had him triple fold and crease the bag and staple it every two inches per Agency regulations.

Thelma slipped the burn bag under one arm and her purse over the other. "Time to get yourself together and get up. I'm going to watch you leave. In fact, I'm going to follow you down the tunnel all the way out to your car. I'll drop this bag in the burn chute on the way to make sure you don't get your hot little hands on it again, and when you get home, Lyle Voth, I want you to think long and hard about what you've done. I expect you to have a better attitude when you get back here tomorrow morning because I will be watching every move you make."

Thus Thelma took care of the Molothrus quickly and efficiently, without anyone else ever finding out about it. Meanwhile, Greyson's Top Secret Molothrus Task Force ground on, consuming resources, and trashing the careers of several innocent employees.

28

My Name is Shelby

I return to the polygraph room to find Virgil, still na-ked, playing air guitar and singing "The Beat Goes On." Words escape me. The bastard sings it through twice before he props the air guitar in the corner and says, "Wel-come back, Shelby. Do you get the joke? Come on, think."

I give him a dumb stare. I have no idea what he's talking about.

Virgil explains. "I'm singing 'The Beat Goes On' when the beat, the heartbeat, has stopped. Get it? Come on, it's brilliant."

Apparently Virgil and I have different definitions of the word "brilliant."

Virgil heeps, snorts, and slaps his naked knee. "I have to thank you, Shelby; you've spurred my creativity. My job was never this fun in life."

"You're not welcome, Virgil."

The bulb of his nose glows cherry red like a Rockwell Santa. "I'm so proud of myself. I'm really developing a *joie de*...what is the opposite of *vivre*?" He waits for me to answer, and then shrugs. "No need to give me the silent treatment. Loosen up, Shelby. I'm going to ask you a few questions designed to gauge your acceptance of embarrassing truths. Allow me to turn the machine on." Virgil turns his backside to me and goes through the motions, adjusting dials and checking styluses.

"Yes or no, did you hate Greyson Earl because you thought you were smarter than he was."

"Yes."

Virgil claps. "Finally, you give me a correct answer on the first try. All right, yes or no, did you hate Arthur White because you feared that he was smarter than you?"

"Yes."

"Two correct answers in a row." Virgil throws up his hands. "Unprecedented progress. That's all the questions for now, Shelby."

Back in my own skull. I was trying to find a parking spot in McLean as the sun set over the tract mansions. I know what night it was.

When I told Esther I was going to attend my first Alcoholics Anonymous meeting, I thought she would be overjoyed. I thought she would cancel the renovation of the basement. I thought she might even cook me my favorite dinner, stringy pot roast. But all she did was tell me to take the garbage to the curb on my way out. Only then did I realize that the meetings would not be enough. I would actually have to stop drinking.

Shit.

I muttered to myself nonstop as I once again circled the Merry Avenue Montessori School, where AA meetings were held in the gym. I imagined walking into a roomful of derelicts smelling of Boone's Farm and unwashed clothing, but then I remembered that I was in Fairfax, one of the most affluent counties in the country. The derelicts probably had their clothing dry-cleaned on a regular basis.

The parking lot of the school was full when I arrived. At first, I was relieved, thinking this an adequate excuse to turn around and go home. Then I realized that for Esther, it would not be an adequate excuse. She might not have reacted much when I told her I was going to the meeting, but she would react if I turned back now. I considered finding someplace else to go for the next hour, but she would know. I didn't know how, but she would know. I might as well have married a damn sharper. So I circled the neighborhood of older split-levels and huge new tract mansions, built almost to the property lines. I finally found a space just large enough for my beat-up Ford pickup. I parked, slammed the door, and kicked the front tire, once, twice, three times until I hurt my toe. I blamed this injury on the universe.

"Blast it all," I said.

The "derelicts" arriving for the meeting all drove much nicer, cleaner vehicles than I. I passed polished BMWs, Audis, and Lexuses, but I didn't covet that sort of transportation. When my pickup died, I planned to buy a newer version of it, as near to the original as I could find. I would travel to dealerships in three states if necessary to find something without automatic windows, heated seats, or other unnecessary gadgetry that would only break and cost money to fix. I wouldn't have dreamed of driving a vehicle that couldn't haul a good load of mulch or manure for my garden. I couldn't imagine why anyone would waste time washing a car. "A good layer of dirt holds down the rust," I used to tell Esther.

I had considered the possibility that I would run into someone familiar at this meeting. I'd heard that's how it was with AA meetings. You always run into someone you know, and it's always a big surprise. As I trudged down the sidewalk toward the school, I tried to guess who it might be. Who would I be most surprised to see here?

Esther. I let my imagination carry me away. Wouldn't it be wonderful to walk in and see Esther waiting for me with an understanding smile on her face? She'd laugh at my surprise. She'd tell me she only pretended to be a tee-totaler all of these years, that she once had a flask of Jack Daniels hidden in the bottom of her Kleenex box. The contractor was building a game room in the basement, not an apartment, she'd say. It would have a pool table and a foosball table and shelves for all the books stacked on my study floor. She'd put an arm around me and say, "It's hard it is to give up drinking, but you're man enough to do it." Then she'd tell me she had a stringy pot roast in the slow cooker for when we got home. By the time I reached the door of the Montessori school, I was sucking my lips and salivating. I paused outside a glass door thickly painted with mutant, pastel-colored mice. Yes, she would be there.

I opened the door to find Greyson Earl sitting on a child-size bench shaped like a zebra. He puffed on a cigarette. His face registered no surprise at the sight of me.

"I've been expecting you for some time, you old sot. If you hadn't come yourself, I was going to have Special Employee Services stage an intervention. Don't look so surprised at seeing me here. You know alcoholism is the number one occupational hazard of the clandestine service."

"I suppose." I struggled to adjust to the sight of Greyson in place of Esther, whom I had so effectively conjured in this spot. No stringy pot roast awaited me at home. Worse, if I didn't attend every one of these meetings, Greyson would refer me to Special Employee Services.

A beefy, athletic woman jogged toward us down the hallway. "I knew I smelled cigarette smoke," she called. "Mr. Earl, once again, this is a no smoking zone! This is a school for small children. Some of them have asthma. Do you want to get us kicked out of here? Now put that out and come in. We're about to start."

The woman noticed me. "Oh, hi. You're new, aren't you? Welcome. My name is Samantha, and I'm the coordinator of this chapter."

"My name is Shelby, and I'm an alcoholic." There. I'd gotten it out. It was over. I could go home.

"Not yet, Shelby," Greyson said, "save it for the meeting." As Samantha hurried away to attend to some other urgent business, he whispered to me, "By the way, there's someone else you'll recognize in here, someone very close to you."

For a moment, my heart leaped. Esther!

"Lyle Voth," Greyson said.

By the time the meeting ended, I was limp with humiliation, relief, depression, a whole host of feelings I couldn't sort. As I shuffled out of the gymnasium to the heavy glass door with the pastel mice, Greyson came up behind me and put an arm around my shoulder.

"Buck up, Shel. Want to go for a beer?" Greyson

laughed at the eagerness that lit my face. "That never gets old. Just kidding. God, you're gullible. I can see from the look on your face that it hasn't come home to you yet that you really can't go out for a drink now when you feel like crap, or when you want to celebrate, or when the stress of an impending rockslide is beginning to get to you." Greyson lit a cigarette, even though we were still inside the glass door, and Samantha would surely smell it. "That's why I started smoking again. Screw the asthmatic brats. Got to toughen up their little lungs some time."

The men and women leaving the meeting frowned at Greyson's cigarette. He smiled and nodded in return.

"Nothing like the self-righteousness of one sort of addict toward a different sort."

Lyle Voth was next out the gymnasium door. He stopped to greet us, looking askance at Greyson's cigarette and then fixing me with a long, appraising glance that made my stomach crimp.

"See you tomorrow morning," he said, "I'll have that memo ready for you promptly by ten o'clock."

"Well, I have no idea what memo you're talking about, but I see it means a great deal to you, so I'll look forward to it," I said.

Lyle returned a sour look and headed out the door.

"Something's off about him," Greyson said. "I don't believe he's even an alcoholic. He always has this look of smug superiority on his face during the meetings. Makes me want to snuff my cigarette out in one of his nostrils."

I looked swiftly at Greyson. Whenever he used one of these colorful expressions, I sensed it was not merely an expression.

"You're right," he said, "I have snuffed out a cigarette in someone's nostril."

By the time I arrived home, I was exhausted. I felt like I'd run a moral marathon. It was all I could do to drag my sorry ass to my front door and open it. Esther, who was watching some silly television program, looked up and broke into a smile.

"You did go! I can tell from your face. I'm so proud." She hopped out of her chair and gave me a hug.

I emitted a series of grumbly, growly, groaning sounds as Esther kissed my cheek.

"I guess I can bring in the stringy pot roast now. I put the slow cooker out on the deck so you wouldn't smell it. If you hadn't gone to that meeting, I wasn't going to give it to you. I was going to freeze it."

Virgil is laughing when I return. "And the only time you ever got smashed again, it was by a concrete portico and not a bottle of bourbon. Hilarious."

"Excuse me, but the humor escapes me."

"You would have made it, you know," Virgil said. "Given a little more time, you would have pulled yourself together, made amends to your wife, and done a creditable job at work. Such a shame." He shakes his head, but quickly perks up. "Okay, enough of that, now I'm going to send you to a really scary place."

Too Late

Another pressurized skull. A terrorist? No, I recognize the coffee breath. It's Maddie again.

She yawned and opened her eyes. Her desktop had grown more chaotic. Cables spilled onto the floor. Something had spilled onto the cables, a whole mug of coffee from the look of it. I find the spatter pattern oddly reminiscent of Brick's blood on mounds of split burn bags and paper. Maddie's computer was so coated with yellow sticky notes that it resembled some ungainly hybrid of Big Bird and Sponge-Bob Squarepants.

She was reaching for one of the notes when a knock sounded at the door. "Who is it?" she yelled.

The door opened to reveal a retired contract escort. "Workmen to install new lighting fixtures," he said. "You need to cover your classified materials."

Maddie jumped up and moved aggressively toward the escort. "I told you three times to go away and never come back!"

"Lady, we have to do this." The escort took a tentative step into the room, but he threw up his hands and backed out as Maddie got closer. "You're the last office we have left on this floor—one of the last in the building—and they have to do it now. They're trying to finish this job up. Don't you want the full spectrum lights? They're supposed to make you happier."

"I don't fucking want to be happy," Maddie yelled. "Get out!"

The escort would have continued his argument, but he was interrupted by the living version of me. I came up behind him and said, "Please come back later."

The contractor recognized me as one of the Horseman and retreated with a polite "Certainly, sir, no problem."

"Hello, Maddie," I said.

She stared at me. I didn't look too bad, at least in comparison to a few weeks earlier. The color had come back into my face, and my expression was more alert, although wary. Anyone walking into Maddie James office would have been wary. It would have been less dangerous to enter a badger's den.

I sat down in the extra chair, even though she hadn't invited me to do so.

Maddie returned to her desk but didn't sit down. "Have you come to kick me out of my office? I don't know what else you could do to diminish my effectiveness any further."

"No," I said. "I've come to tell you that I've approved a budget that will enable you to hire a half dozen alchemists and a secretary. While you're doing the official hiring, I will allow you to borrow a few of my people." I wasn't convinced that her threat was real. I was acting mainly out of guilt, trying to cover my bases in case the worst happened, and starting to catch up on all the things I had neglected.

Maddie was quick to push her advantage. "I'd like a couple of people from the Organ, too, if you can make a deal with Hunter Johnson."

"I'll try to make it happen."

She studied me closely. "What happened to you, Shelby? It's like that scene from the *Lord of the Rings* where the frost finally falls off of King Theoden's face and he wakes up and remembers that the Kingdom is about to get overrun by Orcs and he should probably haul ass."

"I have no idea what you're talking about," I told her, but I did. I remembered that scene clearly and the thought of it made something flop in my gut. "I just want to make sure you have the resources you need in case there's any substance to the threat you've been hyping."

"There is substance, and I'm not hyping it. It's real. You need to send out an alert, have every federal agency in town do a sniff-over."

"Why do you think the target is a federal agency?" I asked. Maddie hadn't seen the latest Westerly cable.

"Because the planner, the Shaker, was working on a plot against a government agency, possibly the Mines, in the late nineties. His focus was Washington. He belonged to the Base then, but they scrubbed his plot and he split with them. I've seen several indications that he's been active recently, and he cleared out of his home base within the last few days. We need to send out an alert and have the bomb dogs go over every agency in town."

"The Shaker?" From Maddie's eyes I see a look of unease pass over my face. I hadn't realized that her threat involved the Shaker, that it must be the same as the Westerly threat.

"Everybody's gone quiet," Maddie said, and her voice grew quiet too as her eyes wandered over the welter of cables. "I can't get a bead on the method of attack. I haven't heard a single thing referring to bombs or explosives or airplanes. Haven't discovered any bomb makers' names. It could be chemical." She leaned forward to study my face more closely. Guilt was clearly written across the doughy landscape. "Shelby, do you know something else?"

"No," I said.

"You do know something," she said.

"I'll send out an alert to all federal agencies." I got up to leave. "I have a meeting. Figure out which bomb dissectors you want to borrow and talk to Lyle Voth. I've told him to give you what you want."

"What do you know, Shelby?"

I turned my back. As my hand fell on the door knob, Maddie hissed, "There's a special spot in hell for people who won't rock the boat."

I fled past the escort, who was waiting outside the door. He stuck his head in and said, "Please, I have to finish this office."

Maddie stared after me.

"Please, ma'am," the escort said.

"Fine, wait a minute so I can cover everything." She took a large link chart off the wall and turned it upside down over her desk. She picked up a few cables from the floor and stuck them under the link chart. Then she taped the edges to her desk to make sure none of the mess spilled out.

"You can go now, I'll be here to watch," the escort said.

"No, I'll stay," Maddie said. She pushed the chair I had just abandoned into the corner and sat down to watch the men come in with their ladders and boxes of lighting equipment. As they removed the old panels over the ceiling lights, Maddie picked up a long box containing one of the new full-spectrum lights.

"Hey, don't touch that," a workmen said.

Maddie ignored him. She opened the box and pulled out a long white tube. She weighed it in her hand, turned it over, and held it up to the light. Her eyes ran slowly from one end to the other.

"The bomb-sniffing dogs go over every package that comes into the building," the escort said.

"Right." Maddie took another long look before she handed it to the workman at the top of the ladder. He plugged it into the new socket he had installed, and the light fluttered on.

And I am back with Virgil. He tips his head to the side. "When Maddie asked you if you knew something else, what were you thinking of, Shelby?"

"The Westerly intercepts, of course."

"In all the cable traffic related to that threat, the only mention of a method of attack was in those intercepts. And that was a single word, 'screamers.' Tell me, Shelby, is that what passed across your face in Maddie's office? Were you remembering that intercept?"

"Yes," I said.

"And why didn't you tell Maddie about the intercept? About any other intercepts on Westerly?"

"I almost told her," I said, my voice barely audible.

"Almost," Virgil repeated. "What a word. Tell me, Shelby, what stopped you?"

"I was going to give Maddie resources to work on her threat. What would Maddie have done if she had found out about Harrison Westerly? If she had found out that we were listening to him? She's not the sort of woman who could let information like that lie quietly in a safe. She would have become ... an existential threat to the Mines."

"What would she have done with that word 'screamers?'" Virgil paced the tiny room: two steps, turn, two steps, turn. "It might have started her thinking in a new direction. Maybe she would have taken a closer look at that light tube. Maybe she would have called the smithies in to examine it. Maybe they would have noticed that it was heavier than usual. They might have taken it apart and found the amplification device. They might have noticed the wires that connected the fixtures to the steel infrastructure of the building, turning the whole structure into an amplifying system." Virgil stopped and leaned down until we were nose to nose. "Or maybe not. It was already rather late in the game. You're right. Probably nothing could have been done. It was too late."

"We're getting close, aren't we?" I said.

"Yes, but there's still time for you to go visit your own skull one last time."

30

Demoted

Sobriety and a headache. A wretchedly clear view of my feet as I trudged up my sidewalk, stepped carefully over the broken area heaved up by the root of an elm, and mounted the cracked brick stairs. I reached for the door, but it opened before I touched it.

Esther stood there with a disturbingly businesslike look on her face. "Your new apartment is ready."

I staggered back a few steps. Esther had to grab my lapels to keep me from falling off the stoop. I righted myself. My voice shook. "But, Esther, I haven't had a drink in weeks."

"When you can say you haven't had a drink in months—at least six—we'll discuss it again. In the meantime, I spent the day moving your things downstairs, so you're all set."

I slumped and let my briefcase drop from my hand. "I've had a horrible day."

Esther showed no sympathy. She picked up the briefcase and led me downstairs to the new apartment, which still smelled of sawdust and fresh paint. A bed, recliner, and dresser stood on one side of the room, and a sink, refrigerator, and cabinets on the other. The big flat screen TV hung above some bookshelves.

The wall on the north side had been redone to enlarge the bathroom. Esther opened the door. "I had them add a shower so you won't have to come upstairs. Didn't they do a wonderful job? They tiled it beautifully. Jesus and his two sons were incredibly fast, and they helped me move your furniture for no extra charge. They cleaned up after themselves so nicely, not like the guy who built the deck and left cigarette butts and empty beer cans everywhere. They were so nice. I hate it that people discriminate against them just because of technicalities."

"Technicalities?"

"Oh, green cards and such."

"You hired illegals? Esther, I'm a government official. You can't go hiring illegal aliens."

Esther waved away my protest. "You make it sound like they're criminals from outer space. They're very nice, God-fearing people—Jesus wears a lovely silver cross—and they're superb at what they do. They build, do electric, plumbing, painting, everything! Jesus has such a great sense of humor, and he's had such an interesting life."

"If they were working so hard, how did you hear about his life?" I asked.

"At lunch. I thought it would be nice to fix the three of them a good meal. I felt like I had so much in common with Jesus because he's a widower."

"You're not a widow."

"I feel like one because you're so out of it." Esther's voice was cross, but then she perked up again. "I'm thinking of hiring them to remodel the master bath. I'd like a tub with water jets, a deeper sink, and a built-in vanity."

"Jesus, Esther."

"Don't use the name of the Lord in vain. You don't even believe in him. Unlike Jesus."

"I guess it's all in how you pronounce it." I looked around, wondering how this bizarre transformation had taken place in such a short time. Jesus and his team must be good. Something about the new space bothered me though. Finally, I put my finger on it. "The walls are purple."

"That's what you asked for."

"I wouldn't ask for purple."

"I asked you what color you wanted them to paint the walls, and you said, and I quote, 'I don't care, paint them purple if you want.' And I thought how lovely that would be."

"I don't remember saying that."

"You don't remember half the things you say. I used to think it was because you drank too much, but now I think you're just oblivious. Well, I have things to do." Esther turned and went back up the stairs. I started to follow her, but she whipped around and said, "No! You stay down here, and you use the basement entrance from now on."

"Esther, you're not serious."

Esther's look softened, but she said gravely, "I've never been so serious about anything in my entire life. When you've been sober for six months …" She paused as her face went hard. "When you're willing to come with me to visit your son, then we can talk."

I swayed a little on my feet. She turned to go and to keep her there a few more seconds, I said, "What about my supper?"

"You'll find a foil-covered tuna casserole in your fridge. Put it in the oven at 375 degrees for twenty-five minutes. Paper plates are in the cabinet. I will keep your refrigerator stocked, but only because I'm old and I don't want to go home to my maker with your death by starvation on my conscience."

"Thank you, Esther, that's a lovely sentiment."

"You're welcome." Esther slammed the basement door shut.

That was the last time Esther and I spoke before my death. We carefully avoided each other and kept to our separate entrances. So the romance that began in a church basement ended in an uncivil exchange on our own basement stairs. How many times will she think back on our last words? At the time, I probably would have been gratified to think she would suffer for it, but now I'm deeply saddened by the load of regret I left her. Such poor repayment for all she did.

Back with Virgil, I shake my head. "When she found out about my death, she must have felt terrible about how she treated me that night."

Virgil nodded. "Yes. She'll be inconsolable for a good six to eight more months. Then she'll start the bathroom renovation to take her mind off it. Then, a year after that, she and Jesus will get married in a lovely ceremony by the fireplace in the living room."

"That's a transparent lie," I said. "Our living room doesn't have a fireplace."

"Jesus and sons are going to build it. They also do stone masonry. You know Esther always wanted one."

She had always wanted a fireplace. I realize that Virgil isn't lying. This feels like the truth, like a bowling ball lodged in my esophagus.

"If it makes you feel any better, they'll toast you at the wedding. There won't be a dry eye in the house."

Oddly, I find this comforting. Esther deserves a good life. "Will Jesus make Esther happy?"

"They'll make each other happy."

"So you can tell the future?" I said.

"When I want to. Don't ask me about anything else because I'm not going to tell you."

Of course, he won't tell me. It would be useless to beg. Might as well get on with it. As the eschatologists say, the end is near. I give Virgil a look of resignation. "Where to next?"

31

Udall

I'm in Senator Westerly's skull. It's fuzzier in here than before, and the smell of decay is stronger.

He sat in his home office, letting his eyes wander over all the traces left by Dirksen. Moths, hatched from the stale seed, fluttered about the room. Fruit flies swarmed over the senator's orange juice.

The phone rang. The senator waited six rings before picking it up. "What?" he said.

"Good morning, Roger here."

"Why do you keep calling me?" The Senator asked with a plaintive note in his voice.

"Because I'm your chief of staff and I'm trying to get you to accomplish at least the bare minimum for the people of Louisiana. Besides, I'm worried about you. You're clinically depressed and you won't take your medicine."

Westerly plucked a well-chewed alphabet block from a bucket and turned it in his hand.

"Senator, are you still there?" Roger asked.

"Where would I go?"

"In fact, there's a place you need to go. I'm just pulling into your driveway now. I'll be up to get you in five minutes."

"No!" the senator shouted, but Roger had hung up. "I don't want you in this room!" he said anyway. Cursing under his breath, he went out into the hallway, closed the door and locked it with a key. The Westerly's home elevator had a mirrored interior. On the way downstairs, he brushed millet hulls from his wrinkled pants, buttoned his jacket, and smoothed a disheveled eyebrow with a licked finger. The effort was in vain.

"You look terrible," Roger said. The maid had let him in, and he stood in the front hallway, looking Westerly up and down with a practiced eye. Roger was somewhere in his forties, clean-cut and wonkish, with the cultivated nondescript look of someone dedicated to grooming others for the spotlight. "Terrible. But there's no time for you to change. We have an important meeting."

"I don't want to meet with anybody. Go away." Westerly raised a frail hand and made a peremptory gesture toward the door. "Go, now."

Roger crossed his arms over his chest and positioned his feet further apart. "I'm not leaving. You have to meet with this guy. He claims to have discovered some irregularities in the financing of your reelection campaign."

"Christ. What's his name?"

"He wants to remain anonymous for now. We have to go talk to him, or he'll go public."

"Christ. All right. I'll go." Westerly followed Roger out the door but balked when he saw the beat-up minivan parked out front. "I don't ride in this sort of thing. It's driving down property values just sitting here. I'll get complaints from the neighbors. Let's take my Lincoln, you can hide this in the garage."

Roger ignored the whining and opened the passenger door. Westerly recoiled as a MacDonald's bag and several Legos spilled out onto the driveway. Roger picked them up and threw them in the back of the van. He swiped some crumbling Goldfish off the passenger seat and all but lifted the protesting senator into the vehicle. He reached across and fastened the old man's seat belt.

As Roger drove, Westerly stared out the side window, focusing on nothing, letting landscape slide by in a blur. Finally, he said, "Maybe jail wouldn't be so bad. No one would bother me there. No pesky maids, wives, staffers. I've already lost my best friend. An additional humiliation would hardly matter. I can't see any disadvantages. Maybe we should just skip the meeting and go home."

"Oh come on," Roger said. "You know you won't go to jail. This guy might make claims, but you haven't done anything wrong that I know of, have you?"

A long silence.

"Have you?" Roger asked.

"Well," the senator said, "I don't tell you everything."

"Christ," Roger said. Twenty minutes later, he turned off Route 50 in Chantilly, and the senator suddenly realized where they were going.

"No!" he shouted and started to open the door of the moving vehicle.

Roger grabbed his arm and almost drove into the side of a parked panel truck. He pulled off the road and stopped the van, trembling.

"Are you nuts?" This ill-considered question gave rise to an awkward silence. Finally, Roger took a deep breath and started the engine again.

"No!" Westerly made another move to open the door.

"If you get out here, what will you do? Hitchhike?"

"I'll call a taxi."

"You've let the battery of your cell phone run down again."

"How do you know that?"

"Because I keep trying to call you. Go ahead, check."

The senator moaned. "All right, take me there, but I won't go in. Do you think you can carry me?"

"Of course, I can. You're skin and bones." Roger maneuvered the van through broad streets lined with low, brick and glass developments for offices and small retail establishments. He pulled into a side road and parked in front of the White Feathers Aviary.

The senator crossed his arms in front of his chest and slumped down in his seat. "I will not go in there, you duplicitous bastard. It was a place Dirksen and I went together. I will not go in without him. And I will not replace Dirksen with just any old bare-eyed cockatoo. Do you think you can just replace a bird like you would replace a …" The senator struggled for an object to his verb.

Roger smiled slyly and supplied one. "Wife?"

"Well, for want of a more politically correct noun, let's say wife. Don't laugh, you asshole. It's much harder to replace a bird than a wife. I taught that bird every word he knew. Whereas I have never met a woman who couldn't talk your ear off with no special training. There's a special bond between a man and his bird. With wives, the bonds are largely legal and social."

"Actually," Roger said, "I'm rather attached to my wife. In fact, I love her very much."

The distinguished senior senator from Louisiana blew a loud raspberry, splattering the dashboard with spittle. "Well, whoopee for you. That's all sickly sweet, but you've never had a cockatoo. I've had more wives than you have, and I've had a cockatoo, so I think I'm qualified to say which one is the truer companion."

"So I guess since you refuse to get another cockatoo, you're going to have to go out and get married again after Adele leaves you."

Westerly's head snapped around. "Adele's leaving me?"

"Don't you know? Everyone knows. She's already hired a lawyer and she has her eye on the Shreveport condo."

The senator closed his eyes and heaved a sigh. "Let her have it. I'm a fair and generous man. I've given every one of my ex-wives a luxury condo."

"I know, you hand them out like party favors." Roger leaned in so close that Westerly couldn't avoid looking at him. "But the point is now you have a choice. You can die alone, staring at petrified bird droppings. You can find yourself another young blond who wants a condo enough to marry an 86-year old, which will probably not be as difficult as it should be, or you can find yourself a good bird."

The senator began to snuffle. Tears blurred his view of the bright parrot flags and toys that decorated the window of the White Feathers Aviary. "I can't have another bird. I'm too old to get a bird. I'll die and then who knows where he would end up."

Roger smiled and patted the senator's hand. "He would end up with Margaret Paulson, a lovely lady who already owns five cockatoos and keeps them in a huge aviary in her home in Maryland. White Feathers recommended her. I visited her home last week. She has a beautiful aviary, very clean, with toys everywhere. She teaches a class on parrot behavior and training. She cooks for her birds. I explained the situation to her, and she agreed to be what she called a 'God-parront.' She even signed a contract that says she will take the bird and care for it in the event of your demise. I wrote up the contract myself. It specifies a very high level of care and bi-monthly visits from me to check on the state of things. I didn't agree to give her any money, but I told her you would leave her something in your will to defray the expense of caring for the bird."

The senator was quiet for a long while. Finally, he said, "What does she cook for them?"

Like a good aide, Roger had anticipated the question and prepared for it. He reached into the glove compartment, pulled out a sheaf of papers, and handed it to the senator. "I had her print out all of her recipes. She uses only organic ingredients. Lots of vegetables, grains, sprouts, that sort of thing."

The senator studied the recipes. His finger made its shaky way down the page as he read through the ingredients for pumpkin birdie bread, winter squash medley with quinoa, and flax seed beet crackers. His finger jabbed at the cracker recipe. "Aha. Beets. Dirksen hates beets."

"This isn't Dirksen." Roger laid his hand on Westerly's shoulder. "Just look at them. It's a clutch of three: two hens and a cock."

Westerly moaned again. "Don't want to see any damned birds ever again. No damn birds. You hear me? Get me out of here right now or I'll call the police and tell them you kidnapped me. That's hard time, Roger, hard time."

"You're cell phone is dead, remember?" Roger spoke softly. "Their mother was Dirksen's sister. These are his nieces and nephews."

This was undoubtedly a lie. Dirksen was thirty years old when he died. The timing didn't work at all, but it must have been a lie the senator wanted to believe. He dared to take a look at the aviary door. "I didn't know Dirksen was an uncle. Are you sure?"

"Yes."

"No, I won't go in. Take me home."

"No. We're going to sit here." Roger reached into the back seat and came up with more papers. Then he reached back again and brought up a thermos. He poured himself a steaming cup of coffee and began to read.

"Think you're smart, don't you?"

"I know I'm smart, sir. Want to know my IQ?"

"No."

Five minutes passed. The senator saw the aviary owner, Jill, standing at the window with a young bare-eyed cockatoo nestled in a towel in her arms. He shut his eyes again.

"Aren't you going to offer me any of that coffee?"

Roger looked up. "I'd love to, but I don't have a mug for you." He went back to reading.

Ten minutes passed, perhaps fifteen. Then the senator heard a voice, heard it as clearly as if Dirksen were sitting on his shoulder.

"Go in," Dirksen said.

The senator looked around the van, but it contained no birds. Roger studiously ignored the behavior. Another five minutes passed, and Westerly's breathing grew rapid and shallow.

"Please take me away from here."

Roger poured himself more coffee, pulled a pad from his pocket, and began to scribble down a few notes.

Westerly took out a wilted handkerchief scented with lavender and wiped his brow. "All right. I'll look at the boy, but only to see how Dirksen's line is faring. I don't expect anything on the order of his magnificence."

"Of course, sir. He'll be a pale imitation, but let's go look." Roger opened his door, poured his remaining coffee on the pavement, and ran around to open the door for the senator and help him out. Roger gripped his arm and propelled him into the store.

When the birdcalls reached his ears, the senator slumped against Roger. Jill rushed forward to take Westerly's other arm. Together they managed to keep him upright until he composed himself. Then they nudged him across the room—past sacks of seed and pellets, toys, rope boings, birdie beds, perches, and swings. The senator's eyes lit here and there. "Oh, the memories," he moaned.

"Sit," Roger said and pushed Westerly into a bright, tropical-print chair under a sign that said, "Expectant Parronts Corner: *We Encourage You to Visit While your Baby is Weaning.*"

"I'll go get him," Jill said.

"I changed my mind. I don't want to see any 'toos. No 'toos. I refuse."

"Channeling Dr. Seuss?" Roger said.

Westerly shook his head vigorously. Roger patted him on the arm and made soothing sounds, while Jill went to fetch the baby. The senator's eyes remained closed. Jill settled the bird in his lap on a towel, and Roger gently placed his hand on it.

At the feel of the warm body and soft feathers, a sob escaped from deep in Westerly's chest. He opened his eyes, and the baby bird lowered and cocked its head to the side and stared up at him with one eye. The senator howled, and two customers quickly moved to the other side of the store.

"Dirksen looked at me like that. Take him away! Take him away now!"

Jill and Roger exchanged looks of defeat. Jill gathered up towel and bird, and Westerly shivered as the warm bundle left his arms. But then, unprompted, the little bird squawked and sprang from the towel, landing on the senator's chest. He began to peck at the knot of Westerly's tie.

"Oh, I'm so sorry," Jill said and reached for the bird.

"Don't touch him." The senator cupped his hand around the bird's snowy white head, and it cuddled into the hand. Tears streamed down his face as he stroked the head. "Look at all the pin feathers! They must itch like crazy. Hasn't anyone helped him with this?" The senator began to gently preen the bird, flicking off the brittle sheathing of the emerging feathers.

"I don't want him," the senator said, "but I'll sit here and hold him for a few minutes because he's Dirksen's nephew, but I'm not taking him home."

Jill tucked the towel under the baby's butt to protect the senator's jacket. "It's time to feed him. I'll go get his food."

Westerly allowed the baby cockatoo to peck at his nose hairs.

"Look at this!" The senator laughed, and his eyes blurred with tears. "Do you see what he's doing? Dirksen loved to pick my nose, too."

"Yes, sir." Roger didn't look to be especially charmed. He turned to Jill. "May I use your restroom? I've had about a gallon of coffee."

"Past the nursery to the right."

Roger rose from the sofa, but the senator put a hand on his arm. "I need to borrow your cell. I have to call ... my lawyer ... to set up an appointment to have my will altered to include Mrs. Paulson."

Roger smiled and handed over the phone while Jill went to the cash register to take care of a customer.

Westerly's eyes scanned the store as he hunched over the phone and dialed.

"Hello?"

"Hello," the senator whispered, "it's me. I have a favor to ask."

"Crap. Get off the line. I told you not to call anymore."

"I need you to call off that thing we were planning."

"What the fuck? You want me to tell our friends 'never mind?'"

"Yes, exactly. I'm not mad anymore."

Deep, measured breathing could be heard on the other end of the line. "Are you still there?" Westerly asked.

"Sure." Gordy's voice had changed, become pleasant. "No problem. I will take care of that for you right now. You have a nice day." The line went dead.

Jill returned with a big plastic syringe and a jar of yellowish glop. Before long, the senator was happily squirting food into the baby's beak, not caring in the least about the dribbles on his tie or the gelatinous baby poop that found its way to his suit jacket. By the time the little bird was full, it had acquired the name Udall.

Back in the polygraph room, a naked Virgil is cracking his knuckles.

I put my hands over my ears to shut out the magnified sound of the bones jumping in their sockets. "I can't believe that really happened," I say. "You're making it up now. A US Senator arranging a terrorist attack on the Mines because we killed his bird? Then trying to cancel it when he gets another bird? That's crazy. Too crazy."

Virgil ceases to crack his knuckles, rests his hands on his cottage-cheese stomach, and begins to twiddle his thumbs. "You spent decades in the Mines and you can still use the words 'too crazy?' What about Castro's exploding cigar? What about hiring prostitutes to drug their Johns and then paying someone to watch? What about the Accustakitty, for gods sake? The Mines implanted a bug in a fucking cat. And despite how badly that turned out, they tried to bug a bird, too. Do you seriously think that Congress is any less crazy than the Mines?"

He has a point.

"Grief, Shelby, does a number on even the sanest minds, and Westerly wasn't that sane even before we killed his bird. That bird was like a son to him, you know."

A son. Grief. I can no longer feel physical manifestations of grief, no constricted throat, no small muscles yanking at the corners of my mouth, no hot welling in the eyes. What I experience now is pure psychic pain without distractions. Grief. How did I never realize that it could be so selfish? So blind? So aggressively misanthropic?

The words rise hot and desperate. They burst from my mouth without warning. "I want to see my son."

"What?" Virgil leans back in his chair and looks down his crooked nose. "This is off subject. I thought you didn't even want to talk about your son, much less see him."

I wish I had the option of crying. I should have done it while I was still alive, like so many other things.

"I want to see my son," I say again. "Edward was so much like me. He loved what I loved. He wanted to grow up to be an alchemist. He ..." I bite my lip and fall silent.

"He what?" Virgil prompts.

"He ... my gentle, perfect son tried to cut Esther's throat. If I hadn't been nearby, if the cut had been deeper, if the ambulance hadn't come so quickly she might have died." I speak rapidly to get it all out on the table. "His behavior had changed, but we tried to ignore it. Schizophrenia stole my son. It had to have been a genetic gift from me. Esther's family was solid as the day is long. My mother spent some time in an institution. My sister Norma suffered from every phobia you could name. I always thought I was the only normal one—except for the depression—but I must have been carrying the gene. It was my fault. I couldn't stand the guilt of it, couldn't stand to see Edward in that institution, so I stopped visiting. That was wrong." I fix my eyes on Virgil's, hoping to connect with whatever humanity remains. "I know you're about to show me horrific things, things that are probably my fault. But first, please, let me see my son."

Virgil doesn't answer, but the polygraph room fades.

32

The Son

I smell Esther's lilac powder.

Her gait was smooth and lady-like. She moved down a long corridor like a camera on a dolly, letting her eyes wander over soft-colored pastoral prints bolted to the pale green walls of the Bright Horizons Recovery Center. That's the sort of optimistic, euphemistic name they give mental institutions these days. Esther stopped at the reception desk of the ward where we had warehoused our only child.

The nurse looked up from her magazine. "Hello, Mrs. Wexler. Edward is doing well. He's calmer. The medications are helping. He's waiting for you in the Florida room."

The Florida room was filled with skylights, wicker furniture, and plants. A nurse sat at a desk in the corner, doing paperwork as she kept an eye on her patients. The sunlight and potted palms remind me of the atrium of the New Shafts Building. An institution is an institution is an institution.

My son looked more haunted than calm as he huddled in the corner of a sofa, arms crossed over his chest, feet propped up on a coffee table. His resemblance to my younger self was startling. He had the eyeglasses; the limp brown hair; the large, naive eyes; the acne; and the tendency to chubbiness. And now he had the haunted look as well. It had replaced the broad, mischievous grin he used to wear. I had once considered him to be myself perfected, made smarter, kinder, gentler, happier. He had a near-genius IQ, artistic talent, and a way with animals that was extraordinary. At the age of eight, he trained our cat to do tricks. A cat!

Esther sat down on the sofa. "I would give my last dollar for a hug right now."

Edward gave her a look of distrust as if he suspected she was joking. "Why would you even want to touch me after what I did?"

Esther's voice was soft as down. "The disease did that, not you."

"I am the disease." Edward looked down, tucking his chin into his chest—something else he got from me.

"You're my son and will never be anything to me but perfect."

Edward rolled his eyes, like any teenager might do. "Mothers," he said. "I don't know how even a mother could forgive what I did."

"I forgave you immediately and completely," Esther said without hesitation.

"That makes no sense." Edward gave her a fierce stare. "I walked up behind you with a knife and laid it against your throat. I cut you."

"Then you stopped."

"Not before your blood was running down your blouse and splattering onto those curtains you were sewing." Edward took a deep breath. "Those curtains you were sewing for my room. All you ever did was do stuff for me, and look how I repaid you. I cut your throat. You cannot forgive that."

Esther regarded the plump, white hands folded neatly in her lap. She took off her wedding ring and rubbed at the dark red mark left behind on her finger. She put the ring back on and raised her eyes to Edward. He wouldn't meet her gaze, so she placed a finger on his chin and turned his head until he couldn't help but look at her. "You listen to me. Forgiveness isn't logical. It isn't a result of weighing evidence. It isn't even a question of whether you deserve it or not."

"What is it then?" Edward asked with a trace of sarcasm. "Magic?"

Esther gently touched Edward's cheek. "Miracle, perhaps. Yes. Forgiveness is the miracle child of grace. Don't question it. Take it."

My son screwed up his face like a toddler. "I don't deserve it. Don't want it."

Esther's voice hardened. "You and your father are so much alike. You think somehow it's noble to punish yourselves, and you don't even have the time to notice that you're punishing me as well. Well I don't deserve that. Forgiveness is as much a gift for the giver as the recipient. It's a gift I can't live without. So you'd better take my forgiveness. You owe me that much."

Esther watched Edward struggling with her words. He chewed his lower lip, shook his head, screwed up his eyes—all things he got from me. Then he finally gave his mother the hug that she longed for, and they both cried.

"Thank you," I say to Virgil when I return. "I never thought I would say those words to you, but I thank you, sincerely."

Virgil belches, and the sound reverberates in the tiny space. "Did you know I've been retasting the same breakfast burrito for my entire afterlife? Anyway, it's time to get back to the attack. No, the day before the attack."

33

The Occipital Bone

I do not want to be in this head on this day.

An elegant, elderly hand tapped slowly on the steering wheel. The line of traffic at the gate was long, stretching out onto Route 123. William cut the air conditioner off and rolled his window down.

Security at the Mines had been stepped up because I had asked that it be stepped up. The SCUDOs were doing "one hundred percent mine tag checks," which meant that every occupant of every vehicle had to have his or her tag scanned by an electronic device. Normally, only the driver's tag was checked. The concrete pop-up barriers were lowered for each car and raised again as soon as the rear bumper had passed. SCUDOs pulled random cars aside for a more thorough check. All of this caused traffic to back up. The line of waiting cars was itself a security problem. No one had forgotten the miners gunned down in the left turn lane on Route 123. After that incident, cars no longer crowded bumper to bumper. Drivers left enough space so that they could pull out of line quickly if necessary. This made the line stretch longer. An armed

SCUDO occupied the humvee that normally sat empty in the grass by the gate. He, and all the other SCUDOs, were authorized to use lethal force.

"Yet borders are not real ..." William whispered.

I had run into him in the hall the day before. He was holding a printed notice from Facilities Management. "Did you see this?" He thrust it at me. It said that in response to employee complaints and worries about rabies and Lyme disease, they had trapped the shakedown squirrel and "disposed of him." William looked at me and said, "Safety trumps kindness and common sense every time these days from the largest matter to the smallest." He continued on his way.

William's eyes wandered to a half-full bag French fries on the floor of his car then returned to the line of cars ahead. Why would a little thing like a squirrel bother him so much?

"I wanted to bring you to this country for a visit," he whispered. "I had so many things to show you. I imagined how impressed you would be."

He must have been talking to Lamplight, not the squirrel. How often did he do this?

As the line inched forward, William continued his conversation with the dead. "I remember how impressed you were when I explained *habeas corpus* and how things are done in America. But how are things done in America? The government incarcerates people indefinitely without access to legal council. Without charges. We torture people. What does it matter? They aren't Americans. But suppose you believe in American ideas for all people? Does that make you un-American? Did I enter the Mines for the wrong reason?"

The light turned red. William was the second car waiting to make the left turn onto the compound. He didn't bother to leave extra space between his bumper and the one in front. He wasn't looking for that kind of exit. He continued his one-sided conversation.

"Everything in the Mines is NOFORN (NF). No foreigners. It pops up at the end of every paragraph. Just try leaving it off. Not for foreigners. They aren't us."

The light turned green, and William made the left turn and joined the line inching toward the gate.

"But borders aren't real. We are them. They are us. The Buddha was right. I felt it as soon as he said it, even though it negated my whole career, my whole life."

The drive leading to the gates was lined with trees on either side. William didn't look at the trees or the blue sky. He focused on the electrified fence, the radiation detector, the concrete barriers.

He continued to talk to Lamplight as if the man were sitting in the passenger seat. "We were told to take the gloves off." William glanced over and I can see Lamplight through his eyes, a memory transported from the chill gray of the past to the sunny warmth of an early summer morning in Virginia. The man had a broad Slavic face with the pasty skin resulting from bad food and scarce sunlight. Blue eyes peered from beneath shaggy gray brows. They were full of an uncanny depth, windows to a Russian soul steeped in fatalism, poetry, and a well-beaten idealism.

"Lethal force," William said. "Extraordinary methods. Sometimes I dream about a face under a wet cloth, terrible in its anonymity. It could be anyone under that cloth, that's what the country has tried to forget. There but for the grace of God ... But what God?"

William reached the series of tire slashers and yellow

cones that forced cars to take a serpentine path. Half-way through, the line stalled. Evidently there was something irregular about the vehicle at the front. The SCUDO motioned for the car to turn around and leave. William watched drivers' heads follow the progress of the car as it moved slowly out the exit lane. The SCUDOs watched with tense faces. A young man of uncertain race. Someone who foolishly took a wrong turn or someone sent to assess entrance security? The SCUDOs took down his license plate, but it would likely tell them nothing.

"I remember how you loved Frost," William said. "Especially that poem about fences. Good fences make good neighbors. You laughed about it, said you would love to inscribe those words on the Berlin Wall. How many years ago was that? Seems like yesterday."

Tears came to William's eyes, blurring the line of cars. "I should never have let you become a friend. Bad tradecraft." He blinked the tears away. "I don't know anything anymore. What would I have done differently? Should I have practiced a Tolstoyan philosophy of avoidance of evil? We talked about that, how neither one of us had the temperament to live like cloistered nuns. It seemed like a selfish escapism." William laughed. "Speaking of escapism, the kind lady at Special Employee Services wants me to take antidepressants. She explained how it was a medical condition, nothing to be ashamed of. But pills seem like cheating, don't they?" He looked toward Lamplight, and the ghost nodded. "In a way you're the lucky one. I've outlived my era."

The cars moved forward again. There were only two between William and the gate.

"Daphne got it back for me: 102774. She stole it. Excuse me." William reached across Lamplight, opened the glove compartment, and took out the old Russian pistol. Lamplight disappeared, and William laid the pistol on the seat where he had been.

William unfastened his seat belt. The SCUDOs were on edge because of the car that had to be turned around and because of the alert. No smiling or nodding or chatting. They peered intently at cars, at mine tags, at faces. They of all people knew that such precautions would be scant protection against a determined attacker and a vehicle full of explosives. Men and women such as these are the first to die in attacks. On days like this, that ranked higher in their minds than the good benefits and job security.

William placed his Mines tag in the glove compartment and snapped it shut. He pulled up to the SCUDO.

"Where's your tag?" the SCUDO asked. He leaned into the car and caught sight of the Tokarev pistol.

William studied the SCUDO's face, watching the alarm rise. Our SCUDOs were not like street-hardened city cops. They worked in a campus-like environment among law-abiding bureaucrats who smiled and said "good morning," as they presented their tags. It took more to push a SCUDO over the deadly force threshold. William waited until he judged the threshold had been passed, then he jammed the accelerator to the floor, just as the car ahead was passing over the spot where the concrete barrier had retracted into the pavement. William's car leaped past the SCUDO. A concussion, both external and internal. Sound pressure nothingness. He could not have asked for better than to have the bullet pierce the occipital bone and to be killed, like his friend, by his own colleague.

34

The Final Inspection

I arrive in a new head, one filled with nervous energy and the smell of tension sweat mixed with something oily and industrial. A terrorist, I can feel it.

He was inside the Mines, striding along a basement tunnel. By the dimmed lights and emptiness, it was after hours. He glanced to his left to a gray-haired, green-tagged security escort. The man huffed with the effort of keeping up, but his face bore an immensely self-satisfied expression—the look of a man earning good compensation for easy work. My host glanced to his right and caught the grim, cold eye of a man wearing grey coveralls emblazoned with the orange sunburst logo of Kreative Industrial Sunlight Solutions. His name tag indicated he was a supervisor. The name, John Summers, seemed wrong for him.

"So this is it," the escort said, "your final inspection?"

My host grunted. He clearly wasn't in the mood for small talk.

The escort was unfazed. "Too bad. I'll miss you guys, but thanks to all the nights you've been here, I've earned enough for a barefoot cruise in the Caribbean with my wife, Florence. We leave next month. A windjammer through the French West Indies. Waterfalls, volcanoes, beaches, and enough rum to drown whatever ails you."

Another grunt. My host glanced down at the over-sized toolbox in Summers's hand, then at the matching toolbox in his own.

"Those are some big toolboxes," the escort said. "What have you got in there?"

"Testing equipment," Summers said.

They arrived at a door deep in the bowels of head-quarters. The sign said, "Electrical Control Room." The escort pulled a slip of paper from his pocket and turned his back to study the numbers. He made a gesture for the workmen to turn around while he worked the combination. He opened the door and disarmed the security system.

"Come on in. All clear. So what do you have to do in here? Just turn the main switch on and off and see if everything still works?"

My host didn't answer. He set and his companion set their toolboxes on the floor and opened them.

The escort looked around. "I wonder if there's a place to sit down in here?" He spied a wooden crate in the corner and took two steps in that direction.

The wrench came down on his skull with speed, precision, and a sickening crack. The escort crumpled to the floor, and Summers hit him once more for good measure.

The men from Kreative Industrial Sunlight Solutions moved as quietly and deliberately as priests preparing communion. They disabled the electrical cutoff switch and the vault's alarm system. Summers opened the door and squirted industrial-strength glue into the locking mechanism. Then they drilled holes into the door and the wall and screwed on a heavy metal plate. Clearly, they didn't plan on leaving that room alive.

When that was done, the men bent over their toolboxes. They each removed a broken down AK-47 They assembled and loaded the guns in silence. Then they prostrated themselves on the floor and began to pray.

35

The Screamers

"Ready to die again?" Virgil asks when I return. He sits in an attitude of the utmost unconcern, his feet propped up on the polygraph table. He's still naked and will likely be so for all eternity.

The light in the room flickers, and I grip the arms of my chair. "Is it time?"

"Yes."

"Whose head will I occupy?"

"I think for this day I'll give you the panoramic view. After all, you hardly got to see anything that day under the concrete. Maybe a few stars, but that was it."

The first thing I see is a cloud high in the blue, blue sky. It resembled a whiskey bottle knocked on its side, emptying out the last, sad drop. Below an old green pickup drove through the willow oak shadows that fell across the perimeter road. It pulled into a reserved space in front of the Old Shafts Building. I barely recognize the man who got out. The foreshortening from this angle makes him even squatter and more turtle-like. Yet it must have been me. My bald head caught the sun and acquired a crystalline glint as if one could have read the future in it. Fat chance. I swung my hip against the door it to engage the latch. I stood for a minute with head tilted and gazed at the Old Shafts Building. I remember thinking it looked strange.

A silver Corvette pulled up, and I hurried to get out of the way. The car slid into the adjoining space, and the tall, slender figure of Arthur White emerged. We exchanged words and then spread a canvas cover over the car.

From this vantage point, it is our shadows that stand out as we walked toward the building. The sun behind our backs threw the shadows in our path. They stretched toward the Old Shafts Building, giving a funhouse mirror view of our interaction. My shoulders were hunched; chin tucked into rolls of neck fat so that I appeared headless in silhouette. Arthur was even taller and thinner than usual. One hand was anchored by a briefcase while the other gestured emphatically to illustrate his words. Even from this angle it's clear that he was in love with his words. I'm glad I don't have to hear them again.

Our shadows disappeared beneath the concrete portico head first, followed by our bodies.

My angle of view shifts. Now I'm at ground level.

Arthur and I walked beneath the center of the concrete portico, balanced on its four tapering, top-heavy columns.

Then came the high, shrieking, pulsing noise. It was siren, jackhammer, dentist's drill. It tore at the tympanic membrane; shook the hammer, anvil, and stirrup; and roiled the liquid of the cochlea, throwing the cilia into violent and suicidal motion. Noise to unmoor the sanity from the most phlegmatic head.

Arthur and I looked up, dropped our briefcases, and covered our ears with our hands. Arthur's mind was quicker than mine. He saw what was about to happen. He shouted something that I would never hear and ran back in the direction from which we had come. His normally cool and bloodless face was contorted in a scream. I stood transfixed and watched concrete move like water above my head as the portico began to rock and shift. I had time to save myself, but wisely chose not to. I stared at the concrete until it crested and broke, the portico listed toward the north, collapsed, and I was gone beneath a pile of rubble.

My angle of view changes. I move effortlessly over the collapsed portico toward the main entrance, which was blocked by the fallen concrete. I get a glimpse through the upper portion of the crumbling glass doors to the inside, where the noise echoing off the marble walls, the granite Mines seal, and the square marble columns of the foyer must have been ungodly. I see SCUDOs turning back miners hoping for an escape out the front doors.

I begin to rise up the side of the building.

Out of the clear blue sky, it began to rain in brilliant, sparkling drops. Glass. It fell from seven stories worth of windows. With each pulse of the screamers, cracks grew and spread until panes shattered and fell. The lower floors had high narrow windows. Then I reach the seventh, which was set back and walled in glass.

The window wall of the BOM's office had already shattered. Dashiell was slumped forward, head resting on his desk. Daphne and two SCUDOs burst through the door. He didn't move. Daphne felt for a pulse at his neck. She looked up at the SCUDOs and shook her head. They pulled him off the chair, laid him on the blood red carpet, and began CPR, but his fragile Chihuahua heart would not start again.

I pass into a seventh-floor tunnel packed with half-crazed employees struggling against each other like cattle in pens. Two burly SCUDOs had Greyson by the arms, propelling him through the chaos. Nearby, I saw Thelma. As she tried to make her way to the stairs, she wrapped a blue and gold scarf twice over her ears and knotted it under her chin. Her face held a look of determination, not panic. I didn't need to be inside her head to know that she was thinking about her family. She would do anything necessary to get back to them.

I want to stay with Thelma, but I have no control over my movement. I continue down the tunnel toward the south end of the building and pass into Slinky Nardovino's office.

He was bent over his computer, face glowing with purpose, right hand flying over the keyboard, hook beating a slow rhythm on his desk. He was messaging subordinates—no one could talk over the screamers. The words burst across the screen: "cut power ... guide pple to loading docks ... bsmt exits ... south emerg exit NSB ... block off Atrium, glass-intense areas ... Why hsn't pwr been cut?"

I pass through walls until I reach Maddie James's office.

She stood on top of her desk. She chomped gum furiously as she removed the frosted plastic panel that covered the lights. She threw the panel to the floor, removed the gum from her mouth, divided it in two and stuck it in her ears. Then she took off her sweater and used it like a hot mat to remove the same light tube she had examined a few days earlier. She sent it flying out the broken window. The second tube soon followed.

I drift out that window, over the building, and down into the interior courtyard, which was off limits to employees, being devoted solely to saucer magnolias, shrubbery, and decorative stone. Now it was frosted around the edges with broken glass. I pass through a window and arrive in the BOM tunnel. The painted BOMs danced a wild bopping line dance to the rhythm of the screamers. Bits of gilt flaked off picture frames and scattered like fairy dust. Cracks snaked through walls. The painted Vaughn Sutter Wayne shook loose and fell face forward to the floor.

From the west, the ghostly Wayne came running. His fists waved in the air. Powdered sugar puffed from his tuberous nose while his rubbery lips puckered, stretched, and contorted with a gush of invisible, inaudible invective.

I sink through the floor and escape. Then I move swiftly along the crowded main basement tunnels and make several turns through a labyrinth of near-deserted side tunnels. Ahead I see a maintenance man and three SCUDOs clustered around the door of the main electrical control room.

One SCUDO motioned for the others to step back. He aimed his gun and shot several times through the cipher and combination locks. He tried to push the door open, but it was held by the heavy metal plate installed by the men from Kreative Industrial Sunlight Solutions.

I begin to rise again, upward and westward, arriving in the cafeteria with its high, arched wall of glass facing the dining courtyard.

The cafeteria always had a steady stream of customers at this hour of the day. The extroverts stayed to break-fast with their colleagues. The introverts took styrofoam bowls of oatmeal with brown sugar and craisins back to their desks. I see that most of the diners had already es-caped out the emergency exits, although a couple had been caught by falling glass. Their colleagues were drag-ging them out, leaving trails of blood. Glass continued to rain down on empty tables and abandoned trays of food.

I pass out into the courtyard with its picnic tables, trees, and Kryptos sculpture.

A few diners crouched under the tables, having wise-ly decided not to risk going through the building to get to the outside. Their eyes turned toward the New Shafts Building.

It was an unusual structure built into the side of a hill. Its two, six-story towers were doubled walled to block electronic emissions. The inner wall was concrete with wide, rectangular windows while the outer wall was a sol-id curtain of blue-green glass. A four-story glass atrium connected the towers and faced the dining courtyard. Es-calators zigzagged to the top of the atrium, where a long glass tunnel led to the exit atop the hill.

The towers appeared to be palpitating as their blue-green curtain walls disintegrated in rhythmic bursts. Meanwhile, the glass of the atrium was shattering in spectacular fashion.

I move inside and look up.

The fragmenting glass against the morning sun had a searing, crystalline beauty. Glittering shards broke as they hit the floor, lending the atrium a look of polar des-olation strangely ornamented by a couple of wrecked pot-ted palms. I saw one body, fast disappearing under the rain of glass.

The wounded had tracked blood into the wave guides, the oddly bent corridors lined with sound-blocking material that led to the workspaces.

The one-sixth scale models of the U-2 and SR-71 aircraft still hung from the atrium ceiling, but they had begun to shiver and jerk. A large chunk of glass hit the U-2; its cables snapped; and the plane nosedived to the floor.

I rise past the deserted escalators, which had stopped, jammed by crumbling glass or the movement of the building. I can see the movement here. The whole structure was beating. Was it about to collapse?

When I reach the top, I see the body of a SCUDO near the badge machines. Beyond the machines, in the long green glass tunnel, I see two more bodies.

At eight o'clock in the morning, the tunnel must have been full of people arriving for the workday. The majority of employees use this entrance because it's near the parking garage and the largest parking lot. The people near the entrance would have had time to get out, those near the badge machines, especially those who had just gone through the machines, were in the worst position. I find myself muttering an apology, "I'm so sorry. I'm so sorry. I'm so sorry." Are the shades of these people nearby or are Vaughn Sutter Wayne and I the only ghosts trapped here?

I move slowly along the tunnel and stop before the Windwalker sculpture, a bronze eagle turning in flight, at a right angle to the floor, delicately balanced on one wing tip. The Windwalker was walking. The vibration moved sculpture on its base to the edge of its black marble pedestal. Balance shifted, and the Windwalker crashed to the floor.

The whole building trembled. With the atrium and fourth-floor exit blocked, the bottleneck to the basement emergency exits must have been severe.

I imagine the weight of the building crushing down on all of those people, my colleagues, my friends. After a few decades in the Mines, with its late hours and restrictions on talking to the uncleared, you find your outside connections fading away. Even my marriage to Esther had faded. These were my people, the bureaucrats.

Then the screamers fell mute, and the vibrations stopped. SCUDOs must have somehow gained entry to the electrical control room or figured out how to otherwise kill the power. No whoosh of air through ventilation systems or hum of lights. Just the diminishing sound of breaking glass. Screams from deep in the building. Then the whine of approaching sirens. Emergency vehicles were probably already clogging the perimeter road, but they would keep coming from miles around.

I wonder what the people in the basements heard. Probably the ringing of their own ears. How many were temporarily or permanently deafened?

I rise through the shattered tunnel until I have a bird's eye view of the compound. Nothing had collapsed, but smoke poured out broken windows in three places. Evidently the vibrations had broken wires and caused electrical fires. Windows were gone, but walls still stood, albeit chunks of concrete had broken off here and there. People still poured out the ground floor exits and the loading docks. Some were limping, others were being half-carried by colleagues. I see one of my office chiefs administering CPR to an older woman. I wonder if he learned it in the classes I arranged.

Emergency vehicles pulled onto the lawns; EMTs spilled out and ran toward those who lay bleeding on the grass. Firemen donned helmets as they prepared to enter the buildings.

I see a flash of blue and gold in the northeast parking lot and then I am at ground level next to her. Thelma bent over a woman with a severe leg wound. She shook out the scarf she had just removed from her head, then knotted it around the leg just above the bleeding gash. She removed a long, gold metal pin from the clip that held up her hair and used it to twist the knot tight.

News crews set up just outside the compound. Polished and perky commentators donned their tragic faces and began to speculate in their usual irresponsible fashion. Police deployed to direct traffic.

I float about the Mines campus for hours, watching recovery operations. I've come full circle now, returned to my death for a second time. I watch the recovery of my body, see the crane lift the slab of cement to reveal a very flat bureaucrat. When I was a teenager, I wished a thousand times that my nose was not so prominent. My wish came true.

A cry escapes my lips, but it's not horror over my ugly corpse; it's a sudden fear that I will end up like Vaughn Sutter Wayne. I'll pace the tunnels for all eternity!

I no longer flit. No longer return to the polygraph room. I drift aimlessly about the compound like a stray dog.

36

Key Judgment

On the third day after the attack, I join Vaughn Sutter Wayne and the Buddha atop the Bubble, the freestanding Mines auditorium that looks like a mammoth golf ball half buried in the ground. We watch as the rosy morning light illuminates the battered Old Shafts Building. Work crews have already arrived to continue the task of clearing debris. Investigators are gathering evidence. All bodies—thank God only a few—have been recovered.

"Don't you look like shit," Vaughn says to me.

"Is that powdered sugar up your nose?" I ask.

"Fuck you."

The Buddha smiles his Buddha smile.

"Damn fucking idiots," Vaughn says yet again. "Look what they did to my Mines. Damn fucking idiots." Vaughn waits, but sees that we don't intend to respond, so he goes on. "Damn, damn fucking idiots. Can you believe the idiocy? I knew it. Knew something was going to happen. Got the instinct. Don't these idiots—IDIOTS—have the instinct anymore? What the hell were you doing?" he says to me. "Aren't you White Mines eggheads supposed to be clairvoyant?"

I don't answer.

The Buddha closes his eyes and listens to the sound of jackhammers on concrete, shouted instructions, the tinkle of glass being swept into piles. He turns to Vaughn.

"They're awake, aware again. It's time for me to go. I wish you peace."

Vaughn's face clouds with rage. "Who's awake? You're checking out now? Hell of a time. You wish me peace? Hell of a thing to say. What do you mean by that? Who's awake?"

The Buddha looks at me, smiles, and turns away. *I know who's awake and I understand why it's time for the Buddha to go.*

I look towards the buildings. When I turn back, the Buddha is gone and in his place is Virgil, grinning broadly, still naked as a jaybird.

"Hey, Shelby. Look at me! I'm out of that damnable polygraph room." He throws out his arms as if to embrace the world and spins in a slow circle, laughing.

"So you're not the devil?" I ask.

"No," Virgil says, "I'm just really obnoxious."

I sink to my knees and plead. "Can you explain it to me now? Where we're going? Who was your management?"

"Shelby," Virgil says, "I don't know. I never knew. You think you'll find out all these mysteries when you die, but it's just like life. You don't know." He starts to sing "The Beat Goes On," accompanying himself on air guitar.

I turn my eyes away from Virgil's nakedness to the Old Shafts Building, which looks blind with all of its empty window sockets. I think of the Congressional hearings that will follow this tragedy, of the pompous pronouncements, snide accusations, and public shaming of selected scapegoats. What are the chances that they will lay the blame where it belongs? On blind grief, blind hatred, distraction, misplaced priorities, and all of the other human frailties that infect our enemies and ourselves? No chance. The Democrats will blame it on the Republicans, and the Republicans will blame it on the Democrats. They'll set in place a raft of ill-considered "reforms" and no one will be wiser in the end.

I notice then that I can no longer hear Virgil singing. I turn around, and he's gone. It's only Vaughn Sutter Wayne and I now. I do not want to spend all eternity with this bitter, sugar-coated ghost.

Then I see it. The light. The blinding shattering light. It inflates my being, and I rise like a bubble. Could it be that Esther was right about forgiveness? Could it be that I've been forgiven, despite not deserving it? Despite everything?

Vaughn looks up and screams, "And where do you think you're going?"

I have no idea. I rise above Vaughn's screaming and hear another, stranger voice. A white bird swoops and circles, muttering it's nonsensical incantations.

"Guns kill pee pee ... billion here billion there pretty soon ... pretty bird pretty pretty bird pretty bird ... hey, hey hey

Glossary

alchemist - analyst.

Black Mines - the operational sector of the Mines responsible for clandestine intelligence gathering.

bomb dissector (BD) - counterterrorism specialist.

Boss of Mines (BOM) - the presidentially appointed director of the Mines.

BOM Tunnel - the corridor in the Mines where portraits of former BOMs hang.

drones - administrative personnel.

Ear, the - see National Audio Collection Agency.

diplomatic service (DipServ) - the agency responsible for foreign diplomacy.

grouper - foreign asset, agent.

Internal Investigative Organ (IIO, in the Mines known simply as "the Organ") - the agency responsible for domestic law enforcement.

Main Shaft - the executive wing of the Mines, headed by the Boss of Mines.

Mines - the agency responsible for gathering and assessing foreign intelligence for the President.

National Audio Collection Agency (known in the Mines as "the Ear") - the agency responsible for the collection of audio intelligence from satellites, wiretaps, etc.

New Shafts Building (NSB) - built in the 1980s, it lies to the west of the Old Shafts Building at Mines Headquarters.

Old Shafts Building (OSB) - the original headquarters building of the Mines.

President's Intelligence Update (PIU) - daily "newspaper" of the most critical intelligence for the President and a few top officials.

rockslide - an unfortunate public incident involving the Mines.

sharper - operations officer or, less politely, spy.

smithies - technical experts who make spy gadgetry.

Special Employee Services (SES) - a unit within the Mines responsible for helping employees deal with personal and psychological problems, as well as substance abuse.

Strikes, the - the 2001 attack on the World Trade Center and Pentagon.

White Mines - the analytical sector of the Mines.

About Susan Hasler

Susan Hasler spent twenty-one years in the Central Intelligence Agency. She began her career as a Russian linguist and moved on to become a Soviet analyst, speechwriter to three Directors of Central Intelligence, and finally a counterterrorism analyst. She served in the CIA Counterterrorism Center before, during, and after 911. In 2013, Hasler appeared in the Emmy-winning HBO documentary *Manhunt: The Search for Bin Laden*. Ms. Hasler's work has appeared in literary journals, magazines, and anthologies. She lives with her husband in Virginia.